THE BIG GAME IS EVERY NIGHT

THE BIG GAME IS EVERY NIGHT

A NOVEL

ROBERT MAYNOR

HUB CITY PRESS
SPARTANBURG, SC

Copyright © 2023
Robert Maynor

Cover image: Tom Rooney
Cover design: Kate McMullen
Interior book design: Meg Reid
Author Photo © Amanda Pennington

Library of Congress Cataloging-in-Publication Data

Names: Maynor, Robert, 1993- author.
Title: The big game is every night / Robert Maynor.
Description: Spartanburg : Hub City Press, [2023].
Identifiers: LCCN 2023002583 (print)
LCCN 2023002584 (ebook) ISBN 9798885740159 (paperback)
ISBN 9798885740166 (epub)
Subjects: LCGFT: Domestic fiction. Novels.
Classification: LCC PS3613.A96285 B54 2023 (print)
LCC PS3613.A96285 (ebook)
DDC 813/.6--dc23/eng/20230209
LC record available at https://lccn.loc.gov/2023002583
LC ebook record available at https://lccn.loc.gov/2023002584

Hub City Press gratefully acknowledges support from the National Endowment for the Arts, the Amazon Literary Partnership, South Arts, and the South Carolina Arts Commission.

HUB CITY PRESS
200 Ezell Street
Spartanburg, SC 29306
864.577.9349 | www.hubcity.org

FOR A.P.

It is an honor to thank the songwriter
Jason Molina, whose songs from the
album *The Magnolia Electric Co.*
helped shape this story.

PART ONE

On a warm Saturday morning after a game, floating in a jon boat on Lake Moultrie with my cousin Marcus, I tried to explain how it felt. The hard breaths I pulled at the end of a long run. The glow of the floodlights shining over the aluminum bleachers, hotdog steam rising from the concession stand. The sound of the marching band. It felt like being born. Opening new eyes to a world I'd never known. How it was all worth that, whenever it came, brief and strange as it was. Mornings sprinting stairs until my eyes went blurry, two-a-days in July, temperatures in the high nineties. When I got home after a game, I'd shower, lie down in my bed, and reach back for that feeling only to find it hidden. Not like a memory or a dream, but like a story someone told me I didn't even fully believe.

"First love is always like that," Marcus said. "Enjoy it." He weighed three hundred and fifty pounds, bore a patchy red goatee on his chin, and smoked mentholated Pall-Mall cigarettes. He was a fireman and possessed the type of grocery-store knowledge and blind self-confidence that can make a normal man seem wise to a fifteen-year-old boy. "Talk to me again when y'all start losing. Or when you get a girlfriend."

We'd won our first four games that year and people were getting expectations. Marcus came to all my games, even though he hated football. Sat up in the top of the bleachers and sipped from a smuggled-in pint of Wild Turkey 101.

He reeled in his line and the hook was clean.

"Fishing on credit," I said.

"More often than not." He pinched a wad of stink-bait out of the plastic tub between his feet and balled it up on his hook, then dropped it back down to the bottom of the lake.

We caught eight or ten fish before lunch, mostly the native channel cats with long whiskers and mossy yellow hide, speckled down their spines with brown. A few transplants too, Arkansas blues, fat from lip to tail. Reeling them in, you weren't sure whether it was a fish or an old tire, just dead weight all the way.

Marcus motored us back to Arrowhead Landing, ospreys flying overhead, outboard Johnson humming, the wind a thick wet tongue against my cheeks.

Marcus liked putting in at Arrowhead because they had a paved boat ramp and a little store where you could buy bait and cigarettes. There was a campground on the bank there too, so people had their campers and trucks parked by the lake, little fires burning. An old concrete swimming pool was dug behind the store, empty but for some rainwater.

We coasted up to the boat ramp and Marcus let me off. I went to the truck, a rusty Ford Ranger, and backed it slowly down the ramp. I was getting pretty good at driving forward, but backward was another thing, and with the trailer attached, I couldn't always remember which way to turn the wheel to make the trailer go the way I wanted. Finally, I got it straight and we got the boat out of the water. Marcus lumbered into the store for a bag of ice while I strapped down the stern. He came back out and dumped the ice over the fish where they were croaking in an orange bucket. "Got to feed the pigs," he said, chewing on an unlit cigarette.

We took Mudville Road toward Highway 76, the asphalt blanched nearly silver by the sun and pitted with holes that made the boat rattle on its trailer. Marcus drove and I looked out the open window at the pine trees and the ditches choked with litter, thinking about a play in the second quarter the night before where I was supposed to run behind Conrad, the right guard, but instead bounced outside and got tackled for a loss. I almost always followed the plays how they were drawn, but sometimes I got in a groove and wanted to wing it. Test the water, explore possibilities. But Coach Hendrickson hated that, and I knew he'd bring it up come Monday.

Marcus slid a disc into the CD player and a rambling, lo-fi guitar riff began to play, some homecooked recording from one of the obscure bands he always listened to. When he wasn't fishing or working at the fire station, he was watching live performances on YouTube.

We pulled into the parking lot of Henry's Grocery at the crossroads of Mudville and Highway 76. Went inside and ordered two cheeseburger baskets and a plate of fried okra to share. We waited at the counter until the food came out, then carried it to a table in the back, beside the drink cooler. The walls were hung with cheap fishing tackle and at the end of one of the shelves sat three bins of late-season vegetables for sale by the dozen.

"Careful you don't get fat now, hanging around with me," Marcus said.

"I'll work it off." I took a bite of my burger and warm juice ran down my chin. I wiped it with the back of my hand.

"Who y'all play this week?"

"Gadsden."

"Whom the world haft left behind." Marcus shoveled a few pieces of fried okra in his mouth.

"They ain't that bad this year. Got a decent linebacker, Fifty-Six. He's supposedly getting recruited. Even Alabama wants him."

"That ought to drive up the price of real estate."

Marcus lived alone in a ramshackle singlewide trailer off Black Tom Road. He picked up lost hubcaps from the roadside and leant them against the tattered skirting of his trailer. Had been doing it for years. He said it was so folks could come back for them, but none ever did that I knew. They shimmered with sunlight as we pulled into the drive. It was like the trailer was hovering just over the land.

We cleaned the catfish at the piecemeal skinning table Marcus had built against the back of his trailer, a porcelain sink basin set in a stainless tabletop, mounted on four-by-four posts and fed water by a garden hose. We'd been cleaning fish together since I was old enough to hold a knife. It was second nature. I sliced the fish vertically behind the head, then ran the tip of the knife horizontally along the dorsal fin until I hit the ribs. Glided the blade around the ribs, then drug it tight along the backbone, separating the meat from the spine, all the way down to the tail. I flipped the fish over and the did the same thing to the other side, then slid it down to Marcus. He cut the skin off each filet and trimmed any belly meat I might have left before dropping the carcass in the orange bucket.

Yellow-jackets hovered around the table, lapping at the spilt blood and slime. Marcus's cat, Spooky, wandered out of the stand of pines and gums behind us. Black with one little patch of white on the top of her head. She rubbed up against Marcus's legs and chirped. He fed her little pieces of the trimmings.

"We got them trained, the whole kingdom, ain't it? They hear that Ford pull in the yard on a Saturday, they're hitting the chow line. Bees lining up on the table, Spooky wandering up out of her hole. Buzzards is probably back there around the gut pile licking their beaks." He dug a Pall-Mall out of his breast pocket and lit it up, fingers still bloody. "Bringing the wildlife up by hand."

"Lydia likes cats," I said. "But her daddy won't let her have one."

"Still talk to her?"

"Sometimes."

"I seen her at the game." Marcus smiled. "Working for the Peanut Man."

Lydia's father, Ronald Proveaux, owned a boiled peanut cart he towed to gas-station parking lots and special events, like high-school football games. The rig was really just a steel box on trailer tires with a rough-cut window, *Proveaux's Peanuts* painted on the side. He sold original and hot by the pound. Cooked them right there in the trailer over propane fires in two enormous aluminum pots, sweat beading on the steel. Sometimes Lydia worked the till.

One afternoon over the summer when they were parked at Henry's, me and Marcus pulled in for peanuts. Lydia was at the window, a string of fake pearls around her light brown neck. Ronald was slumped over in the corner on a folding chair, asleep.

"We'll take a pound of hot," Marcus said.

Lydia took a sip from a can of Mountain Dew. "You ain't even going to make any small talk first? Bitch about the heat. Ask about business. Pretend I actually want to be here talking to you."

"I don't play make-believe," Marcus said.

"I like that." Lydia turned, lifted the lid off one of the pots, and dipped out a batch of peanuts with a big slotted spoon. "You go to Sandridge too, don't you?" she asked me as she poured the peanuts on a vegetable scale hanging from the ceiling.

I was surprised she recognized me. She was a grade ahead and we didn't have any classes together. "Yeah, I go there."

She checked the scale and ladled on a few more peanuts, then poured them in a plastic bag and twisted it closed. "Play football or something, don't you?"

"Running back."

"Couldn't tell you the difference," Lydia said. "But that's cool."

Marcus handed her a five-dollar bill and she gave him the bag of peanuts.

"Thank you," Marcus said. We turned to leave.

"Hold on a second." Lydia tore the edge off the bill and wrote her phone number in blue ink. Handed it to me through the window. "Text me sometime."

I did that night, but I didn't know what to say, so I just wrote *Hey this is Grady Hayes from today.* We started texting fairly regular and about once a week she'd call me with some crazy dilemma. Whether a dent in a can made the food inside go bad, should she check the oil in her Oldsmobile with the motor running or not. But anytime I saw her in the hallway, those fake pearls against her tan neck, I got too nervous to speak.

I brought the last fish out of the sink, a channel cat, maybe three or four pounds. "Reckon she saw any of the game?"

"I don't know," Marcus said. "Them boys was lining up for peanuts. Seems like everybody got a thing for them light-skinned girls."

"Her daddy is white."

"I didn't say there was nothing wrong with it. Shit, if I was you, I'd be birddogging that little honey too."

I cut the fish quickly and slid it over to Marcus. He finished it off and I took the gut bucket without saying anything and walked into the woods. The tall trees shaded out most of the sun, thick trunks gnarled with knotty growths. Mosquitoes whined in my ears. Marcus made everything into a joke. Usually it was all right, but sometimes it got under my skin.

At the gut pile, the brush was packed down from the scavengers rooting. Dirt covered in bones. Mostly catfish, their thick gray skulls and dark eye sockets. Even the guts we'd dumped the weekend before were already picked clean. You had to watch where you were walking because the vertebrae were thin and sharp, scattered from the birds and the possums shaking spines. I emptied the bucket and headed carefully back to the yard.

Marcus was waiting for me. "You helping me cook tomorrow?" he asked.

It was Meemaw's seventieth birthday, so we were having a fish fry at her and Shorty's place. Marcus was handling fish and potatoes. His mom, Aunt Gail, was bringing coleslaw. My Mom had agreed to make a coconut cake. That way, Meemaw wouldn't have to cook. Marcus had arranged all the plans the week before.

"Figured I would."

"Good, you can do the taters. I already got a bag inside." He took his cell phone out of his pocket and looked at the time. "I got a shift starts in four hours. I'm going to sleep a little while. You want to go home now, or you want me to drop you on the way?"

"Guess now."

We unhooked the boat from the Ranger and Marcus handed me his keys so I could drive. We took Black Tom Road back to Highway 76, past the Methodist church and Sandridge Fire

Station, where Marcus worked. We had the windows trimmed down and I was resting my elbow on the ledge, steering with one hand. I'd had my restricted permit for about three months and I loved to drive. The feeling of the hard, grainy steering wheel. I could turn it any which way, and that's where we'd go. I controlled the destination and the path. Even if I was just going where Marcus or whoever else told me, it was my hand on the wheel, my choice to follow. That's what I loved most.

We crossed the little bridge over Wassamassaw Swamp. Below, two old men in wide-brimmed straw hats fished with cane poles. A couple miles further, I turned off onto Lantana Lane, where me and Mom lived in a yellow house. Pulled into the driveway and shifted into park.

"Not bad," Marcus said. "You're getting the hang of it."

I nodded and got out of the truck. Marcus scooted over behind the wheel. "Pick you up tomorrow at noon."

"Be careful tonight."

"Always am." He winked and started backing down the drive. "Just putting out fires."

The house was dark. It smelled stale, like no one had been moving around in it enough to dust up a scent. I walked through, turning on lights and spraying air freshener from under the kitchen sink. It left a sheen on the pictures hung crookedly on the walls, mostly of me from elementary school, but one new one they took for football. I was wearing the green and yellow home uniform, helmet and all, my eyes like two pin holes through the facemask. It was stamped with a watermark that read SAMPLE. I opened the front room windows, despite the lingering early-autumn mugginess outside, and went to my room to start on my weekend homework.

I had bunkbeds my whole life, like some careless joke. I slept on the bottom and piled dirty clothes on top. A large, empty aquarium loomed in the corner of the room on a metal stand, an old tinge of green algae clouding the glass. I'd had fish in it once, but they died easy and I never got any more. I unzipped my backpack and laid my books out on the floor. I had a Geometry set to finish and a chapter to read for U.S. History. Geometry was easy for me because it was all about angles and planes, like football. Coach Hendrickson talked every day about pad level and getting into space. "Low man wins," he said. "Get to the edge, you better disappear." History was harder to invest in because the pieces didn't fit together clean. I was driven by scores. How the truth could be found.

It was getting dark when I finished my homework and Mom still wasn't home. She took extra shifts whenever she could get them at the old folks' home in Pineville, so her schedule was un-predictable. Sometimes after work when it wasn't too late, she'd go to the Mexican restaurant for margaritas with the other nurses too. I tried to call her cell phone, but she didn't answer. She'd made it to the game the night before. I saw her walking carefully up the bleachers in her wedge sandals with her hair all curled. So I wasn't worried at all.

I packed up my books and went to the kitchen. Me and Mom had been redoing parts of it whenever she got extra money. The refrigerator was new, shiny and metallic with an ice dispenser in the door. It stood beside the dented stove. Only three elements worked and they glowed orange when you put them on high. Linoleum floors stained and peeling up in places. Mom had re-cently come home with a new table in a cardboard box and we built it together. It looked like the nicest thing in the house, but really it was just pressboard with a fancy finish.

I boiled a couple eggs for dinner, peeled them over the trash can, and took them to the front room wrapped in a paper towel.

Sat in the recliner and turned a college football game on TV, Georgia versus Kentucky. I never had a favorite team because I didn't watch football for pleasure. I watched it like work. Studied the running-backs, how they lined up, how they took a handoff or faked the play-action pass. I loved the way some of them put their hand on their lead blocker like they were feeling his muscles, reading a map by Braille, which cut to make.

Studying the college players filled me with a mix of dread and excitement, because they were bigger and more skilled than me. Every movement was made with confidence. I wanted that. To stand in the heart of a stadium packed with eighty thousand people watching and know I was strong enough, fast enough, tough enough, good enough. It was hard to imagine those same men in school desks, reading history chapters in their bedrooms. Then the camera cut to the sidelines and I could see some of the players with their helmets off, their faces more recognizable as boys somewhat like me, if a few years older. I wondered if playing in front of all those people made the experience feel more real, or less. I wanted to find out.

The game was close going into the fourth quarter, but Georgia took the lead and pulled away in a matter of two minutes. A few good plays and a lot of luck. The game ended quietly and another one came on the screen immediately afterwards. It was a lazy, formless contest. I fell asleep in the recliner. Woke up past midnight to a West Coast game. Groggily watched a few plays before stumbling to bed with the TV still on. Boys hugging leather, men talking.

I counted my bruises in the late morning sunlight, birds in the yard, bickering over seeds. The color always took a day to come

THE BIG GAME IS EVERY NIGHT

on good. My ribs on both sides were tinted yellow. Arms dotted black. Beneath my left hip were two purple squares, the imprint of a facemask.

I took a shower and dressed in khaki shorts and a cutoff T-shirt. Looked in Mom's bedroom to make sure she'd made it home and saw her sleeping on top of the covers. I wrote her a note on the back of a torn envelope to remember the coconut cake and leaned it against the coffee pot, then went outside to sit on the porch steps and watch the cars pass, heading for church.

Marcus pulled into the yard right on time, power-steering pump whining on the Ranger. "Beautiful morning," he called out the open window. "Wish we were headed back to the lake."

I climbed in the passenger seat. "Any action last night?"

"Not even a burnt bag of popcorn," Marcus said. "A smokeless Saturday night."

It wasn't far to Meemaw and Shorty's place, a one-story brick house off Starline Drive. Marcus pulled into the yard and backed up to the carport.

"Did you bring a present?" I asked.

He killed the engine. "She's seventy years old, Grady. It ain't that kind of party."

We went inside without knocking, the door always unlocked. Flames threw shadows around the house. Meemaw and Shorty kept their gas logs burning day and night from September all the way to May. We went to the kitchen and found Meemaw bent over the sink, snapping beans.

"Happy birthday," I said.

She turned around smiling, short gray hair stuck to her forehead with moisture. "My two handsome boys."

"You ain't supposed to be cooking," Marcus said.

"I know. I just couldn't help it." She turned back to her beans.

Breaking off the ends, rinsing them, dropping them into a silver pot.

I went over and rubbed her back. "How's it feel to be so old?"

"Useless, really."

"Stop."

"Aren't you hot in here?" Marcus said.

"You know, I don't even ask myself that anymore."

I went to living room to see Shorty. His bald crown was shining in the light from the gas logs, and his rocking chair was pulled up close to the TV screen like always. The room was dark with the blinds closed, lit only by the television and the fire. From inside, you couldn't even tell what time it was, what season, what year. I walked up to Shorty and patted his shoulder.

"Hey, buddy." He didn't look away from the screen. New England was playing Miami. Brady completed a pass to Gronkowski for a first-down. "I love to see those white boys catch the football," Shorty said.

Me and Marcus were under the carport setting up the propane fryers when Aunt Gail pulled up in her little Mazda. Marcus's stepdaddy Peter sat squashed in the passenger seat with his hair slicked back. He got out and came over carrying a big glass bowl of coleslaw. Aunt Gail followed behind him, eyelashes clumped with poorly applied mascara. She held a single yellow balloon tied to a string. She looked much older than my mom, but it was only six years between them.

"I never know what to do." Aunt Gail gestured at the balloon. "She's so hard."

"She's cooking beans," Marcus said.

"Of course she is."

Peter coughed and readjusted the bowl of coleslaw against his round belly.

"Right," Aunt Gail said. "Let's take this inside."

The day was warm and still. Folks drove by with their windows down, little bits of music drifting from their radios. Marcus reached into the toolbox of his Ranger and pulled out two cold cans of Natural Light from the little cooler he kept stashed there. Offered me one, but I waved it off.

"Sooner you start, sooner you can quit. You don't want to be one of them old alkies, do you?"

Mom showed up over an hour late in her green Jeep with the top down. Me and Marcus were finishing up the last batch of fish and potatoes, both dripping sweat from standing over the fryers. She had her cake on a dinner plate, covered with tinfoil.

"I forgot the stuff to make icing." She was wearing a flowy white blouse and gold earrings. Her hair was pulled back in a ponytail. She didn't have on any makeup. "So I just used whipped cream."

"You're late."

She rolled her eyes. "I'm sure I didn't miss anything important."

I didn't respond.

"Anyway, I'm the adult. Just because you're getting some muscles doesn't mean you can start minding my business."

"Don't be fooled," Marcus said. "He might be getting bigger, but he's still just a baby."

Mom nudged my arm. "Is that true?"

"Quit playing." I couldn't stand when she acted like that. Like she wasn't the last one to show up, an hour late, toting a half-assed cake. She thought she could talk her way out of anything. We were quiet for a minute and she went inside. Marcus spooned the last pieces of fish out of the fryer and onto a paper platter covered with napkins.

"How much longer on those taters?"

"Five minutes."

He went to his toolbox and got another Natural Light. "What is more significant, sharing the womb, or sharing all of this?"

"I don't know what you're saying."

He laughed and cracked his beer.

Meemaw was leaning against the counter beside the stove when we came inside, watching her beans boil. Mom and Aunt Gail were sitting across from each other at the table. The yellow balloon was tied to a chair. I laid the platter of fish and potatoes on the counter and washed my face and hands in the sink. Meemaw gave me a clean rag to dry with.

We all gathered around the table except for Shorty. Aunt Gail fixed him a plate and he ate in front of the television.

"I can't believe my mother is seventy," Mom said, squirting store-bought tartar sauce over her fish. Marcus was eyeing her.

"Our boys cooked the food," Aunt Gail said.

"I don't know how the cake turned out."

The sound of loud cheering came from the TV and Shorty groaned.

"Just please don't sing," Meemaw said. "Okay?"

We ate until we were full. Mom took the cake out of the fridge, uncovered it, and stuck in seven candles. She lit them with a match and brought it to the table, wax dripping. Meemaw extinguished the flames without ceremony. Mom cut thick slices and laid them on fresh paper plates. Passed them around.

"The icing is just whipped cream," she said. "Sorry."

It tasted better than I thought it would.

We stayed around the table for a little while talking until Marcus got up and cleared the plates. The two of us went outside and cleaned up our frying station. It was almost six o'clock, air cooling off, bugs starting to hum. I dumped the oil in the backyard and Marcus threw the potato peelings into the trees. We loaded the fryers back in the Ranger.

Marcus left me there to ride home with my mom. He was tired from his shift. I didn't blame him. The rest of us gathered in the living room around Shorty on the couch and in the two wingback chairs beside the fireplace. Peter fell asleep. Meemaw turned on a lamp.

The Patriots won by seventeen. As soon as the game was over, Shorty pulled the remote out of his pocket and switched the channel to the news. Mom got up to leave and I did too. She kissed Shorty's head and we hugged Meemaw and Aunt Gail, mumbling about getting together again soon. Outside, there was just a tinge of pink and orange left in the sky.

"Can I drive?"

"It's almost dark."

"Jeep's got headlights, don't it."

"Just not tonight."

We rode the first mile in silence. The radio was tuned low to an old country station. We passed a yellow fire hydrant, a wooden cross.

"Why you so quiet?" Mom asked.

"I'm not."

"Feels like we haven't talked in forever."

"You've been busy."

"So have you." Mom flicked her blinker and slowed down to turn. "We're short-staffed at work. Almost everybody's getting overtime. Seems like we're on backwards schedules. You're at practice when I'm home, or at school, or whatever. Things will slow down soon."

"Season goes until December if we make the playoffs."

Mom turned onto Highway 76. "That's not so long. Anyway, I know you love it. You played good the other night."

"Thanks."

"It's weird seeing you from the bleachers. I can hardly tell it's you."

"That's what the numbers are for. I'm Twenty-Eight."

"I didn't give you a number," she said. "I gave you a name." She adjusted the seatbelt against her throat. "Feels too much like sharing."

We were quiet. I wondered how much of the game she actually watched or understood. She didn't sit with Marcus. She sat with a group of women who wore green T-shirts, their sons' names ironed on the backs. Mom didn't wear one of those, thank god. I don't know how she met those ladies, but that was just her way—to insert herself in a club, then refuse their customs.

"We play Gadsden next week. Away. Coach Hendrickson thinks it will be tough."

"I'm so proud of you," Mom said, like she hadn't heard me at all.

Coach Hendrickson told us you start each day with your most important business, so first period was weight training every semester. Monday morning, I dropped my bookbag in the bottom of my locker and changed into the clothes hanging from the rod. Green shorts and a gray T-shirt worn rough from too many washings, the vinyl numbers peeling away from the cotton.

Little talk in the mornings, just grunting with sore muscles, everybody rubbing sleep from their eyes. It was cold from the air-conditioning and every sound echoed off the tile floors, the steel lockers. Coach Hendrickson sat at a plastic card table in his office. Situated at the head of the locker room and separated by a clear Plexiglas partition, he could see everything. But sometimes I'd look in and watch him work too. See him study his three-ring binder and dissect film on a tablet. Scribble notes on graph paper with a pencil and sip coffee from a purple Thermos. Dark hair always perfectly combed. He never looked anything but calm. Features of a man with authority.

Coach Ellis, the strength trainer, was waiting for us on the basketball court where we warmed up. Tall and shiny bald, he always kept a whistle in his lips. I was one of the first ones there, so the gym was calm and mostly quiet.

Others slowly drifted in through the double-doors. My shoes felt loose on my feet, so I bent over to tighten the laces. Someone pushed me lightly from behind and I stumbled forward. It was Seabrook, so pale and toned you could see every curve of his muscles and the thick blue veins bulging beneath his skin. He looked like a squirrel with the hide peeled back.

"Too early for that shit."

"Ease up," Seabrook said. "I come in here to find you all poked up, you know I got to touch it. You sore at all from Friday?"

"Me?" I shook my head.

"That's right." He patted my lower back. "That's what I like to hear."

Coach Ellis blew his whistle three times and we all formed lines. Laid on the hardwood and moved silently through the stretching routine. I studied the mural over the double-doors. *Sandridge High – Home of the Stags*. A cross-eyed deer was painted above the letters, horns cartoonishly mean. We moved to the edges of the court for calisthenics. Ran high-knees, lunges, Carioca. Sweat dripped down the backs of our necks. We blew our untamed breath.

In the weight room, every wall was a mirror. The day's workout was written neatly on a little A-Frame chalkboard propped up in the corner. Leg day—squat, calf-press, power-clean, deadlift—three sets of twelve. Smell of old sweat, like spoiled tea. We paired off by size and position. The other two running backs,

Quinton and Fritz, lifted together. Fritz was a sophomore, small but easily the fastest player on the team. He wore his hair in cornrows and spoke almost as quickly as he ran, so that sometimes his mouth tripped over his voice and he stuttered. Quinton was a senior, the starting running back for two years until I somehow beat him out that summer. Hard to tackle, he had excellent balance and a devastating spin-move. The letter Q was tattooed on his forearm in dark ink, decorated with what looked like an ivy vine. He disliked me because he thought I stole something from him. His job as the starter, his pride, and in some ways, I guess, his future. I tried to push all that out of my mind and focus on myself, the role I had to fill.

I lifted with Seabrook. He played safety. We were about the same size, but he was stronger. He could tackle hard but was bad in coverage and busted a lot of plays. He didn't really understand the game and I don't think he wanted to. He didn't love it, you could tell. It was just an excuse to lift weights and hit people.

We went together to our station. A Godsmack song blared out of the stereo, the singing like a chant, guitar chords deep and driving. Seabrook loaded the squat bar with weight, ducked beneath it, and lifted it off the rack. I stood behind him with my arms wrapped around his waist and moved in unison with him as he bent his knees and drove the weight back up. I watched us in the mirror. His face turned red and his jaw shook. When he finished the set, he grunted and thrust the bar back on the rack. Shuffled immediately over to the dumbbells, picked up a pair of forty-fives, and began curling.

"Curls are not on the board," Coach Ellis called.

"I'm sculpting a masterpiece," Seabrook said.

Our shirts were mottled with sweat when we finished the workout. Seabrook took his off and flexed in the mirror. He turned back and forth, studying his body from every angle. Quinton came by us on his way out the door. "Your bitch got nice titties," he said, pointing with his thumb at Seabrook. I tried to think of something smart to say back but couldn't.

"If you worked as hard as you run your mouth, maybe you'd still be starting," Seabrook said.

Quinton sucked his teeth. "Right. Cause that's what it's all about. Ain't it, Hayes?" He walked out the door and it slammed shut behind him.

Seabrook wrapped his sweaty T-shirt around the back of his neck. "Asshole. He don't like none of us, but he especially don't like you."

"I wouldn't like me either if I was him."

"Whatever. Just keep doing you."

I nodded and we headed back to the locker room.

At the end of summer practice, a week before the first game, Coach Hendrickson taped the depth chart to the Plexiglas partition that separated his office from the rest of the locker room. Everyone lined up to see where they fit. I'd had a good summer. Worked hard, run well. Held my own against Quinton, even though he was older and more experienced. Quinton was ahead of me in the line and he saw the sheet first. I heard him laugh. It made me pay attention.

"I ain't believing this shit," he said. There were whispers down the line. Quinton turned around and came toward the back. He stopped close in front of me and leaned forward, so his face was level with mine. "You starting now, Hayes. Go figure."

I didn't say anything back. I thought he was messing with me. But when I finally got up there to the paper, I saw my name at the top of the page and swallowed hard.

I changed back into my jeans and T-shirt without showering. Boys passed cans of body spray around the locker room. Tinny music blared from cell phone speakers. Seabrook mixed a protein shake. I put my bookbag on my back and headed out into the hallway.

I had to cross the whole school to get to my Geometry classroom. I passed Lydia working the dial on her locker. She had her hair in a thick braid and the silver clasp of her fake pearl necklace glinted under the fluorescent lights. Both back pockets were ripped off her jeans, and the denim where they should've been was dark and intimidating. I worried I might stink of sweat, so I just put my head down and walked by without talking.

My seat in Geometry was in the back corner of the class under the air vent. The teacher, Mr. Farmer, was a thin man with hearing aids. He spoke in a monotone and made math sound, for the first time to me, like something that helped explain the world, not confuse it. He drew diagrams on the whiteboard and we seldom used our textbook for anything other than problem sets. I wanted to learn the shape of everything.

At lunch, I got two chili dogs and a spoonful of sweet peas on a Styrofoam tray. Sat at a round table near the middle of the cafeteria with Seabrook and his girlfriend, August. She wasn't eating anything, just chewing gum. Seabrook emptied a packet of ranch on a slice of pepperoni pizza, then topped it with hot sauce.

"Why even bother?" August said.

"Ranch is my zodiac sign."

August had recently gotten her bellybutton pierced, so she kept lifting her shirt and fidgeting with the jewel. I looked around the cafeteria to keep from staring. Hambone Daniels was sitting by himself at a table nearby. A lanky kid with dark shaggy hair and a pointed nose, he was a year older than me but in the same grade. We accidentally made eye contact. He snarled his lips and nodded. I looked away.

"Something is wrong with that boy," August said. "He gives me the creeps."

"Don't sweat the peasants," Seabrook said.

Coach Molina taught U.S. History, but he spent most of the time behind his computer, leaving the class to discuss the assigned reading. He coached both baseball and football and always insisted on being called Coach in the classroom.

I stayed in my seat and looked at my cell phone, staring down at the screen to avoid having to talk to anyone. I went to MaxPreps, the recruiting database for high school athletes, and typed in my name. A page came up with a square where there should've been a picture, but there was just the gray silhouette of a boy with a question mark over his face. All my stats were there, even from Friday's game. Every rushing yard, every touchdown, every fumble. Below that was a ranking system. I was ranked 1,943rd in the nation and 37th in the state for my position. I had to get better.

With about ten minutes left in class, Coach Molina stood up from his desk and walked to the front of the room. "Okay," he said. "All right. Let's get started." I put my phone in my pocket. The rest of the class kept talking. Coach Molina cupped his hands around his mouth. "Hey. Mark Twain to Thomas Jefferson. Strike." He clapped his hands together loud, but still no one paid him any attention.

Between the end of school and the start of practice, me and Conrad met up behind the locker room with a can of Grizzly and filled our lips with wintergreen-flavored snuff. Conrad was a senior, almost done with all his credits, so he only came to school for half a day. He had thick legs and broad shoulders. Cheeks heavy with freckles. He lifted by himself in the weight room after lunch and took Government and Economics with the other seniors last period.

We stood with our backs against the cement building, watching Coach Ellis drive around the practice field in a green utility vehicle, throwing blocking pads on the ground in stations. Conrad played right guard, so in many ways, my football fate was stitched to his. If he missed a block, I got hit hard behind the line. If he laid one, it gave me a chance to get in the open field and make us both look good. We understood this strange symbiosis without ever having to discuss it, which is why I think we got along well enough.

Conrad spat a brown glob on the sidewalk. "Got a call from the Citadel on Saturday," he said, squinting in the late afternoon sun. "Gave me an offer."

"No shit. Full ride?"

Conrad shook his head. "Preferred walk-on."

I nodded consolingly. The big schools turned out Conrad's sophomore season. They were calling all the time, sending him stuff in the mail. Then he had to have hip surgery over the off-season and came back stiff and weak in his core. The calls from recruiters quit coming, but he'd been working hard and was having a better start to the season this year.

"My parents ain't paying for school."

"I know." The snuff made me dizzy, but not sick anymore. Conrad's wanting to go to college was, I think, like my own, just more immediate. We wanted to play under the big lights, sure. Compete with the best. Get a degree. But really, there was no choice. It was the only way to go. We'd put in all that time, all that work. Every day, football was the center of mass we revolved around, and the choice come senior year, if it even was a choice at all, was play college ball or nothing, just drift loose from our unique gravity. We approached the game with a disciple's zeal and a bookkeeper's practicality.

We emptied our lips of the snuff and went inside. I changed quickly into my practice pants and jersey. Coach Ellis came in and blew his whistle three times and we all made our way to the classrooms where we watched film in the dark, offense in one classroom, defense in the other.

Coach Hendrickson stood in the back of the room behind the computer desk, playing the film and narrating the action. He referred to us only by number. He skipped over my touchdown run in the first quarter, but when he got to the play I busted in the second, he slowed the video down and replayed it three times without commenting. "Hat on a hat. Handoff is clean. What happened?"

I cleared my throat. "I felt an opening off the edge."

"Oh, you felt something."

"Yes, sir."

"Well, you felt wrong. See?" He replayed the linebacker stepping up and hitting me at the line of scrimmage. Quinton snorted behind me.

"The play call is not a suggestion, men," Coach Hendrickson said. "It is a command." He played the clip one more time, then moved on.

The practice field had a smell all its own. Cut grass, boys' sweat, hot plastic. The sky was cloudless, so light blue it was almost white. We started out in position groups, running drills. Quinton and Fritz harassed me over the busted play.

"He skipped my touchdown," I said. "But I know y'all didn't forget about that."

"Shit," Quinton said. "Anybody could've scored on that play. I could've run backwards into the end zone."

At the end of practice, Coach Ellis blew his whistle three times and we all gathered in a tight circle at midfield, helmets off. We locked arms and Coach Hendrickson said the Lord's Prayer. *Our Father, which art in Heaven, hallowed be thy Name.*

In the parking lot, bugs hovered around the streetlamps and a sunset wind blew through the lot. Seabrook was showing off his new fishing rod, casting a white rubber worm across the asphalt. A group of guys were gathered around Quinton's Chevrolet Impala, listening to a song bump from his new speakers.

Conrad drove me home. We kept the windows down and the radio on and didn't talk much. Commercial for a car dealership. Commercial for the county boat show.

Mom was at the house when I got there, sitting cross-legged on the floor in front of the television. She was watching *Wheel of Fortune*, a plate of half-eaten food in front of her. A lamp was on, but mostly the house was dark, and it smelled of cooked onions and peppers. "Takes one to know one," Mom said to the television. "Takes one to know one."

I dropped my bookbag by the door.

"I made spaghetti," Mom said. "Couldn't wait to eat though."

She was wearing her scrubs, but I wasn't sure whether she was coming off a shift or getting ready to go on. I went to the kitchen to fix a plate. The spaghetti sat on the stove in a disposable aluminum pan, topped with slices of Kraft cheese. Beside the stove was an open bag of premixed salad and a bottle of red wine vinegar. I fixed a plate of mostly spaghetti and a little bit of lettuce. Went back to the front room and sat on the couch. There was a new puzzle on the screen.

"Empire State Building."

"That's too many letters," I said.

"Shit," Mom said. "You're right. You're too good at this."

"Just count the squares," I said. "It's right there."

We started practice on Wednesday by watching film on our opponents. Gadsden's defense was impressive. Their best player, the outside linebacker, Fifty-Six, looked even better on film than I expected. He blitzed just about every play. His timing was excellent, and he almost never missed a tackle. A brown beard hung out of his facemask.

"He will be playing college ball next year," Coach Hendrickson said. "No doubt about it. But we will rise to the challenge. He can be beat."

The practice field was covered in goose shit. We installed a new play where I ran a short passing route out of the backfield and the quarterback hit me with the pass over the middle. The football felt warm and moist in my hands when I caught it, a newly born thing.

The play was a decoy to draw Fifty-Six into pass coverage. Keep him honest. At the same time, a wide receiver was running a deep route, and the idea was that if we ran the play a few different times, eventually he would come open for a big gain. Coach Hendrickson named it 341 Hatch. We ran it eight times against the scout team defense. No contact, but it was obvious I was going to take a hard lick if all went as planned. Most probably from Fifty-Six himself.

The second string came on for their reps and the first string jogged to the sideline. I went to the water cart with Conrad and Seabrook.

"How you like playing tackling dummy?" Conrad said.

"It's a smart play."

A flock of geese came flying over the field, squawking.

"Especially if you ain't the one getting hit," Seabrook said.

That night when I got home, Mom wasn't there. I ate leftover spaghetti standing at the kitchen counter. Stuck my dirty plate and fork in the sink. I took a scalding hot shower, got two bags of frozen lima beans from the freezer, and lay down in my bed with one bag on either side of my ribs. The bruises were turning black. I stared up at the wooden slats on the bunk above me and rehearsed the new play in my head. A few minutes later, my cell phone started ringing. It was Lydia. I let it ring a couple times before I answered.

"Hello?"

"Can you use Comet to clean the toilet bowl?" she asked.

"I think Mom does."

"Ronald don't even wipe his feet at the door." She always called her dad by his first name.

"I feel like our house could use a clean," I said. "It don't look dirty though."

"That's the worst kind."

I bit my thumbnail. I could hear the noise of wire rubbing against porcelain through the phone. "Got a game Friday."

"So I heard."

"Y'all tow the peanut cart to away games?"

"God, I hope not."

I heard the phone hit the floor, the toilet flush. I rearranged the lima beans on my ribs. The feeling was going from burning to numb.

"Hello?" Lydia said.

"I'm here."

"I could come just to watch."

"Yeah."

"You wouldn't know either way."

"I'd know."

"Well, toilet's halfway clean."

"Glad I could help. Maybe I'll see you tomorrow."

She laughed. "Yeah. Maybe you'll speak."

I didn't know what to say back.

"Bye," Lydia said.

"Night." I hung up the phone and stayed laying there in the bed a little while longer, letting the frozen beans work on my bruises. I thought about what I'd said on the phone and tried to come up with better ways to say it, or just better things to say generally. I imagined Lydia walking around their trailer in her underwear. I wondered if her thighs were the same dark tan as her neck. I pictured her stretching for something on a high shelf and her T-shirt riding up her back, exposing the sweet skin just above her panty line. I reached down and squeezed myself gently. Started rubbing. But it felt all wrong in my head, wanting her that way. Dangerous and against the rules, even if it was possible, like passing a slow car on a double yellow line.

I got out of bed and went to the kitchen. Tossed the lima beans back in the freezer, washed my dirty dishes, dried them with a rag, and put them away in the cabinet where they belonged.

I woke up the first time my alarm went off Friday morning. Dressed in Wrangler jeans and pulled my jersey on over my head. Rolled the sleeves up, just above the elbow. I got my Wolverines from out of the closet and pulled them on my feet. Laced them up through all the eyes and tied them with double knots. I wore them every game day because Dad once told me that a man in boots looks like he has a purpose.

We didn't lift on game days, just stretched for longer than normal and sat in our lockers, sipping water. The whole day was nothing but biding time. Everything calm and regimented to make up for the nervousness. Staying rested and hydrated. Getting ready to pour it all out come kickoff.

My locker was right was beside Quinton's. We both usually made it a point not to be there at the same time if we could help it, but on game days, it was hard. Him and Fritz were squeezed into his locker together, listening to music on Fritz's cell phone.

"Play that one y'all were listening to last week," I said.

"F-F-Fuck you," Fritz said. "This ain't all request hour."

"Come on."

"Learn the name," Quinton said. "Then talk to me."

In fourth period, Coach Molina was even more jittery than usual. It was obvious he couldn't lecture or even speak coherently at all. He played us a fictional movie about a secret mission during the Vietnam War.

"We ain't even got through Reconstruction yet," somebody said.

"Time is an ocean," Coach Molina said, turning out the lights.

✣

After school came the worst part of waiting. From the locker room, you could hear the cheerleaders and the marching band in the hallway, laughing. We sat in our lockers, taping our joints, cleaning our cleats with toilet paper. There were no windows to the outside. No way to tell the time other than to check your cell phone, and even then, it was like you couldn't remember. You had to just keep checking and checking.

"You look nervous," Quinton said. "You ready for that new play? Hatch?"

I nodded.

"That linebacker going to fuck you crooked."

"We'll see."

"Sure will," Quinton said.

I went to the bathroom to check my bruises in the mirror. My ribs were still discolored. I pushed on them hard with my fingers and it didn't hurt much. I pulled down my jeans and looked at my hip. The mark there was almost gone, and it wasn't tender at all. When I got back to my locker, Quinton was gone and Conrad was sitting in his place.

"How much longer?" I asked.

"I don't know. I think I heard the buses pull up."

"I wish we could just play now."

"There's going to be recruiters there, Grady."

"There's always recruiters."

Conrad shook his head. "More than normal. They come to all Gadsden's games now. To watch Fifty-Six."

I patted his shoulder. "It's just another game."

Conrad went back to his locker and I changed into my uniform. Checked my phone again. I had a message from Dad, like every Friday during football season. It was our most constant communication.

Good luck. Play mean.

THX

I stashed the phone on the top shelf of my locker. A few minutes later, Coach Ellis blew his whistle three times near the back door. We all stood up and marched in a line carrying our shoulder pads and helmets to the parking lot, where two yellow school buses waited for us, coughing up diesel fumes. *McCleod County School District* stenciled in black down the sides. I walked up the stairs and nodded to the driver. It was two to every seat, filled back to front. I squeezed into a seat against the window and Fritz pushed in beside me. He had earbuds in and didn't speak. We arranged our gear between our knees.

Coach Molina was the last one on our bus. He stood at the front, looking back at us, dark sunglasses covering his eyes. "Hold on, magnolia," he said. "Hold on."

The swinging doors closed and we pulled away.

III.

The lights at Gadsden were dull and the field was poorly manicured. Holes worn in the turf, bleachers on the visitors' side made of wood. Our marching band sat in their tattered uniforms like chickens waiting for a rain. During the pregame warmup, music played on the PA system. Kid Rock clumsily rapping about all his heroes at the methadone clinic.

Gadsden wore burgundy jerseys with black pants and made a show of tearing through a paper banner and running through a tunnel of cheerleaders. Things we never did, even during homecoming, because it was against Coach Hendrickson's philosophy. He didn't even make speeches. We just huddled on the sideline in our white jerseys with green numbers and prayed the Lord's Prayer, our elbows interlocked.

"This is what we have prepared for, men," he said at the end. "Now, let's execute."

We grunted in agreement and broke out of the huddle. Spread

along the edge of the field. I looked to the stands. Marcus was there, alone at the top of the bleachers, easy to spot in the crowd at his size. I saw Lydia with two other girls I didn't know. Couldn't find Mom, but folks were still wandering in.

The weather was humid and no wind blew. I sweated lightly under my pads. The sun was just starting to set as the clock on the scoreboard ticked down to five minutes until kickoff. Smell of popcorn and mud, the feel of grass beneath my cleats. It made me less nervous than I'd been in the locker room and on the bus.

Conrad came up beside me carrying his helmet in his right hand. "See any recruiters? Can you tell them apart?"

I shook my head. "It doesn't matter. Just execute. They'll see."

He nodded. Seabrook approached from my other side. He was wearing his helmet, but he had it unstrapped. "Ready to bust some fucking heads," he said, punching my shoulder pad with his fist.

A voice came over the PA and asked everyone to stand for the national anthem. The song played, people clapped, and then Coach Hendrickson walked onto the field for the coin toss. As he came back to the sideline, he shouted for the receiving team, and they trotted out. All that time healing, preparing, waiting, now here it was, simple as anything. Handshakes, coin flip, a few words spoken.

Fritz was the kick returner. He stood with his heels on the edge of the end zone. At the opposite side of the field, the Gadsden kicker arranged the football on the kicking tee. The other players lined up alongside the ball. The kicker backed up a few yards and measured his approach. He held up his hand, took three exaggerated steps, and booted the ball into the air. The rest of the team started running, following the ball's trajectory. Fritz caught it cleanly and made a nice return before he was tackled. The small crowd clapped. Our band played a tune. Fritz stood up, tossed the ball to the referee in his striped shirt, and came jogging to the sideline. I pulled my helmet over my head, strapped it up, and stepped onto the field.

The first play call was simple, a run behind Conrad. I didn't even look at the defense, just took the handoff and tucked it into my chest like a secret. Conrad laid a clean block and I ran for a short gain before I was tackled. It felt good to hit the ground, to feel another person's weight on top of me. I jumped up and went to the huddle. The next play was another run, this time to the opposite side. We took our positions. I surveyed the defense to find Fifty-Six. He was in a good spot to make the tackle. I didn't look at his face, just his body, those numbers stitched on his jersey. He wore black armbands around both biceps. I stared at his chest and envisioned hitting him so hard his pads fell apart and his breastbone split open. Standing over him, looking down at his insides.

I took the handoff and Fifty-Six read the play perfectly. He stepped into the hole to tackle me. I ran straight for him, lowered my shoulder, and drove my feet. He squatted, grabbed me around my waist, and let my momentum carry me over his shoulder. We fell together. No gain. His beard brushed against my arm. He stood up before I could and held out his hand. I took it and he pulled me up off the ground. Then he headbutted my facemask and ran to his huddle without a word. I returned to mine, slightly dizzy. Coach Hendrickson signaled for a pass play. I stayed in to block. Fifty-Six came on a blitz from the right. I blocked him, but the quarterback had to rush the pass and it fell incomplete. The punt team came on and I jogged to the sideline, past Coach Hendrickson. He didn't speak, just nodded his head.

I scanned the stands and still didn't see Mom. Lydia was

peeling the wrapper off a piece of candy. Marcus took a bump from his pint of Wild Turkey 101 and slipped it back in his pocket.

Conrad came from behind me and handed me a water bottle. I turned back to the field and took a sip. It tasted like bleach.

"That's a mean motherfucker."

"He can be beat," I said.

The defense stopped Gadsden and they had to punt. Our next drive started with decent field position. The sky grew dark and the moon rose behind the home bleachers. The crowd was quiet but for chatter.

First play, I ran a counter away from Fifty-Six for a solid gain. Then Coach Hendrickson called a play-action pass, which gained a first down. The next play was same one I'd messed up the week before, and I swore to myself to run it as called, regardless of the defense. On the snap, Conrad threw a nice block and I ran behind him. I got across midfield before Fifty-Six came in from the side and hit me hard in my bruised ribs, leading with his helmet. The pain felt cleansing. I lay on my back, ball in the crook of my arm, and took a deep, difficult breath. Blind bats swarmed around the floodlights, picking bugs. It felt like I could hear their wings beating. All week, I'd been nursing my ribs for that moment. Not so they wouldn't hurt, but so they wouldn't break. Break me. I stood up and jogged to the huddle.

"You good?" Conrad asked.

"Hell of a block."

He slapped me tenderly on the helmet.

The next play was a quarterback run. I blocked. Punched a defender hard in the armpit and watched him wince. We picked up the first down. I had climbed to a rare space I could only seem to find on game days. No care for worldly concerns, only run fast, inflict pain. Another rush up the middle. Fifty-Six charged through the line and tackled me for a short loss. Quinton came onto the field and pointed me to the sideline. I jogged off.

"Got to keep you fresh," Coach Ellis said.

I stood beside him with my helmet still on and strapped up. The defense stopped us twice and we had to punt. I stayed beside Coach Ellis, not talking, just watching the movements of the game, impatient to get back on the field.

Gadsden was moving the ball well. They completed a long pass and the receiver made it past the forty-five-yard line before Seabrook finally tackled him. A collective shout of acknowledgement came from the Gadsden bleachers and their cheerleaders went streaking down the sideline, legs glimmering from across the field.

The next play was a run for another big gain. I felt useless standing there, watching them drive down the field. More than anything, I wanted the ball back in my hands. To be in control. They ran another good pass play, taking them into the red zone, about to score. Coach Molina ran six steps onto the field. I could tell he felt as helpless and angry as I did.

"Hey," he screamed, getting the defensive players to look at him. "Unite is to bury," he called. "Unite is to bury."

Whether that was a play or just something he thought was inspirational I'm not sure, but the defense made a stand and Gadsden was forced to kick a field goal. We went down 3-0.

The stakes for that game against Gadsden were no higher than any other. That's not to say they were low, only that the stakes were always high. We had a decent team and played eleven games a season. Winning was not an achievement, but an expectation.

Coach Hendrickson called the offense together before we took the field. He looked at his play sheet. "All right, men," he said. "Need a good drive here. We've got to move the football." He called the first three plays of the drive. The second one was the new play, 341 Hatch.

We broke the huddle and ran onto the field. My helmet sat heavy as a stone on my neck. I heard nothing but the sound of boiling blood in my ears. My muscles tingled. I took the first handoff and bolted straight up the middle. Hit the boy who tried to tackle me hard with the crown of my helmet and drove through him for a short gain, a mere formality.

It was called with nonchalance, but I had a sense that 341 Hatch was a fulcrum the game would rest upon. It would reveal whether Fifty-Six could truly be beaten. Whether Coach Hendrickson really knew as much as I wanted to believe.

I lined up in the backfield. When the center snapped the ball, I ran my route as fast as I could. Palms open, breathing heavy. Fifty-Six covered me, just like he was supposed to. He stayed a couple yards away, giving me a cushion. I looked back for the pass and the ball was there, already thrown. I reached out my hands and squeezed it in my fingertips. Pulled it into my chest and bent my knees for impact, which came as expected. Hard. Facemask to earhole. I went to the ground and Fifty-Six landed on top of me. I could feel his lungs throbbing. The whole thing went exactly as Coach Hendrickson had anticipated, and as I stood up and trotted back to the huddle, I had a feeling of being as solid and efficient as metal.

Next play was a counter away from Fifty-Six. The blocking was pristine. I outran the middle linebacker, stiff-armed another would-be tackler, and sprinted up the sideline. Sixty yards, not even daring to look back. Just running wide open, breeze blowing in through my facemask until I hit the end zone. I sucked in that special air as our marching band played a song with heavy cymbals. No sound from the PA system. The Gadsden stands were quiet. Conrad came running up the field with his arms raised. We jumped toward each other and bumped chests.

"That's right," Conrad said. "Give 'em something to see."

We jogged to the sideline. I looked to the bleachers and Marcus held up his thumb. Lydia was laughing happily. Mom had finally gotten there. She was sitting with the group of other mothers, earrings glinting in the light. They were all clapping.

"I swear you're faster on Fridays," Conrad said.

I didn't respond because I didn't want to dirty the atmosphere with words. I went to the edge of the field and watched our kicking team prepare to concede the football in what seemed at that moment a gesture of supreme justice. Sweat dripping down my legs, I reached down the front of my pants and adjusted my girdle. The kicker struck the ball and I watched it soar through the night, like everyone in that pitiful stadium, tracing a single rock's movement through space.

The kick returner caught the ball and ran up the middle of the field before slanting toward our sideline. He juked a kid. Broke a tackle. I could see the tendons working under his skin. Muscles moving. The beauty of the ball and all its gravity had transferred to the boy. He crossed the thirty and it seemed he was running directly toward me on the sideline. Closer and closer he came. I couldn't move my eyes or my feet. Would not. I just watched. Saw his lips quivering like a catfish's with each step, each breath, until he was so close, I could have reached out and touched him.

Then there was a collision—the noise reached me before anything else—and the boy was on me with all his beautiful momentum. Another came with him. Even through the chaos, I realized this was Seabrook, finally making the tackle. They crashed into my legs there on the sideline and I heard another noise, only this one came from inside of me, like the crunch of a bicycle chain slipping from its gears. I fell to the ground and standing bodies parted. My left leg hurt like hell. It felt heavy. I couldn't move it. Seabrook and the kick returner lay on the ground beside me. They stood up and moved away. A horde of faceless helmets looked down on me. The pain in my leg was not cleansing. I howled. Coach Ellis appeared amongst the helmets, bald head shining, and asked me if I could move. Then Conrad was there too. The freckles on his face seemed to swirl. He and Coach Ellis grabbed me under my arms and drug me away from the field, behind the bench.

"What happened?" Conrad said.

"You've got to pay attention," Coach Ellis said.

I sat on the grass against the chain-link fence that separated the playing field from the outside world. Pain was radiating up my leg to my hip. I was dazed with it. I felt cold, like the sweat on me was starting to freeze. Then from somewhere behind me, I heard Mom's voice. She must've run down from the bleachers. "Is he okay?"

"He's fine," Coach Ellis said. "Please stay in your seat. I'll have the trainer take a look."

"Are you okay, Grady?"

"I think so."

Coach Ellis walked away, and I didn't hear Mom anymore. Conrad stayed squatting beside me, not talking, until I heard Coach Hendrickson call for the offense.

"Make sure you get Quinton," I said.

Conrad nodded and left. My knee was the source of the pain, I could tell, but it was running all the way up the side of my body, into my teeth. They started to chatter. I had a bad grasp on time and its passing.

I watched the backs of my teammates, identifying each of them by their number. Listened to the noises on the field, trying to determine what was happening, but it was hard to focus. All I could hear was incoherent shouting and whistles. The trainer approached. I'd never spoken to him. I always believed if I could ignore his presence, I could ignore the need for him there at all. He wore a green polo shirt and had gel in his hair. Knelt beside me and asked what was wrong. I gestured to my leg.

"Your knee?"

I nodded my head.

The trainer put his hands around my shoulders and guided me into a prone position on my back beside the fence, sending currents of pain through my bones. He picked up my leg and bent my knee toward my chest. I growled.

"That hurt?"

I nodded again. I still had my helmet on.

"How bad?"

"Real bad."

"One to ten."

"Fucking bad."

He tilted my leg to the side and straightened it out. I screamed again. Piss leaked from my bladder.

Another voice came from beyond the fence. "Quit screwing with him." It was Marcus.

The trainer laid my leg down easily and stood up. Moved out of my sight. "I don't feel any damage to the ligaments," I heard him say. "I think he's sprained his knee."

"Too bad you're no fucking doctor," Marcus said. "We're taking him to the hospital."

"I don't think that's necessary. Regardless, you're going to need to wait until halftime."

"Says who?" Marcus's voice had an edge I hadn't heard before.

"It's fine," I said from the ground.

"You sure?"

I leaned up on my elbows and looked over at him. He was clutching the chain-link fence. "Yeah," I said. "Till halftime."

Marcus nodded and went back to his seat. The trainer walked away. I looked into the stands for Lydia. She was watching me, hands in her lap, biting her bottom lip. I hoped she hadn't heard me holler. When I saw a person injured at a game on TV, it seemed heroic. The camera cut to their face, the crowd became silent, the other players kneeled. But I didn't feel heroic at all looking at Lydia. I felt shame on several levels, and above all, pain that was making it hard to think in sentences.

The trainer returned and handed me a plastic bag of ice. "Put this where it hurts," he said.

At halftime, we were up 14-6. I don't know how we scored the second touchdown. Conrad and Seabrook came over to check on me on their way to the locker room.

"Real sorry, bro," Seabrook said. The black paste he wore under his eyes had run with sweat and dotted with pieces of grass.

"Not your fault."

Conrad was scanning the bleachers.

"They're going to see you," I said. "Just keep working. They see everything."

He nodded. "You'll feel better by Monday. Can't nothing keep you down." Then he and Seabrook ran together down the sideline.

A few minutes later, the trainer came driving across the field in a green utility vehicle. I was still cold, but the pain had become almost manageable if I held very still and didn't think about it.

The trainer pulled up beside me and climbed down from the vehicle. "Think you can stand?" he asked.

I held out my hand. He took it and helped heft me up off the ground. I used only my right leg, leaving the left one to dangle, but when I got stood up and the blood started moving around, my knee felt like an overripe fruit about to bust. I gritted my teeth and leaned against the trainer. "Now what?"

"Just lay down in the bed."

He opened the tailgate and I sat down on it. Planted my hands on the steel and prepared to hoist myself back. "Pick up my leg," I said. "Hold it steady."

I finally got situated and he closed the tailgate. We drove across the field, into the parking lot. Some people in the home stands looked at me. Arranged their faces concernedly. Most didn't notice. The smell of exhaust coming from the tailpipe made me want to puke. My teeth chattered louder. When we rode over the curb in the parking lot, a noise escaped me, and more piss. I hoped it wouldn't show through my pants.

"What's the car look like?"

"Green Jeep Wrangler," I said.

He found it quickly. Mom and Marcus were waiting with the motor cranked and the doors open. The trainer pulled up beside them and switched off his vehicle. I sat up and looked blankly into the Jeep.

"I guess you're going to have to ride up front," Marcus said. "I don't know what else."

"Are you sure we shouldn't get an ambulance?" Mom asked.

"No," I said.

The trainer lowered the tailgate and helped me out of the bed of the utility vehicle. I tried to put some weight on my left leg, but it wouldn't hold me. I almost fell.

"You're going to have to help out a little bit," the trainer said to me.

"Could you be any more useless?" Marcus said. He pushed the trainer out of the way. Put one arm around my shoulders, one behind my legs, and lifted me off the ground. When my knee was forced to bend, I groaned again. I couldn't control the things that were coming out of me. The pain now was worse than the collision on the sideline. I put my knuckles in my mouth and bit down. Marcus placed me in the passenger seat and closed the door. I still had all my pads on, but I'd left my helmet on the field. I leaned my head against the glass, closed my eyes, and saw pure black.

When I opened my eyes again, Mom was behind the wheel, Marcus was in the backseat, and we were on the highway. I could feel the vibration of the tires on the asphalt, the steel body of the Jeep shaking in the wind. I couldn't stop my teeth clicking together.

"We've got to get gas," Mom said.

"Christ," Marcus said.

"I know, but we'll run out."

I felt the Jeep slow down. When Mom made the turn into the gas station parking lot, my knee bumped against the dash. I bit down on my knuckles again. The light over the gas pumps shined through the windshield and I could feel the heat on my skin. Mom got out and began to fill the tank.

Marcus leaned in from the back seat. I smelled the bourbon on his breath. "Are you making that teeth sound on purpose?"

"I don't know."

When we finally got to the emergency room, Mom parked in front of the electric doors and went inside. She came back out with a man wearing blue scrubs, hair cut in a speckled gray mullet. He looked into the car, then went back inside. Returned rolling a wheelchair. He knocked on the window where I was leaning.

"About to open up," he said. "Don't fall out."

I leaned the other direction and he pulled the door open.

"Hey, brother. You're here." He smelled like men's deodorant and disinfectant. "It's almost over now."

Marcus climbed out of the backseat and stood beside the nurse. They mumbled to each other, then I felt a warm hand on my upper arm.

"Ease back."

They helped me out of the Jeep and into the wheelchair.

"I'm taking him straight to a room," the nurse said. "Y'all can give them his information at the desk."

He wheeled me through the sliding glass doors and down a long white hallway. We turned a corner and passed the nurses' station. My hands felt like they were shriveling up, like I'd kept them under water for too long.

"What position do you play?"

"Running back," I said.

"Birds of a feather. I played running back in college." He patted my right shoulder pad. "It's a rite of passage, this. We'll get you patched up." He led me into a room and helped me into the bed. I sat on the edge while he unstrapped my shoulder pads and helped me pull them over my head. I laid down and he lifted my hurt leg, moved it onto the bed, and propped it up on spare pillows. He took scissors from the counter and carefully cut through my pants and kneepad, exposing my pain to the cold air. I didn't look down. He covered my torso with a blanket.

"Just sit tight now. The hardest part is over. I'm going to go check on your people, make sure they've got all the paperwork filled out. When I come back, I'll have something to ease the pain."

He left and I closed my eyes. The hurt was becoming bearable again, idling at a reasonable frequency. My teeth were still chattering, but only a little. I pulled the blanket up over my chin.

Mom and Marcus came in quietly sometime later. I didn't open my eyes. Mom took my left hand and held it. "I'm so sorry," she said.

Marcus tapped the toe of his boot on the tile floor.

The nurse came back a minute later, whistling. I opened my eyes and pulled my hand away from Mom.

"You're all set up in the system," he said. "Now I can give you the good stuff." He tapped the syringe sticking out of his breast pocket and smiled. He retrieved the scissors from the counter and cut my pants even further up my leg. Wiped an area of my thigh with an alcohol pad, then pulled the syringe from his pocket. He took off the cap and flushed out the air. A drop of medicine dribbled down the needle. "Here comes the bee sting," he said. "Doling out nectar."

I didn't feel the stick, but I felt the medicine flow in cold and spread.

"What is that you gave him?" Marcus asked.

"Dilaudid."

Within seconds, I felt the medicine go from cold to hot. Blood warming, lungs expanding, muscles relaxing. My teeth quit chattering. I closed my eyes and listened to the nurse shuffle around the room, talking quietly to Mom and Marcus, taking my blood pressure, wiping my face clean with a rag. I kept my eyes closed the whole time, fading almost into sleep, but not quite. The pain in my knee waned slowly like a late-morning dream. Its absence was the best thing I'd ever felt. Better than a touchdown run. I forgot to be scared. Forgot to be ashamed.

"Thank you," I mumbled.

"It won't last forever," the nurse said. "But it'll get you through tonight."

IV.

Six days I laid in the bottom bunk of my bed, leg wrapped in an Ace bandage. Got up only to travel to the orthopedic clinic. I rode in the backseat of Mom's Jeep, stretched sideways across the bench. Anytime we hit a pothole, pain like a pointed jackhammer hit my knee and echoed all the way up the side of my body. I cussed from deep in the back of my throat, like I was hocking up the hurt. Mom never got on to me. She just turned the radio up loud, even it if it was just a morning show with stupid jokes or an advertisement for a DUI lawyer or whatever.

The doctors couldn't figure out what was wrong with my knee. X-rays didn't show a break and evaluations didn't make them think I had any torn ligaments. All anybody seemed to know was what I could have told them myself. It was swollen up big as a basketball and hurt anytime I tried to move it.

My bedroom was hot and musty. Crotch and armpits stayed

sticky with sweat. My only baths were wiping down with a soapy washcloth. I took the pain medication they gave me in the Emergency Room every four hours. Lortab. Kept the bottle under my pillow in between. It seemed to dull the pain a little bit, loosen the muscles in my neck, behind my eyeballs. I ran through the first bottle in about five days, but Mom went to the pharmacy and got another. She told me not to worry, to take it when I needed it. She told me not to let myself get miserable, but even with the pills, I didn't really have a choice.

Marcus took my football equipment back to the school and picked up my clothes, bookbag, and cell phone. He and Mom sat with me between shifts, often wearing their uniforms. I made them keep the blinds closed.

Lydia called a couple times, but I didn't answer. I was embarrassed, and I could hardly talk coherently through the pain and the medicine haze. I slept more than I thought was possible and watched shitty daytime television on a little set Marcus hooked up for me on the floor. I began to measure time by shows. *The Price is Right* meant it was between eleven and one. *According to Jim* meant it was somewhere between three and five.

One afternoon Marcus came by with a plastic five-gallon bucket, his forearms all sunburnt. He took the lid off my empty aquarium and dumped the contents of the bucket inside. Murky water and two largemouth bass, each dark green with a jagged black stripe down its side. "To keep you company when I ain't here," he said.

"Where'd you get them from?"

"The lake."

"How the hell am I supposed to feed them?"

"Bugs. I'll do it when I come." He took the bucket to the bathroom and started filling it with water from the shower. "It ain't

48

good for recovery to be sitting alone in the dark like this," Marcus hollered. "You need to be stimulated."

"You're a doctor now."

"I got the internet, fuckhead. I know you need stimulation like fertilizer, you're trying to heal."

"I'm trying to watch TV, but you won't shut up."

"That's no good either." He came back in and dumped the shower water in the tank. "I got some magazines for you in the truck. You need to read and shit."

Aggravating as Marcus was with all his internet remedies, being alone was worse. I hated myself for getting hurt. Not even on the field, but beside it. I deserved to suffer. I deserved whatever shit they were talking about me at school.

It was Friday again when they finally figured out what was wrong with me. A full week gone by, just floating on pills and pain. The doctor was a man named Hughes, the third one I'd seen. He was gray-haired and pale-skinned with busted blood vessels all over his nose. Wore loafers without socks. His exam room was decorated with soccer posters. It took countless X-rays and two MRIs, but he finally discovered my bone was broken. Femur, two places, through the growth plate and across my knee joint. I was lying on his exam table when he told me, staring up at the drop-tile ceiling. Mom stood beside me, her hand on my shoulder.

"It's pretty rare," Hughes said. "Outside of automobile accidents. That's why it took so long to find. But your growth plate was just beginning to close. It was brittle. And you took a lick in just the right place. It's almost like a miracle," he said. "Or whatever the opposite of that is."

Me and Mom didn't say anything.

"But this is good news, actually," Hughes said. "Considering the alternatives. Ligaments have to be surgically repaired. Bones, often, do not."

He and his assistant put me in a fiberglass cast from my toes up to my groin. They both groaned and sweated as they did it, talking the whole time about how long and heavy my leg was.

With the cast on, the pain subsided, but I still couldn't put any weight on the fracture, else I'd disturb the healing. I went home with another prescription for Lortab, refillable for a year, and instructions to stay in bed with my leg propped up above my heart as often as possible.

The team was playing Pineville that night. All week, I'd been thinking about the game. I was ashamed to admit it, but I was hoping they would lose without me. I knew that wasn't right, but I needed vindication. I never said it out loud to anyone, but I whispered it in my head over and over again like a prayer, trying to will it to happen.

That evening lying in bed, Dad texted me like normal to say good luck. He didn't even know I'd gotten hurt. I didn't respond. Just dropped my phone on the floor and let the pills rock me to a restless sleep.

I woke up in the middle of the night, house quiet. I could hear the wind moving through the trees outside, frogs squalling in the ditch. I picked up my phone and the light from the screen made me squint. Messages from Conrad and Seabrook. It was the first time they had texted me all week. I didn't even open the messages. I couldn't fall back asleep, so I turned on the TV and flipped through the channels until I found a black and white Western. Halfway over, but those things ain't hard to follow.

✤

Saturday morning, Mom was off work. She drove down to Henry's and came back with two sausage biscuits and fried potatoes in a Styrofoam container. Bottle of Pepsi and a newspaper. She wore a T-shirt and a pink baseball cap with her ponytail threaded through the back. Makeup on from the day before. She probably hadn't slept since her last shift. She sat on the edge of my bed and we shared breakfast from the box. She flipped through the news pages to the sports section. Pulled it out of the stack and handed it to me. "Figured you'd want to see the score and all."

I turned to the third page, where the high school games were listed. Sandridge 32, Pineville 28. Quinton had a huge game. Over a hundred yards and two touchdowns. Pineville's defense was weak, anyway. "They won."

"Oh, good," Mom said through a mouthful of potato.

I dropped the paper on the floor and picked up my phone. Read the text from Conrad first. *We won. Wsh u wuz here.*

Then the text from Seabrook. *Sry again man. We won. Gone do r best wid out u.*

I turned the screen off and put my phone on the bed beside me. Took a bite of my biscuit. "You off all day?"

"Thank god. I was sleeping on my feet last night. Stomach bug's going around. It's like an orchestra of vomit walking down the halls."

I looked at her with my biscuit in my hand.

She laughed and stood up from the bed. "Sorry." She picked the newspaper up off the floor and started cleaning up some of the other trash that had started piling up too. Gatorade and soda bottles. Cardboard Hot Pocket sleeves. "You want to sit outside this afternoon?"

"For what?" I took one last bite of biscuit and dropped in in the container. "Take this too," I said. "I'm done."

She took the container. "Get some sun on your bones."

"I'm good."

"You going to watch the college games?"

"Probably."

"Okay. Just let me know. I'm yours all day." She walked to the kitchen. I heard her stuffing trash in the can.

"Hey," I yelled. "Dad texted me yesterday." I picked up my cast with my hands and shifted it over in the bed to try and get more comfortable, but it didn't feel any better. "I just remembered."

"What for?"

"About the game. You didn't tell him?"

Her footsteps shook the floor. She came to the door and leaned against the frame. "I forgot."

"What do you mean, you forgot?"

"To tell him. Why don't you just tell him now?"

"It's your *job*."

"No, it's not. He's *your* father. Just answer him back."

"He'll be mad."

"For what?"

"Just tell him. Please."

She adjusted the bill of her hat and scratched her arm. "Okay," she said. "For you." She turned and went back to the kitchen.

Since I'd gotten hurt, she'd been saying stuff like that. Making herself out to be a martyr. It pissed me off. Everything pissed me off.

At noon, I turned ESPN on the TV. Popped another pain pill. Ohio State was playing Syracuse. I watched the first half, but not closely. It seemed less urgent than before, like reading the manual for a machine you don't have. Like watching *The Price is Right* on a Tuesday during school hours.

❧

Meemaw called later and said she was coming over to see me. Mom brought me a rag to wipe down with. Sprayed my hair with dry shampoo and handed me a comb. I brushed my hair back blindly.

"That's better," Mom said. "But you really need to shave. You're getting little wisps."

I felt my face get hot. I'd never shaved before. "Come on," I said.

"I'm serious. You don't feel them? It's just a few long hairs dangling off your chin and your neck." She made a face and shook her head like it disgusted her.

"Okay," I said.

Mom walked away and came back a few minutes later holding one of Dad's old battery-powered razors she found in her bathroom and a plastic mixing bowl from the kitchen. She handed me the bowl first. "Hold this under your chin," she said. Then she handed me the razor. "Just run this all over your face."

I flicked the switch and the razor started vibrating in my hand. "I don't need any shaving cream or anything?"

"Not with an electric razor. I don't think so."

I nodded and started to buzz the razor along my neck. Over my lip and down my chin. I didn't have a mirror, so I couldn't really tell what I was doing.

"Hit your right cheek again," Mom said. "You missed a spot."

When I was done, she went back to her bathroom and came back with a bottle of lotion. She squirted some in my hand and I rubbed it over my face. It smelled like rotten flowers.

"Does it burn?" Mom asked.

"Not really."

✢

Meemaw brought me a Ziploc bag full of homemade chocolate chip cookies and a thick paperback book full of crossword puzzles. Her gray hair was curled meticulously. She wore a men's dress shirt unbuttoned over a white T-shirt, and brown shoes with gold buckles. Mom brewed a pot of coffee and they came to my room with cups. There wasn't any place to sit, so they just stood around, looking at me, slurping their coffee.

"You got fish in that tank?" Meemaw asked.

"Bass. Marcus brought them."

"What an angel."

I laughed. "That's one big angel."

Meemaw hid a smile and took a sip of her coffee.

"You want me to pull in a chair from the kitchen?" Mom asked.

"I'm fine standing," Meemaw said. "Prefer it, actually."

I looked at her feet. They were swelling out the tops of her shoes. "How's Shorty?"

"He's Shorty. Same as ever. Getting pickier though, to where now he don't even want to eat pork twice in the same week, not even different cuts like a chop and a loin. I said, 'What are you, turning Jewish? You go to the store then. You cook.' But he don't, of course. That's about the extent of his changing, his whole activity really. Just bitching." She scratched the back of her hand. "We been praying for you, though, darling. Both of us."

"Thanks," I said.

Meemaw walked to the fish tank and tapped on the glass. The bass swam to the surface and the water made a small noise as it broke. "Can you go back to school now?"

"Not yet," Mom said. "He's supposed to stay in bed as much as he can. The bone's fragile while it heals."

"Going to get awful far behind."

Mom rolled her eyes. "He's smart."

"Even still," Meemaw said.

✤

Dad was angry when Mom called him that night, like I knew he would be. I couldn't hear what he was saying, but Mom had on the timid voice she used only for him, when he was yelling. Meemaw was gone but Marcus was there. He'd come over after work with a twelve-pack of Natural Light, shirt untucked, fireman's badge gleaming over his breast. He yanked the blinds up and dropped a handful of writhing nightcrawlers in the fish tank. The bass opened their lips and sucked the worms away, leaving nothing but bubbles.

The sun was orange, sinking level with the house, beaming in the windows. Marcus sat on the floor with his back against the bottom rail of the bunk bed, a fresh beer in his left hand and two empties on the floor beside him. He smelled like smoke and asphalt. We watched a show about chainsaw carvers in Canada. Marcus's choice.

"If your dad's so worried about what's going on with you, he ought to be around to find out. Call you about something other than a fucking football game."

"That's just how he is," I said.

"Just like my old man. Pretends like he cares, but he don't. It's just a show for himself."

Marcus's father left before Marcus was born, but he still tried to come around sporadically for special occasions a long time after, until Aunt Gail married Peter. Marcus was about fourteen then. Dad left when I was nine. I remember him being with us only in flashes. Riding to a deer hunt in his old Dodge truck, eating boiled peanuts on the front porch and tossing the shells on the ground, fights with Mom in the middle of the night.

"He sends us money sometimes."

"Well," Marcus said. "Let's sanctify the bastard."

Dad started living with another woman in north Georgia less than a year after he left us. They had a baby girl named Rebecca. I met her once, right after she was born, but she didn't feel like my sister. Meemaw and Marcus and Aunt Gail always acted like having that family somehow made Dad's leaving worse. They never cut him any slack. But I didn't feel like that. You can't really get any further away than gone.

"Is what he is," I said.

"That's true both ways." Marcus drained his beer and smashed the can.

Mom came in a little while later, took a beer out of Marcus's box, and cracked it open. "Well, it's done." She took a sip and glanced at the TV. A man with curly blond hair was carving a piece of red cedar into the shape of a rabbit. It was snowing heavily outside, and the camera kept cutting from his work to the weather.

"He says he's real sorry. If he would've known sooner, he would've called, or even come to see you. Now he's too embarrassed. But if you need anything, you should call him." She took another sip of beer. "Oh, and I'm a spiteful bitch. He wanted me to tell you that too."

I didn't say anything. The show cut from the carving process to an interview with the carver. *I told the client I would have this carving to him by Thursday, so I'm going to have it to him by Thursday. No snowstorm is going to stop me from keeping my word.* The camera cut back to him working, snow falling.

"My word is my bond," Mom said in a deep, gravelly voice. "Please don't grow up to be men."

"Shit is fake," Marcus said. "And stupid." He turned the channel.

✠

Marcus left after he drank all his beer. Mom went to the kitchen to fill out some evaluation forms for work. I turned onto my side and watched a little bit of the prime time game. Auburn versus LSU. It felt far away. I couldn't see myself in it, and I didn't want to, because every time I thought back to myself as a football player I was standing on the sideline, transfixed by the ball. All I had to do was step out of the way.

My phone started ringing. It was Lydia. I let it vibrate in my hand, staring at her name on the little screen. Finally, I just answered it.

"You know how to use eBay?" she asked.

It was nice to hear something like before, something almost normal. "What you selling?"

"Last week I found a peanut big as a potato. Probably need a hammer to break the shell."

On television, one of the Auburn receivers caught a screen pass and spun away from a tackler. Made twenty yards before someone finally pushed him out of bounds.

"You're going to sell it?"

"Thinking about it. What else?"

"I don't know. Plant it?"

Lydia laughed. "Now there's an idea. Start a whole new breed of monster peanuts. Why sell one when I could sell a thousand?"

"You think it's any good to eat?"

"I don't know," Lydia said. "I just been looking at it."

We stayed on the phone for almost forty-five minutes, the longest we'd ever talked. She never mentioned my leg, barely anything about school. She told me about seeing a cat at the SPCA she wanted, an orange one with yellow stripes. She couldn't wait until she got her own place. I told her about a woman on *The Price is Right* who got so excited when her name was called that she passed out cold on the floor. The football game ended, and I didn't know who won. Eventually I remembered why Lydia had called.

"Well, sorry I don't know anything about eBay," I said.

"That's okay. You got better ideas." I heard her yawn into the phone. "Getting kind of late," she said.

"Yeah." I didn't want to stop talking to her. It was the best I'd felt since I got hurt.

"But I can call you again tomorrow. I figured I might could even come see you."

The thought of her in my bedroom made my heart beat hard. The messiness. The wrongness of it. All the quiet little differences between us. And me laid up with my cast, basically useless. I wondered what Mom would say. Whether she would approve. It almost seemed better not to know.

"If you wanted," she said. "I mean, I thought you might get lonely."

"Yeah, no, I do. I would. I mean, you should definitely come over if you want to."

"Just forget it."

"No, seriously, I want you to come. I just got to ask my mom."

"Okay. Well, let me know what she says."

We talked awkwardly for a few more minutes until we found a good way to hang up. I couldn't believe she wanted to come over, and already it had my guts upset. I convinced myself she was just saying that to be nice, and that even if she had wanted to see me at first, I ruined it by talking like an idiot. I looked around my room. TV on the floor, largemouth bass in a dirty tank. I couldn't even take a proper shower.

Suddenly I missed Geometry. Perfect lines, measurable angles. And football, not the playing so much but the rhythm of it, the structure. *Play call is not a suggestion, men. It is a command.* Out here it was too much like history. It wasn't just you, it was your family and your ancestors. Forces beyond your control. You had to think about motives, and how other people would react. You had to read between the lines.

Mom stuck her head in the door. "Who were you talking to on the phone?"

I thought about telling her the truth—Lydia Proveaux, her father is Ronald Proveaux, her mother is unknown; seventeen years old with skin as deep and smooth as the creamy sandbank of Lake Moultrie; long, coarse, shiny black hair; always wears a strand of fake pearls, but not like she's trying to be someone she isn't, more like she's proud of exactly who she is—but the thought of saying her name made me shiver. I'd never had a girl over before. I wondered what Mom would think if Lydia was the first one. It was all just too much.

"Nobody," I said.

The days began to run together. I moved periodically from the bed to the couch. Looked at different screens. Sometimes Mom convinced me to go and sit on the front steps, which I didn't care to do because it was hard to get comfortable out there and it made my bedroom smell nasty when I went back inside. I could feel my muscles softening. Marcus brought over an old boom-box and a stack of his CDs. Said music was supposed to help with recovery. I never listened to them unless he was there.

Sandridge beat Hobcaw, then St. John's, an out-of-conference team. There was an entire paragraph about Quinton in the paper, how well he was doing. Reading that was like looking in my own casket, and I started to understand how Quinton must've felt when I took the field for that opening drive every week. Planted my cleats where he knew his should've been. The question never was whether he was good, only whether I was better. But that didn't matter now.

Seabrook quit texting after I didn't respond to his first message, but Conrad kept on. I never answered him because I didn't feel a part of that life anymore. I knew what they were doing. Lifting weights, watching film, installing new plays. All without me. I read their names in the newspaper. Football was a fantasy. I couldn't even walk. How could I ever have run?

One evening while I was watching *According to Jim*, there was a knock on the door. I figured it was the UPS man or something. Mom was always ordering clothes online because she could find the good stuff she liked cheap enough to buy. I'd just taken my afternoon Lortab and was zoning in on the television, not paying attention to the goings-on, but the colors, the camera angles. I was feeling a little tingle at the corners of my eyes.

Mom answered the door. She'd been home all day, doing bills and taking little naps, preparing for the overnight shift. I heard her talk, and a deep voice respond, but I still didn't think anything of it. Then she called for me. "Grady, honey," she said. "Someone's here to see you."

I could tell she was flustered. I thought for a second it might be my dad and I got a little bit excited. I hadn't seen him since Christmas two years earlier. I sat up in bed and got my crutches off the floor. I was wearing sweatpants and a black T-shirt. As I stood up on my crutches, I could smell myself, and I stunk badly. I hobbled down the hall to the front room, but instead of Dad, sitting on the couch was Conrad, Coach Hendrickson beside him. They were both wearing khaki pants and golf shirts like two different versions of the same person, young and old. Mom was standing beside them, still wearing her hoodie and pajama bottoms, grinning forcedly.

"How are you, son?" Coach Hendrickson said.

"Doing okay." I hobbled over to him and he stuck out his hand. I shook it.

"Ain't heard from you in a while," Conrad said.

"Yeah."

"Can I get y'all anything?" Mom asked. "Coffee, tea, glass of water?"

"We're just fine, ma'am," Coach Hendrickson said. "We know you weren't expecting us, and I apologize."

Mom's face turned red. "Oh, it's no problem at all. I'm sure Grady is thankful for some company other than me and his cousin. But if you will excuse me for just a minute." She winked at me and walked toward the hall. There was a dirty cleaning rag on the back of the recliner, and she snatched that up on her way.

I maneuvered over to the recliner and sat down. I had to sit on the very edge to keep from sitting on my cast and grinding the fiberglass into the back of my leg. My knee was already starting to ache from moving around. Just that, from bed to front room, was all it took. I laid the crutches on the floor beside me.

"That's a hell of a rig," Conrad said.

"Took 'em like forty-five minutes to wrap it."

I could smell the grass of the practice field on them. Residual locker room body spray.

"Recovery is hard." Coach Hendrickson ran his hand through his hair. "I tore the ACL in both my knees at Clemson. Two years in a row. It's a damn lonely process."

"Yes, sir."

"Lonely enough that you need all the friends you got. Do you know what I mean, son? You're still a part of our team."

"We're playing for you," Conrad said.

"That's right," Coach Hendrickson said. "We're playing for every one of us. And that means you too."

Conrad was leaning forward and looking at me hard, like he was trying to see the impact those words were having on me, like my cast was going to break in two right then, leg fully healed. But it sounded like bullshit. Like Marcus said about Dad, this was a show for them. I'd played football once too. I'd seen people get hurt, and I'd put them immediately out of my mind. Because that's all you can do. If you start thinking about injuries, it's hard to suit up and step out on the field.

"Thanks," I said.

Mom came out of her bedroom with her hair quickly combed and lipstick on. She'd changed out of her pajama bottoms into jeans. Coach Hendrickson looked at her and smiled. She put her head down and walked to the kitchen.

"Got some good news too," Conrad said. "Thought it might cheer you up. The Citadel upped their offer to a partial scholarship."

"That's great," I said.

"You'll have plenty of time for all that when you get back," Coach Hendrickson said. "You just focus on getting better right now."

I looked at my toes sticking out of my cast. They were numb and turning red from the way I was sitting.

"Well, I guess we'll head out. Just wanted to stop in and let you know we were thinking about you." Coach Hendrickson stood and brushed the front of his pants. The sun was low and the house was dark. He was just a shadow. "But if you would, I'd like to pray before we go."

Conrad stood and came over to me. Locked his left arm in mine and his right in Coach Hendrickson's.

"Ma'am, would you care to join us?"

Mom came out of the kitchen. When she saw how we were,

she wrinkled the corners of her eyes. Outside, the frogs were wailing again. Coach Hendrickson offered Mom his free arm, and she locked her elbow in his. He said the Lord's Prayer. *Thy Kingdom come, thy will be done in Earth, as it is in Heaven.*

I realized for the first time that was the only prayer he knew. When he finished, he shook Mom's hand and mine. Conrad did the same. Then they left, feet stomping down the stairs.

"I'm so embarrassed," Mom said.

"They shouldn't have come here."

"He's a good man."

I picked up my crutches and stood, maneuvered back to my room, and closed the door behind me. I sat down on my bed, dug the medicine bottle out from under my pillow, and shook two pills into my hand, even though I'd just taken one an hour or so before. I didn't want to feel good. I wanted to disappear. I wanted to forget the things outside those walls that once had meaning but now did not. I tossed the medicine in my mouth, closed my eyes, and swallowed. Felt the pills roll dry down my throat and sink to the pit of my stomach. I laid down and waited for them to slowly dissolve.

PART TWO

V

On a moonless Thursday night in February, me and Hambone Daniels were out hunting coons on his uncle's property, the old Allendale Plantation land. The weather was cold enough to keep the mosquitos off and we wore long sleeves. Stood side by side on a skinny dirt road near Hambone's silver Nissan Frontier. He was taller than me, but real thin with long legs like a scarecrow. His dark hair curled out from beneath his hat. We had our guns laid on the dog box bolted to the bed of the truck. Hambone was using his Remington twenty-two caliber rifle and I had Marcus's old Weatherby twelve-gauge shotgun he was letting me borrow.

We'd turned Hambone's dog out about thirty minutes earlier. Merle, a long-legged blue tick. He opened a few times but nothing convincing. We drank cans of Bud Light. Hambone held his up and drained it. Threw the empty into the trees. "Finish yours yet?" he asked.

"Still working on it."

"Nursing."

People said every week Hambone's daddy gave him a box of bullets, a case of beer, and a tank of gas. That was his allowance. They said his mom kept logs of Copenhagen in the freezer for him all the time. I never asked, but he always had beer, always had bullets, and he always had Copenhagen.

In the distance, Merle started barking more consistent, deep and drawn-out, like it was coming from his belly. It made the hair on the back of my neck stand up, my bones start to shake.

"He treed?"

"No," Hambone said. "But he's seen a coon now. That howling there, that ain't exploratory." He could tell by his bark what the dog was doing, what he was thinking. Put his fingers in his lips and whistle one time, if Merle could hear him, he'd come right to him, even if he was on a coon. Hambone opened the cooler behind the dog box and pulled out two more beers. Opened them both and pushed one my way. "Drink up."

"Yeah, all right." I wasn't feeling drunk at all, but I didn't want to. Not yet. "You got rubber boots on?" I asked.

"No, just my short ones. You'll be fine."

I was wearing my Wolverines, the ones I always wore on game day. They were better suited for the woods, anyway. I adjusted the knee brace under my jeans. I'd been out of the full cast since before Christmas, but my muscles had withered, and the knee joint just didn't seem to swing as easy as it should. More like grinding.

Merle changed his bark again. The sounds came faster and more frantic, echoing across the swamp and through the timber. Hambone opened the driver's side door and pulled out two headlamps. Tossed one to me. "Now he's treed," he said.

I adjusted the straps to fit my head and turned on the light. It shined on the trees in front of me. I looked down and the lamp lit the sandy road. It was hard to see because it only shined a narrow beam, so I had to choose where to look. Down at my feet, or up at what was coming. I'd have preferred a regular flashlight, but Hambone was certain the headlamps worked best because they freed your hands.

I picked up Marcus's Weatherby, made sure the safety was on, and put it on my shoulder. Hambone strung an orange dog leash around his waist. He got his Remington and walked to the edge of the road, leaving his open beer on the dog box. He pushed aside a tangle of vines and walked into the trees. I followed him, leaving both my open beers too, one half-drank and one not at all, feeling excited and a little bit nervous, but steady. Hambone beat the brush with the stock of his rifle and stepped heavy on the fallen leaves and pine needles, crunching them as he went. Coon hunting, it wasn't really like hunting at all. The dog did all the work, finding the coon, running him up a tree. Didn't need to be quiet or sneaky, just patient. Mostly it was a way to kill time, and I had more than I could stomach.

I trained my headlamp on the back of Hambone's legs as we walked toward the sound of Merle's barking. Tried to put my feet exactly where his had been just seconds before, because I knew it was solid enough ground. Being in the woods at night was like being in a hole. Stars blocked by the branches. Merle's barking, low and rhythmic like church organ notes.

The ground turned from leaves to mud as we came to the swamp. Cypress knees jutted from the ground. Our feet made small splashes and sucking noises as we pulled our boots out of the muck. Merle's howls grew louder as we drew closer. Echoed over the water like the whole woods were ringing.

"Too cold for cottonmouths, at least," Hambone said. He

stopped walking and I ran into the back of him. He cupped his hand behind his ear and listened. "Hard to tell. But I think he's this way." He started walking again toward the deeper middle of the swamp. Water was starting to leak in my boots.

I trusted Hambone. But I didn't trust him. He seemed to know more about coon hunting and training dogs than any grown man I could imagine, but it was hard to tell if he really knew it, or if he was just making it up as he went along.

It wasn't until I went back to school in late November that me and Hambone first spoke to one another. He kept to himself since he got held back, mostly by choice it seemed. He always acted like he was above it all.

Doctor Hughes cut me out of my cast and let me go back to school on crutches. First period, first day back, I was supposed to go to weight training, but I couldn't stand to face the team. I hadn't seen anyone except Conrad and Coach Hendrickson since I got hurt. Never returned Seabrook's text messages.

Quinton ended up being the most productive offensive player on the team. Rushed for over nine-hundred yards and eleven touchdowns. The team made the playoffs and won their first-round game. They were preparing to play Stono Ferry in the second round. I didn't want to be a distraction.

When the first bell rang, I went inside the building and wandered around on my crutches until everybody filed into their classrooms, then snuck out one of the side doors and found a bench where I could sit, blocked on both sides by thick holly bushes. My armpits were tender from rubbing on the crutches and my knee was throbbing. I loosened the straps on my brace. The joint was red and swollen. I was sweating. Wore out already.

I thought about calling Marcus and asking him to come pick me up, but I knew he'd tell me I needed to stick it out.

Hambone came out the same door I had and walked quickly along the side of the concrete school building, looking around. When he saw me sitting on the bench, he startled a little bit, then smiled. "I'll be damned," he said. "I thought you were dead."

Those were the first words he ever said to me, even though we'd been in school together for years.

"Yeah, I did too."

He sat down beside me and pulled a can of Copenhagen from his pocket. Packed it loudly with his right hand. He opened the lid and offered the black snuff to me. "Dip for the formerly dead, then? Guess there's hope for me after all."

We shared a dip, spitting on the roots of the holy bushes. The weather was gray, almost chilly but humid and heavy. There were no birds, just the sounds of the cars passing on Highway 76. I hadn't done a dip since I'd gotten hurt, so it made me dizzier than it used to, and almost sick, but not quite. Hambone talked about Merle, how he'd gotten him as a pup, how he fed him boiled pork ribs after a hunt, how sometimes when it was real cold, his daddy would let him bring the dog inside.

"That nearly ruined him the last time," Hambone said. He rubbed his hands on his knees and adjusted his chaw with his tongue. Spat a loose thread of tobacco. "That cold snap we had a couple weeks back, he slept on the floor beside my bed. On top of a blanket. When I had to put him back out, he didn't want to go. Didn't even want to hunt. Wouldn't hardly leave my side at all. I had to beat him with a pine branch to piss him off, make him sniff coons."

A lady came out of the door, a teacher or someone from the front office. She wore a long sweater over a floral-patterned shirt. Held a tall stack of paper. She came right by us. I looked at Hambone. He smiled at her without showing his teeth. I did the same.

"Good morning," Hambone said.

"Good morning," the lady said. She looked at Hambone, then at my knee, strapped in a brace, the crutches propped on the bench beside me, and kept right on walking.

When she got around the corner of the building, Hambone pulled out his dip and threw it on the ground. "Told you," he said. "Like seeing a ghost. Them crutches and that brace going to get you out of a whole lot of trouble." The bell rang for the next period and Hambone stood up. "Somebody I want to see in my next class. Think I'll go. Talk at you later."

"Thanks for the dip."

"Anytime," he said. "Seriously. Like tomorrow. I can't stand fucking English."

I laughed and nodded. He went inside the building. I tightened my brace back down and hobbled to Geometry. I was the first one in the class. I made my way back to my old seat in the corner under the air vent and sat down. Leaned my crutches against the wall. Mr. Farmer sat at his desk, scribbling at a piece of paper with one hand and adjusting his hearing-aid with the other. He waved to me and I waved back, but thankfully he didn't say anything. The other students didn't notice me when they came in. They were talking to each other, messing on their phones, getting their notebooks out. The lesson was about proofs. Mr. Farmer stayed mostly at the whiteboard, drawing these crazy diagrams, talking about bisectors and postulates. I didn't understand a thing.

As me and Hambone got closer to Merle and the tree where he'd bayed the coon, the water in the swamp got deeper, up almost to our knees, gritty even through my jeans. My knee brace was wet and heavy. We held our guns up by our chests and waded through the swamp. It stunk like mold and rot. I heard water moving, and, over everything, Merle's howling.

"I thought you said my Wolverines would be fine."

"Well, aren't they?" Hambone said. "You're walking. Must be all that rain last week why the water is so high. Wouldn't matter what boots you was wearing. My feet are wet too."

I looked for snakes, even though Hambone said it was too cold for them. It just seemed like they should be there, winding through the water. The beams of our headlights cut deceitful strips of sight. What I could see seemed more detailed and out of place in the dark. The knotty, peeling bark of the cypress trees, the green leaves of the swamp palms draped with moss and spackled with white bird shit. I stumbled on a log hidden under the water. Bumped into Hambone, wetting us both up to our waists.

"Careful there, cripple boy."

My whole body tensed when he called me that.

In early January, Doctor Hughes had told me I was healed. I could go back to working out, even take a hit on the football field. That evening, I strapped up my brace, pulled on a pair of gym shorts, and went for a jog down the driveway and along the edge of Lantana Lane. I was out of shape. My lungs burned more than they should've. I'd gained some weight. But it felt good to be working again, to be doing something productive. The roadside weeds brushing against my ankles, folks waving as they passed in their cars. After about fifteen minutes, though, my knee started throbbing. A few minutes later, it was hurting so bad I had to turn around. By the time I got to the house, it was swollen as a cantaloupe, turning purple. It hurt to put weight on it, to bend it at all. Mom was at work. I got a bag of frozen corn out of the freezer, laid down on the couch, and put the cold bag on my knee. Turned on *Wheel of Fortune*. When I woke up the next morning, my knee was so stiff I could hardly walk. I didn't tell Mom or anyone else. I didn't want her saying not to run, taking me back to the doctor. As bad as it hurt, nothing was worse than those weeks in bed. The boredom, time slowly dripping. The stink of my body. It was like a miserable lifetime of its own. I swallowed a few pain pills and suffered through. Figured I'd wait out the pain, work it away. After three days, the swelling subsided and I tried to run again. Didn't make it half as far before I had to turn around. I was worried something was still wrong and might always be.

Me and Hambone walked a few minutes further, Merle's barks reverberating across the swamp. It wasn't like something I was hearing, just something that was.

"There he is," Hambone said.

I followed his light where it shined and saw Merle, standing on a little patch of dry ground, his front legs mounted on the trunk of a thick pine tree. His muscles bulged beneath his spotty blue fur. Long black snout pointed up toward the branches of the tree, howling. His ears hung torn and bloody from his head like two pieces of old rag. He turned his head and looked at us coming. His eyes flashed solid green, almost like neon in the headlamps. He turned back to the tree and howled, the longest and loudest of the night. He started circling the tree, snapping at the trunk, digging toward the roots, growling. When we got up to him, Hambone put his hand on his back. The dog's hair raised up and he cowered down a little bit. Whimpered.

I shook what water I could out of my boots.

"You see the coon?" Hambone asked.

I looked up and my headlamp shone toward the top branches

of the tree, cast in shadow. I took a step back, looked up and down the trunk, then started circling, looking for any sign of the coon. Hambone patted Merle's flank and he started growling again. Put his front legs up on the trunk and bayed.

On the back side of the pine, about fifty feet up the trunk, tucked into the crotch of a thick branch, I saw the eyes of the coon reflected. "There he is." I pointed at the coon with Marcus's Weatherby.

"Have you got a shot?"

"I don't know. He's kind of high."

"Let me see." Hambone came around the tree and looked at where my lamp was shining, adding his to the beam. "Yeah," he said. "Might be a stretch for that shotgun. Good thing I brought my Remington." He smiled and checked to make sure there was a bullet in the chamber. "You want to take it?"

"No. You go ahead."

Hambone nodded and put the rifle in his shoulder. He pointed at the coon and took aim through the iron sites. Merle saw him and came creeping over, still growling. The dog turned his head toward the tree and bared his teeth. Long, pointed and white. Hambone clicked off the safety and pulled the trigger. Fire blew from the barrel of the gun and the sound of the shot rang through the swamp. The green eyes of the coon went black as it fell out of the light. There was a thump as it hit the dirt. I trained my lamp where I heard it and Merle was already there, on top of the coon, half-growling, half-barking, tearing at its throat. The coon, not yet all the way dead, was making quiet noises and tearing weakly at Merle's lips with his claws. They rolled in and out of the light, eyes and teeth flashing. Merle barked one full bark, then bit down hard on the coon, and it was still.

"Good man," Hambone said. "Come."

Merle came dancing from the kill, his hips twisted and his tail wagging frantically. Blood dripped from his mouth onto his chest. Hambone unlatched the orange leash from around his waist and clipped it to Merle's collar. He squatted and rubbed the dog on the head.

"Grady, tell him good man," Hambone said. "Let him know you're proud of him."

"Good man," I said.

"That's right."

Hambone stood and led Merle back to the coon. I followed behind him. The swamp was silent, no humming from the bugs in the chilly air. Even our voices sounded muffled. The animal was laying with its eyes open and its throat torn, fur matted with blood and slobber.

Hambone told Merle to sit and the dog obeyed. Hambone pulled out his pocket-knife and knelt. Cut off the coon's left ear. "Beg," he said to Merle. The dog whimpered. Hambone tossed him the ear and Merle caught it in his mouth. Chewed quickly and swallowed. It made me feel strange, the way they were together. How they anticipated each other's moves, how they communicated, how they seemed to act on pure instinct. It gave me gooseflesh beneath my wet jeans.

Hambone cut off the coon's tail and put it in his back pocket. He saved all his tails and dried them out. Hung them on a wall in his bedroom. He stood up and looked at me, his headlamp still on, almost blinding. I couldn't see his face behind the light. "Am I missing anything?"

"I don't think so."

He tilted his head to the sky and howled until he was out of breath. Started walking in the direction of the truck, leaving the dismembered carcass of the coon lying on the ground. Merle walked beside him, strung from the orange leash. Six steps and they were back in muddy water, wading through the swamp. I followed close behind.

At lunch that first day back in school, I didn't know who to sit with. I was exhausted from being on the crutches, navigating through the crowded halls. Wasn't hungry. I just wanted to go home. I sat by myself at a table right by the door. Everyone else was waiting in line for food. I took my phone out of my pocket and texted Marcus: *School fuckin sucks*

He replied almost immediately, like he'd been waiting on me to text: *Nothing new. Take your meds and power through.*

I knew he'd say something like that. I put my phone in my pocket and rummaged through my bookbag until I found my orange pill bottle. I slipped one pill out, then another. It seemed like they'd quit working good. One wouldn't do anything for me at all. Two was just a little bit better. I popped them in my mouth and swallowed them dry.

Seabrook was standing in the pizza line, August beside him, both hands clutching his forearm. Coach Hendrickson sat in his normal spot, eating a salad. He wore a purple collared shirt with white stripes, all three buttons undone, his dark hairy chest showing through. It made me feel weird, seeing them all there, like I was somewhere I wasn't supposed to be. I put my bookbag on my back and gathered my crutches. Stood and maneuvered out of the cafeteria, toward the vending machines. Bought a Coke and a bag of pretzels. Ate them alone, leaning against the wall, my knee turning red and splotchy in my brace. After a little while I could feel the pain meds kicking in a little, the soreness in my muscles and the aching in my knee subsiding just the tiniest bit.

The bell rang and I staggered on my crutches to U.S. History even though I didn't want to, even though I felt like I was going to be sick with nerves having to face Coach Molina. I thought he might not even remember me. I wasn't sure if that would be better or worse. I sat in the back corner of the room and stared at the screen of my phone as the other students filed in, just making myself look occupied.

Coach Molina walked over and rapped his knuckles on my desk. I looked up at him. Dark green eyes under curly brown hair. He put his hand flat against his chest. "It breaks this heart, your broken leg," he said. "It breaks this full-moon heart."

"Thank you."

"See you next season, though. You'll be back by next season." He walked across the room and sat at his desk. Pecked roughly at his keyboard.

When we got back to the truck, Hambone put Merle in the dog box and we took up with the beers we'd left lying, no longer cold but not exactly warm either. Kept our guns loaded on top of the box. The sky was like a blanket, the stars just light peeking through the seams. I checked the time on my phone. It was a little after ten o'clock.

"Got somewhere to be?" Hambone asked.

"Just curious."

He pulled a can of Copenhagen from his back pocket and thumped it with his forefinger. "You want to move spots and turn him out again?"

"I don't know." I poured out the last fizzy swig of Bud Light from my emptiest can.

"You don't even like beer." Hambone put a pinch of snuff on his tongue and tucked it into his bottom lip.

"Just foam. But I mean, the taste ain't great anyway."

"But you like to get drunk."

"I don't know," I said. "Sometimes. Anyway, I got this whole one you opened for me earlier." I threw the empty can in the woods, picked up the fuller one, and took a long sip.

Hambone put the can of Copenhagen back in his pocket and spat on the dirt. "You'd rather eat them pain pills," he said.

My ears got hot. "Just when it hurts."

"Yeah, but it always hurts, don't it?"

Across the road from us and a few dozen yards down, an owl hooted. A clear loud noise. Sounded almost like it was blown through glass. I looked in the direction from where it came. Hambone seemed like he hadn't noticed the sound at all. "Come on," he said. "I'm hurting too."

"It's not like that."

"So, you do have some."

"Not with me. Anyway, it's medicine."

"Oh, I know about medicine. All the different purposes. Cause and effect. Effect and side effect. Lawful distribution. Unlawful. My momma got a whole goddamn drawer of them things."

The owl hooted again. This time Hambone turned and looked at the noise. "No need to be scared," he said. "Just a bird."

"I ain't scared."

"I saw you."

He got like that sometimes, ornery in a crooked, sneaky kind of way. I couldn't tell if he was joking or digging, and I don't think he could either. He was used to getting his way.

"Come on." I lifted my beer. "Let's chug." I tipped the can to my lips and poured the bitter juice into my mouth. Swallowed quickly to keep up with the flow.

Hambone turned his up and did the same. He finished before me, smashed the can, and tossed it at my feet. I finished and dropped mine too. Burped up a bit of foam and swallowed it back down.

The owl hooted a third time, short and warbled. It flew from where it was perched, crossing the road and casting a dark shadow on the dirt. It lit in a white oak right beside the truck and shook its feathers. Merle growled softly from inside his box. Hambone grinned. "He got the taste, now." He pointed at the guns. "Get it for him."

I shook my head.

"Grady, he wants it."

"I don't give a shit."

"Well, you ought to. Ain't really got friends to lose anymore, do you? Especially old Merle. You couldn't ask for one better." He put his arm through a slot in the dog box and scratched the dog's flank.

I could've lowered my shoulder, run three steps, and rocked him off his heels, hurt knee and all. Stood over him like he was some skinny cornerback that tried to keep me from the end zone. Watched him wriggle in the sand. But he was right about not having friends to lose, and I knew it. I picked up Marcus's Weatherby and checked the chamber to make sure it was still loaded. It was.

"Shine the fucking light."

Hambone grinned. He clicked on his headlamp and shined it at the owl. The bird blinked its wide black eyes—not glowing in the light like Merle or the coon—and cocked its head slightly toward us. It grunted, opened its wings wide, and clicked its beak. I looked at Hambone. "Shoot it," he said.

I put the gun in my shoulder and pointed it at the bird. Aimed the bead on the barrel right at its chest. Merle growled from the dog box.

"He wants it," Hambone said.

My backbone was hot. My breathing was heavy. It was like the nerves before kickoff, the fear and the anger and the want. I clicked off the safety, held my breath, and pulled the trigger.

The recoil shook my shoulder. The owl fell backward, its wings spread out and ripping limply through the branches, pale feathers flying. Smoke drifted from the barrel of the gun. I clicked the safety back on, laid Marcus's Weatherby on top of the dog box, and looked Hambone right in his eyes. I turned on my headlamp and he squinted from the light. I walked to the edge of the woods and picked up the owl by its feet, scaly-feeling and warm. It was lighter than I expected. Blood leaked from its beak. I carried it to the truck and laid it on top of the dog box. "Give me your knife," I said.

Hambone reached into his pocket, pulled out his blade and handed it to me. I cut off the owl's feet, each with four long toes tipped with sharp black talons. Put them in my pocket. Merle whimpered in the box. I cut off a wing at the joint closest to the body. The knife sawed easy through the tendons, the hollow bones. There was hardly any blood. I pushed the wing through a slot in the dog box. Merle sniffed it once, then picked his head back up and started whimpering again.

"I guess that ain't the part he wanted," I said. Hambone was quiet behind me. I could feel the beer we'd chugged and the others earlier in the night working on my head, mixing with adrenaline. "Let me try again." I laid the owl flat on its back, its eyes like two black rocks, blood staining the white feathers around its beak. I pushed the knife into its breast, past the feathers and through the skin. Drew a line down its middle, opening its warm guts to the air. They smelled different than fish guts, more putrid and somehow more human. I put the knife down beside the bird, reached into its belly, and pulled out a handful of steaming innards. I pushed them into the dog box and Merle fell on them, teeth clicking together as he quickly chewed the meat.

I picked up the remains of the carcass and carried them to the edge of the road. Laid them in the grass where a possum could easily find it. Walked back to the truck. Hambone was staring into the dog box, his headlamp still on, shining a spotlight directly on Merle as he finished eating the guts.

"Seems satisfied," I said.

"Never," Hambone said. "He'd eat till he croaked."

I clicked off my headlamp and looked up at the moonless sky, the space between the trees just a slightly bluer shade of black, stars dim and distant. "I'm ready to go home," I said.

Hambone snickered. "Yeah, I figured."

I picked up his knife from on top of the dog box, closed it, and put it back in his pocket. Wiped my bloody hands down the leg of his pants, dirtying them red.

He pulled his leg away and looked down at the stain. "What the fuck?"

"I wanted them clean," I said without looking at him.

The team lost to Stono Ferry in the second round of the play-offs. Not even close, something like twenty points. At school, I overheard about the seniors crying in the locker room. Most of them would never play football again. Conrad was committed to the Citadel. Quinton had a few offers to walkon at some schools, even big ones, but he was waiting for a scholarship to open up. That's what people said, anyway. But the rest of them were done. Bus ride home, throw your jersey in the laundry, walk into the parking lot and drive off into the rest of your life.

The Monday after, during weightlifting, I was sitting out front the school with Hambone on our bench, sharing a dip. Gnats floated in the air like dust beat from a rug. "You were glad to see them lose, weren't you?" he asked.

I spat and wiped my mouth. "That's still my team."

Hambone laughed. "No, it ain't. Or you wouldn't be out here with me. You'd be in there watching them hump around the weight room and take baths together."

"You don't get it."

"Sure, I do. You think it's special, but it ain't. It's a fucking boys' club. Spend all your time together. Play dress-up and bump chests. Growl and cuss and holler. You were in. You got broke up. Now you ain't." He pulled the chaw out of his lip and tossed it on the grass. "Now you're with me."

We took Highway 76 toward my house. The road was barren except for us. Hambone drove with an open Bud Light between his knees, sipping at it every couple of minutes. Radio dialed to a country channel. DJ talking. I checked my phone. The bright screen lit up the cab. No messages. I put it back in my pocket and looked out the window. A song came through the speakers. Toby Keith singing about both ends of the ozone burning.

I reached for the radio and pushed the button to turn it off. The owl's blood that didn't come off on Hambone's pants had dried on my hands, red and flaky. My jeans were still wet. I could feel the skin on my legs wrinkling.

Hambone turned the radio back on and spun the dial through static. "Don't have to turn it off if you don't like the song," he said. "Just change the station." He settled on another channel playing classic rock and roll. Finished his beer, rolled down the window, and flung his empty can across the road.

A few minutes later, he turned onto Lantana Lane and pulled into my driveway. The house was completely dark. Not even the porch light was on. I gathered Marcus's Weatherby and climbed out of the truck. Patted my pants to make sure I had all my stuff. Felt the owl's feet in my pocket, already stiff. "Guess I'll see you," I said.

"Guess? Merle will be ready to go again by Sunday." He made his lips like to kiss and winked at me. I shook my head and shut the truck door. Went inside. He backed out of the driveway and drove away.

I took my Wolverines off by the front door and walked to my bedroom in the dark. Flipped on the light switch and unloaded the Weatherby. Leaned it in the corner beside the fish tank. One of the bass had died, but the other had grown. It was almost ten inches long. I grabbed the can of goldfish food sitting on the rim, opened the lid, and dropped in a pinch. The bass opened his wide mouth and sucked in the flakes. It was too much trouble to find bugs and the fish didn't seem to mind the store-bought stuff.

Mom was probably working, otherwise she'd have been waiting up for me. I closed the lid on the fish tank and went across the hall to her room. I knocked quietly on the door and when she didn't answer, reached inside and turned on the light. Like I figured, she wasn't there. Clothes lying on the bed. Can of hairspray sitting on her dresser. She was working the night shift again. I went back to my room and turned on the television still sitting on the floor like it was temporary. Tuned it to a criminal show, one of the ones that's based on real crimes, but it's still like a story, and actors play out the murders. Kept the volume low.

I took off my shirt and stripped out of my wet socks and pants. Rubbed my hands over my belly. It was getting soft. Losing muscle tone, adding fat. Months of laying in bed, eating Hot Pockets and sausage biscuits and cheeseburgers. I unstrapped the brace from my knee and rubbed the skin where it'd lain, red and raw from chafing, dented lines where the metal pushed into the meat.

My leg was always aching, and the brace didn't seem to help it much, just made it hurt different in other places. I looked at my hands, still faintly tinted red with blood. Went to the bathroom and washed my hands good with soap, all the way up to my elbows.

Back in my room, I took off my underwear. Opened my dresser, found a fresh pair, and pulled them on. In the back of the drawer, I felt my pill bottle. I pulled it out, twisted the lid, and shook out two pills. Then one more. I swallowed them, then counted the rest. Fourteen left. I had more refills, but the last time I asked Mom to get it for me, she acted surprised I was still taking them. I didn't really want to ask her again. I put the bottle back in the drawer, behind a pair of socks.

The house was eerily quiet and still, the sound coming from the television the only thing making any noise at all. I closed my bedroom door and that felt better for some reason. I picked my pants up off the floor, took out my wallet, and unthreaded my belt from the loops. Laid them both on top of my dresser. Fished the owl feet out of my pocket. They were lighter than they looked, almost weightless in my hand. Hint of soft feather at the top, where they met the body. I held them to my nose and sniffed. Dry and musky. I looked closely at the talons. Traces of dirt. Rodent fur. I sat the feet on the dresser beside my wallet and turned off the light. Lay down in my bed, facing the television. The episode was about a woman stabbed to death in her bathtub. The reenactment was intentionally blurred and shadowy. They only showed bursts of action, cut between interviews with mustached men in brown coats and stock images: the glint of a knife, red blood pooling in a porcelain tub.

The aching in my knee began to subside a little. I could feel the medicine mixing with the beer in the back of my head, at the tip of my spine, a little ball of warmth. The pills made me notice more feelings like that, the parts of my body, the function of them. I felt my heart beating, fluttering like the gills of a fish. Moving toward my throat, stuttering, speeding up. Something was off. I was scared my heart might explode.

I took a deep breath. Focused on the story playing on the screen. Drunk husband. Cheating wife. Money worries. All variations of the same story.

My heartbeat began to slow. I got up and turned the volume all the way down on the television but left the screen playing. Got back in the bed, pulled the covers up around my shoulders, and closed my eyes. Behind my lids, light and shapes played around the room. Just a presence, so I wasn't alone.

VI.

Friday when I got home from school, Mom was in the kitchen ripping up linoleum, exposing the yellow plywood beneath. She was on her knees, using a razorblade and a rusty prybar, slicing at the glue and pulling up the flimsy tiles. Stacking them beside her. Sweating a little bit through her light blue T-shirt shirt, right along her backbone.

"Didn't know you were doing this today." I dropped my bookbag on the couch and stood at the edge of the kitchen.

"Me neither. Till I did."

"You find some new linoleum?"

"No." Mom laid her tools down and twisted around to look at me. "Wood," she said, like it was something precious. "Engineered, but still wood. Molly who works with me, she and her husband Easton are building a house on Katy Hill Road. They got a whole extra truckload. Selling it cheap."

"How cheap?"

"Almost nothing. For what it is. Like three-hundred bucks, I think."

I went to the cabinet, got a plastic cup, and filled it with water from the sink. "Is it enough to do the whole kitchen?"

"I mean, it's a truckload."

"Guess it depends on the size of the truck." I took a sip of water. "But it sounds good to me."

"Glad you approve," Mom said, taking up her tools again.

"Let me help you."

"I got it for now. I enjoy it. Tearing up this ugly shit. Soon we'll have a whole new kitchen."

I took another sip of water and sat the cup by the sink.

"Anyway, I'm about to quit for now. I won't be home this evening."

"Work again?"

"Can't I go anyplace else?" She picked at another tile with her razorblade.

I rolled my eyes. She loved to act like that, especially since I'd gotten hurt. Like she could never do anything she wanted. But truthfully, she hardly ever did anything but. Ripping up the floor on a whim, for instance. "You going to Pineville with the ladies from work, then? Meeting at the Boat House for drinks?"

"Jesus, do you think I'm that predictable?"

I laughed and shook my head. Went back across the kitchen to the front room and picked up my bookbag. "Predictable isn't exactly the word I would use." I walked down the dim hallway toward my bedroom.

"Call my cell phone if you need me."

I gave her a thumbs-up without turning around.

"Love you," she said.

"Love you too."

I closed my bedroom door behind me and sat on the edge of my bed. Took my Geometry workbook from my bag and looked at the problem-set we had for homework. I was far behind the rest of the class, completely lost. Even the directions seemed to be written in a foreign alphabet. Like we weren't studying shapes anymore, but the idea of them.

Not long after I got back, Mr. Farmer stood near the door at the end of class, leaning against the whiteboard wearing a faded olive colored shirt and a deaf man's smile, pleasantly removed from the chatter. As all of us students filed through the classroom into the crowded hallway, he handed us back our latest quizzes. I was still using crutches and sitting in the back of the class, so I was the last to leave. He handed me my quiz paper. Scrawled in purple ink was the score, forty-five percent. Beside that he'd written *negotiable*. I stared down at the paper, not so much caring about the grade—I'd expected as much—but trying to figure out what I could most easily do with it, the physical thing, so I could free up my hands to use my crutches.

Mr. Farmer put his hand on my shoulder. "It isn't your ability," he said. "You just missed so much time."

"I know."

"You'll see I wrote 'negotiable' beside your score." He took his hand off my shoulder and adjusted his glasses. "I'm here every day after school." He spoke so softly I almost couldn't hear him. His talking voice was different than his teaching voice. "I'd be more than happy to catch you up on the concepts. And you could retake the quizzes."

"Yes, sir." I was still preoccupied with how to most respectfully stash the paper. I decided to fold it neatly and put it in my back pocket. "Thank you."

"How about this afternoon?"

"That might work. Yeah, I think it probably could."

"Great," Mr. Farmer said. "I'll see you then." He went toward his desk and I leaned onto my crutches. Maneuvered myself into the hallway, trying to move with the rhythm of the crowd.

I didn't go see him that afternoon, or any afternoon ever. I might've run into Conrad, since he only came in the afternoons, or another one of my old teammates. I'd have to explain it to Hambone why I was staying late. Have to arrange for a ride since the buses would be gone. Anyway, I didn't need tutoring, Mr. Farmer said so himself. I just needed to catch up. I could do that on my own.

Only problem was, I didn't know how far back to go. And I couldn't learn the old stuff and the new at the same time. I kept thinking we'd come to a point where there was a wholly new lesson, not building on ideas I was supposed to know but didn't, and I'd take off from there. Waited and waited. Quiz papers noted with purple failures kept piling up, and soon the *negotiable* beside the score disappeared. I began to feel a different kind of shame, like not only was I incompetent, but I didn't even care, and soon that became more true than not. It almost quit bothering me.

I closed my Geometry workbook and put it back in my book-bag. Took my cell phone out of my pocket and thought about looking for a study site, but, like an instinct, went to the MaxPreps website instead. I pulled up my own profile first: GRADY HAYES, NUMBER 28. But under that, in bold red type, *Injured*. I wondered for a second how they knew, who updated it. Would it stay that way until I walked back onto a football field? Would it ever be changed to *Healed?*

I typed in Quinton's name and his profile loaded on the screen: Quinton Cook, Number 27, Senior, RB, 983 yards, 0 fumbles. Below that, the rankings: 832nd nationally, 19th in the state. Quinton's profile had another section that mine didn't. Recruitment Status:

Quinton Cook, the senior running back from Sandridge High School in South Carolina, put up impressive numbers over his senior season, despite seeing limited action over the first four games. Long body and large hands. Cook has a desirable blend of speed and strength, but perhaps his biggest asset is his ability to make tacklers miss in space. He has drawn interest from in-state schools such as Charleston Southern University, Newberry College, and, most notably, the University of South Carolina. However, no official scholarship offers have been made, which draws questions regarding Cook's academic performance, as well as his character and dedication to the game.

The detail was precise. To think someone was watching so close, tracking our movement to the yard. Three feet. Thirty-six inches. But the end part was off. No one could question Quinton's dedication to the game. Even I could admit that. He loved it as much as anybody. Stuck with it even when Coach Hendrickson moved him to second-string his senior season, behind me, a sophomore. Showed up to every practice, ran hard through every play. And he never got in trouble about his grades, at least not that I knew. Compared to how precise and measured and correct the rest of the information was, down even to the size of his hands, that part was so wrong it didn't even seem like a mistake. It was just a lazy assumption, or even worse, a lie.

I closed the site and dropped my phone on the floor. Looked up at the wooden slats holding the bunk above me where my dirty clothes were piled. I thought about Quinton, and when I really got down to it, I didn't know much about him except he could squat three-hundred-fifty pounds and run forty yards in 4.7 seconds. We spent two seasons sitting in lockers right beside each other, and never got to know any more than a stat sheet about each other.

I remembered a time with my dad, a Friday evening in early summer. I must've been about nine or ten. We rode down to Henry's in his Dodge for him to buy a case of Miller Lite and a bag of ice. He bought me a glass bottle RC Cola from the cooler by the register and I popped the top off with the bottle opener on the side of the cooler myself.

Outside, I leaned against the hood of the Dodge, sipping. Dad was at the tailgate, arranging the beer in his cooler and putting in the ice. A thin man wearing a fisherman's hat and baggy khaki pants with stains on the front walked up to me from the side of the building. He had brown eyes cataracted cloudy blue in the center, spooky against the dark skin of his face, the hint of a gray beard coming through. He held out a plastic bag filled with okra, yellow squash, and underripe tomatoes flecked with dirt.

"You want to buy some vegetables?" he asked. "They fresh. I mean, they can't get no fresher. Picked them this afternoon."

"I love fried okra."

"Whoo," the man said. "Fry it. Stew it. Pickle it. I'll eat it any which way. Makes you strong."

Dad came from around the back of his truck with two cans of beer in his hand. "What you selling, old man?" he asked.

"Your boy said he loves him some okra. I got some here, fresh picked." He held out his bag spread open toward Dad. Behind him, it was getting to be dusk. Fireflies lit up in the yard beside the store.

"Here," Dad said, holding out the beers. "Take these."

The man peered into his open bag, then back at Dad.

"I ain't trading," Dad said. "I'm giving them to you."

The old man smiled. He was missing a tooth on the bottom. He took the beers from Dad's hand. "Thank you, sir."

Dad reached into his pocket and pulled out a crumbled five-dollar bill. "Here," he said. "Take this too."

The man took the money and put it in his pocket. He lifted his fisherman's hat and rubbed his head. "Yes, sir. I sure do appreciate it." He held out his bag for Dad to take. "I hope you and your boy appreciate these nice vegetables. Like I said. Make him strong."

"Nah," Dad said. "You keep them." He held up his hands and walked to the driver's side of the truck. "Sell them to somebody else." He got in the truck and called for me to follow him. I did what he said, and we drove away, leaving the old man standing there in the parking lot with his bag of vegetables and the two cans of beer Dad gave him, the dull lights from over the gas pumps shining on him.

"Why didn't you take the okra?" I asked. "You paid for it."

"I wasn't buying. I was giving him something." He reached for the gear-shifter and pushed it into third. "Anyway, that shit was stole."

"How do you know?"

"Look at him," Dad said. "He don't own no land to grow."

I dozed off on the bottom bunk for a little while. Dreamed fuzzy dreams about Dad and Quinton, like they were there in the room with me, watching as I lay in the bed. Different versions of them, faces faded, ageless. Woke up to my phone ringing on the floor beside me. Picked it up and looked at the screen. Marcus.

"Hello?"

"I'm on the way over." His voice was muffled and crackly. A blowing sound came through the speaker, like he was in his Ranger with the windows down. The radio played faintly in the background.

I wiped my eyes and cleared my throat. "Okay. What for?"

"We'll talk when I get there. Just wanted to give you a heads-up. Didn't want to find you with your hands in your britches."

"Whatever."

Marcus laughed and hung up. I put my phone in my pocket and got out of bed. Looked around the room to see if there was anything I needed to pick up. I didn't want him giving me shit about being a slob when he got there.

The owl feet were still lying on the dresser. I stashed them in the back of my sock drawer, beside my bottle of pills.

Marcus was dressed nicer than usual when he came in. His jeans were clean if frayed a bit around his boots, and he wore a long-sleeved button-up shirt.

"Don't you look pretty," I said.

"Wish I could say the same about you. That long peach fuzz on your lip. We'll stop by the house. I'll put a little milk on it and let Spooky lick it off."

"Shut up."

"Seriously. Damn. I told you I was on the way."

"I didn't know we were going anywhere."

"Well, now you do."

I went to bathroom and undressed. Put on fresh deodorant and fished Dad's old electric razor out of the drawer. Mom had let me keep it. I ran it over my face and down my neck. Rinsed it off and threw it back in the drawer. In my room, I put on a pair of dark Wranglers and pulled a plain black T-shirt over my head. Few squirts of Curve cologne, then out to the front room.

Marcus was sitting on the couch. He had a half-pint of Wild Turkey 101 in his hand. He took a swig and put the bottle in his pocket. "What the hell happened to the kitchen?" he asked.

"Mom," I said.

"She got something else to put down?"

"Supposedly."

Marcus put his hands on his knees and rocked himself up off the couch. "One step ahead is two steps behind." He went to the door and put his hand to the knob.

"Where we going?"

"No questions," Marcus said. "Just close your eyes and follow the ghost."

Marcus drove and I rode shotgun. I hadn't driven at all since I broke my leg. Hadn't even ridden very much. Every now and then out with Hambone. To the grocery store with Mom. At first it was too hard for me to go anywhere with the pain and the heavy cast I had to drag around, but after a month or so, I got to where I had no desire. Didn't want to see anybody, didn't want to talk. I still felt that way for the most part. Though it was good to be out with Marcus, riding in the Ranger. Friday night, weather cool, windows up and the radio off. He puffed cigarettes and flicked ashes on the floorboard. It felt like all of time was laid out there on the road before us.

"So, your mom's working?" Marcus asked, breaking the quiet.

"No," I said. "She went out."

"Who with?"

"Didn't say."

We passed a blue house with a man out front, huddled beneath the hood of a truck, only the back of his head lit by a little electric lightbulb.

"Most likely a date," Marcus said.

"Doubt it."

He rubbed his hand over his goatee. "She's going to have to start sometime. What happens when you move out? She ain't going to want to live alone."

I bit off the white tip of my thumbnail and spat it on the floorboard. "I haven't thought about it."

"Well, you ought to. One way or the other. You don't want her being lonely. But you don't want no shithead living in your house neither."

We crossed the little bridge over the swamp. I looked for ducks but didn't see any in the dark. Water was low. Tops of cypress knees exposed. "It ain't a date, anyway."

We were quiet again until we got to the corner of Highways 76 and 52. Marcus pulled into the BiLo Grocery strip and parked in front of China Taste. The neon sign on the window said *Open*, but the *p* was burnt out.

Brass bells tied to the door jangled together as we walked inside. The air smelled like bleach and cooking oil. Green booths lined the barren walls. Beside the counter sat a fish tank, as grungy as the one in my room. A lighted menu with pictures hung from the ceiling and a boy that looked younger than me stood behind the register, spinning a pencil like a propeller between his forefinger and thumb. Marcus ordered without asking me what I wanted. Shrimp fried rice, sesame chicken and eggrolls.

"Okay," the boy said. "Please have a seat. It'll be about ten minutes." His voice was deeper than I expected, and his English was perfectly clear.

"Y'all don't sell beer, do you?" Marcus asked.

"No alcohol."

"Shame, but I get it." Marcus grabbed a handful of soy sauce and hot mustard packets. Crossed the restaurant and squeezed into a booth facing the door. I sat across from him. His belly pushed against the table. He crossed his arms in front of him to try and hide it.

"I can't stand these tiny little booths," I said, to try and take away some of his embarrassment. "I hardly fit."

"You're telling me."

The boy behind the counter shouted toward the kitchen in Chinese and the two old men who served as cooks started scrambling around, opening plastic bowls, pouring grease in high-sided pans.

Marcus stared down at the table. He arranged the sauce packets in neat rows. "Fire last night," he finally said. "Trailer off Starline Drive, way down past Meemaw's. Call came in around four in the morning."

"You get it put out?"

"No," he said. "It was over by the time we got there. Those trailers go up, they're gone before we can get our helmets on good. Just boxes of kindling." He took a deep breath. "One man living there by himself. Like me in mine. Found him cooked to a crisp on a pile of ash, looked like it was his couch. I carried him out myself."

"He slept through the fire?"

"Probably drunk. Passed out. High on something."

That worried me. Both the death of the man and the way Marcus talked about it. Calm and measured. But I knew the fact that he mentioned it at all meant it was weighing heavy on his mind.

"That's terrible."

Marcus nodded. "But it ain't the worst thing I've seen." He arranged the sauce packets in lines, alternating colors. Black then yellow, black then yellow.

A few minutes later, the bells on the door jangled. I looked over my shoulder at the noise. It was Lydia Proveaux, alone, wearing plaid pajama bottoms and a gray sweatshirt, her hair tied up in a loose bun. She was beautiful even in that. Maybe more, because of that, the way a leaf looks better on a tree than taped to a page in a book. We met eyes right off, watched each other recognize. It was too late to turn away.

"Hey," I said.

"Oh, so you can speak. You do know me."

After Lydia said she wanted to come visit when I was still laid up, I never asked Mom. I wanted to see her, almost more than anything. I must've imagined her a thousand times in my bedroom, her perfume smell on my covers, the way her bare feet would look against the carpet. But I didn't want her to see me. Not like I was, all broke up, stinking from not being able to shower, just laying there in my bed like a cold pale fish. We talked on the phone a little bit more, but Lydia never mentioned coming over again and neither did I. Our talking faded off. I knew she thought I didn't want to see her. I figured that was better than the truth. It'd been over a month since we last spoke.

"What you doing here?"

She walked over to the edge of our booth, so I had to look up to see her face. "Same as you, I guess. Getting food. Taking it home for Ronald and me." She looked at her car keys in her hand like she was surprised to find them there, then stuck them in the front pocket of her sweatshirt. "Y'all looking all dressed up. Big plans on a Friday night? I hardly knew you were walking again."

My face got hot. I looked down at the table. "Not really walking good," I said. "Not all the way. I don't know what we're doing. He just came to get me."

"Just trying to have a little fun," Marcus said.

I cut my eyes at him.

"Yeah, well. Must be nice," Lydia said. "I got to go. Ronald's waiting." She turned and walked to the counter. The boy gave her a paper bag and she gave him money from her sweatshirt pocket. Bills and coins, exact change. He didn't even have to tell her how much. She turned and walked toward the door.

"See you later," I said.

"I won't hold my breath." She pushed the door open and walked into the parking lot. The brass bells clattered as the door swung closed behind her.

The boy brought our food on blue plates shortly after Lydia left. He carried three on one arm like a real waiter. Sat them down on the table between us. "Need chopsticks?" he asked.

"Not even if I knew how to use them," Marcus said. "Forks."

The boy smiled, pulled two rolls of silverware from his back pocket, and laid them flat on the table.

"Thanks," Marcus said.

The boy nodded and walked back behind the counter. He tapped on the glass of the fish tank and the water swirled, but I still didn't see any fish.

"What'd you do to piss off the Peanut Gal?" Marcus asked, tearing the top off a soy sauce packet and squirting it over the plate of fried rice.

"Nothing." I picked up a set of silverware and started slowly unwrapping it.

"Sometimes nothing is just as bad as something."

I didn't answer. He was like a fortune cookie, mostly full of bullshit disguised as insight, but sometimes vague and applicable enough to make you think twice. I put my napkin on my lap and looked at our food. Rice sopped with soy sauce, thick beige eggrolls shimmering with grease, sesame chicken, bright red and steaming. It looked like the guts I'd pulled out of the owl the night before. Bile rose in the back of my throat. I got a twisting tightness from the bottom of my stomach all the way up my throat. I looked toward the fish tank and swallowed hard. Saw a shimmer of black, but still nothing I could tell what it was.

Marcus shoveled fried rice into his mouth. "You all right?" he mumbled, mouth full.

"I'm fine."

"Look like you're about to yak."

I took an eggroll from the plate and bit off the hot, doughy end. Chewed slowly. "See? I'm fine."

Marcus stabbed a piece of the bloody looking chicken with his fork. "Keep saying it." He put the chicken in his mouth. "Just keep saying it."

We took Highway 52 toward the Santee River. The night was dark. We pulled off the blacktop onto a long dirt driveway. After about a mile, the road opened into a field. A tall fire burned in the center, reflected on the shallow water of the river running beyond it. Few dozen yards to the right sat a hayshed hung with Christmas lights, under which people stood, clutching cups and cans, facing a group of men working instruments. Two six-string guitars, a bass, a set of small drums. Marcus parked along the tree line behind an old Pontiac with rusted out fenders.

"Some kind of party?" I asked.

"That's Harrison on the drums," Marcus said. "From the station."

"But whose party?"

"It's a bonfire. Relax."

As we walked toward the fire, I could hear the music drifting out from under the aluminum roof of the hayshed. Mostly sounded like kick drum and cymbals, but I could hear faintly the warbling of an electric guitar and the deep, driving thud of the bass too. Folks sat propped in camp chairs around the fire, their faces flickering in the light. I didn't recognize any of them. Near the fire stood a fold-out table covered with two-liters of soda and handles of booze. A metal horse trough sat on the ground beside the table, filled with ice and cans of beer. Marcus waved to the people in the chairs. They smiled and waved back. He went to the trough and pulled two cans of Natural Light from the ice. He offered me one and I took it.

"Ain't afraid to drink now?"

"Who invited you here?"

"Christ," he said. "Pull the stick out your ass."

Marcus walked toward the hayshed and I followed. The closer we got, the clearer the music became. I started to hear a man's voice, just barely audible over the instruments. I popped the tab on my beer and took a long gulp. First sip was the worst. I hoped it would calm my nerves. I never really liked being around people I didn't know, but anymore, I almost couldn't stand being around anybody at all.

Marcus stood at the corner of the shed, leaned against a thick wooden pylon that braced the roof. I settled beside him and looked at the others standing in the small crowd. Some swaying to the sounds. They were all about Marcus's age. Some men with sideburns and some with mustaches, most of them wearing baseball hats embroidered with the names of beer brands, construction companies, mechanic shops. Women all beautiful in the partial darkness, hands holding drinks or shoved into their pockets. I took another long swig of beer. The band finished a song. People clapped. Some whistled. The band began another song, slower than the one that came before it but with a big, driving guitar sound. The man began to sing again, shaky and sincere.

From the start this very heart's been on the table
Where you sit with knife and fork in hand

Marcus took a long, desperate slug from his beer. I couldn't see the band past the crowd. There was no stage. They were just standing on flat ground. But I could feel the kick drum vibrating in the cavity of my chest. Inside somewhere, the words, that voice, rattling around, spun together by the low, distorted twang of the guitar. The hair on my arms stood up. I closed my eyes and rolled my shoulders. Ground my heels in the dirt and sipped from my beer. Tasted salty, better than it had before.

Marcus leaned over and spoke into my ear. "Sound good."

I nodded. Didn't want to talk. I closed my eyes and focused only on the music. The people around me all faded away. My body vibrated with noise like a corn stalk in a thunderstorm. Though I heard the words, I didn't understand them. Somehow, I still knew the story I was hearing was a sad one, even if it didn't make me feel that way exactly.

> It's hard to make a living when you're trying not to die.
> Hard to shoot the breeze, just aiming at the sky
> I don't know if this ride is over, but it's broken down for now
> I got some tools, lord, I hope I got the know-how

The words faded to the sound of a guitar solo, fuzzy and imprecise, drawing visions from my mind, distant and close, seen and imagined. A football flying through the air, tumbling end over end. Shorty slumped in his dark living room, the television screen lighting his face. My mother, younger, with a swollen bloody lip. Lydia standing naked in my bedroom, her waist and breasts many shades lighter than the rest of her. Merle eating hot owl guts, the fur around his lips matted red. Quinton's tattoo, hands folded in prayer, green ink against—beneath—his skin.

The song ended. People clapped. I opened my eyes. The crowd was dispersing, moving toward the fire. I could see pieces of the band. The drummer, Harrison, wiping sweat from his forehead with an oily looking rag. The bass player squatting to put his instrument in a case, pushing his long blonde hair from his face. The crowd continued to thin, and I saw the singer with his back to me, an electric guitar strung over his neck. He wore baggy Carhartt work pants, dirty boots, and a plain black sweatshirt. It didn't seem possible that those words, that song, had travelled through him. Seemed too plain, too small. He turned around and unstrapped his guitar. His face looked familiar—tan and wrinkled, not like he was old, just like he'd seen a lot of weather—but I couldn't place him.

"Come on," Marcus said, putting his hand on my shoulder. "Let's go talk to Harrison. He can introduce us to the rest of the band."

"No," I said. "Not me. You go ahead."

Marcus laughed and drained the rest of his beer. "Just tell them good set. They love to hear that. All bands do. Everybody is too scared to say it. They're just dudes from around here."

"I need another beer. You go ahead. I'll be right back." I walked off toward the drink table before he could respond.

More people were crowded around the fire and the drink table now that the band had quit. A man with a long, dark beard tossed a wooden pallet on the blaze. I tossed my empty can in a plastic trash barrel and took another beer from the horse trough. I watched as the bearded man brought an old Christmas tree to the fire and tossed it on, the dry needles crackling and sending up a shimmer of sparks. A man bumped into me as he approached the beer trough. I backed away from the bustle, to the very edge of the firelight. Cracked my beer and took a sip. Looked back to the hayshed. Marcus was standing in a semi-circle of people. The bass player, Harrison, and some others I guessed were friends. Marcus put a Pall Mall in his mouth and lit the tip. Handed his lighter to a woman standing beside him. The singer was moving around behind them, hunched over, rolling up cables and packing them into a red milk crate. He seemed oblivious to Marcus and the others.

Oblivious to everyone. Just meticulously packing his gear.

A woman approached me from the drink table holding a plastic cup in either hand. Back to the fire, I could barely see her face. She wore a long-sleeved flannel unbuttoned over a T-shirt and jeans tucked into tall brown boots. "Have a drink and join the party." She offered one of the cups to me. "We're all good people here."

"I've got one." I showed her my beer.

"A real one," she said.

I took the cup from her hand. The bottom was full of golden-brown liquor. She bumped her cup against mine. "Cheers." She downed the whiskey. I drank mine too. It was nasty on my tongue and burned all the way down my throat. I sipped my Natural Light to wash it down.

"Not bad," the woman said. She took the cup from my hands and walked back toward the table. After a few steps, she stopped and turned around. "Come on," she said, gesturing with her head. "I'll pour another one for us. I promise, we don't bite or nothing."

I followed her back to the table. I could see her face better closer to the fire. She had dark curly hair, faded around the roots, and thin lips. She lifted a bottle of Evan Williams and tipped it over the cups, spilling some down the edges and on the table. "To new friends," she said, handing me my cup. "May we not be scared to meet them."

She tossed back the shot. I looked down at mine. It was a heavier pour than the last.

"Drink it," she said. "It's a gift. An offering of peace."

I poured the whiskey in my mouth, but I couldn't swallow. I just held it in my mouth for a second until I finally forced myself to choke it all the way down, like bitter heat. I gagged and burped at the same time, fumes coming out my nose.

The woman laughed. "Don't worry," she said. "You'll learn." She turned and walked shakily toward the fire. I took a swig of beer, sloshed it around my mouth, and spat it on the ground. Took another sip and swallowed. Marcus was still under the hayshed, talking to the band and the people with them. There seemed to be more now, but the singer wasn't with them. I saw Marcus laugh. Teeth shining, belly shaking. He didn't seem too concerned, like he was looking for me or anything. I took another beer from the horse trough and walked past the fire, toward the river, with quick, measured steps, both to keep me steady after the whiskey and to make it look like I had a destination, so no one else would try to stop me or talk.

At the bank of the river, the party behind was just a figment. Faded fire, muffled voices. The current hummed. Water trickled and swirled over fallen limbs and rocks. I sat on the ground, thick grainy sand and patchy brown grass, dead with winter. I crossed my right leg and stuck my left out straight. I could feel that my knee was swollen. I knew if I bent it too far, it would feel like thick rubber bands popping, gears grinding.

I finished my beer and smashed the can. Laid it on the ground beside me and cracked the fresh one I'd brought. A cold wind blew across the river, shaking the leafless treetops on the opposite bank and sending chills up my bare arms. I watched the river run black and blue, a long shallow bruise across the county. Head swaying from the booze. It was different than the pills. I felt it more in my head than my body, a heavy kind of calm. I was angry at myself for the feeling. Even more for enjoying it, if that's what you call it, because it didn't feel so much like joy as relief.

Footsteps sounded behind me, crunching against the sandy ground. I looked over my shoulder. It was a man approaching, too small to be Marcus. He came to the riverbank beside me, just a few steps away, and stared out over the water. I thought he hadn't seen me, and I worried if I spoke now it would startle him. He pulled a pouch of cigarettes from his back pocket and fished one out. Stuck it in his lips and lit it with a Zippo lighter, cupping his hand over the flame. It was the singer. The lighter echoed over the water like a firecracker when he flicked it shut. "I can't tell if it's any quieter over here." He didn't look at me when he spoke, just stared out over the river. "My ears are ringing."

"Not as loud," I said. "But still."

"It's the amplifiers. I'll be deaf before I'm fifty." He stood very still, just his elbow swinging mechanically, bringing his cigarette to his lips, then dropping it back down by his side.

I drank from my can of Natural Light. "Like your song," I said. "The last one you played. It's the only one I heard all the way. But it was real good."

The singer didn't respond. He just stood stone still, smoking. "Sometimes I wonder if the closest we'll ever hear to true quiet ain't actually so much noise you can't decipher it."

I picked at a piece of dead grass. Flicked it at the water, but it didn't make it all the way. I worried I'd offended him somehow.

"Worst thing about a song is you've got to sing it. I'd rather be at home tonight, playing guitar by myself." He finished his cigarette, flicked the butt on the ground, and crushed it in the dirt with his heel. "But a song you don't sing don't exist. Guess that's a drawn-out, fucked up way of saying thank you. For listening."

"You're welcome."

The singer took three short steps down the bank, unzipped his pants, and pissed into the river. It was an extended, voluminous piss that sent a tremor down his spine. When he was done, he shook his member dry, zipped his pants, and walked back toward the fire, the crowd, without another word.

VII

I woke up on Marcus's couch Saturday morning with my clothes still on. My head was sore and my throat was dry. The sun was just starting to break outside. I pulled the musty blanket Marcus gave me up to my chin and tried to go back to sleep, but I couldn't. I was stuck in some waking worry, like I was just treading water in a lake of deep, heavy dread. I started to feel sick, the worry and the booze boiling in my stomach. I got up off the couch and went to the kitchen for some water. The sink held a few dirty forks and cups. I washed one of the cups with dollar-store soap and a crusty sponge sitting on the rim of the sink. Filled it with water and drank.

I could see the road from the window over the sink. Thought I saw something shiny and silver near the asphalt, lying in the grass. I took one more sip of water and went to the door. Pulled on my boots and walked outside. The air was chilly, but the sun was beaming warm, right into the yard. I walked to the road and found the thing I'd seen. A hub cap, solid like a trashcan lid, no spokes. Bent along one edge. Chevrolet cross stamped in the center. I looked back to the trailer. The other hubcaps Marcus had found still leaned against the trailer skirting, glistening beneath a thin film of dew. He had at least twenty. I figured there must be a pothole nearby knocking them loose. I looked up the road but didn't see anything. No traffic. I started walking, straddling the center yellow line, carrying the hubcap under my arm. Strange to walk on the highway, rocks crunching beneath my boots. Felt like the dimensions were changed. Wider. Asphalt thicker. I walked a good distance without finding the pothole, just beer cans and Styrofoam cups and cigarette butts in the ditches. Rounded the corner and saw something dark near the edge of the road, I figured it was the pothole, but as I approached, I saw it was just a patch of dried blood and fur, the remnants of a roadkill. Probably a possum, but I couldn't tell. I turned and walked back toward Marcus's. A car approached, and I moved to the edge of the road. Waved, still holding the hubcap under one arm. They didn't wave back.

Spooky was waiting by the front door. She chirped as I walked up the rickety wooden stairs. I rubbed down her back. She turned and bit my hand softly. I opened the door and she ran inside. I followed her. The heat wasn't on, but it was still warmer than outside, almost stuffy. Marcus was standing in the kitchen near the stove in boxer shorts and a cutoff T-shirt, heating a pot of water. Spooky rubbed her teeth against his bare leg.

I held up the hubcap. "Got another one for your collection."

"It ain't a collection. I told you. It's a lost and found."

I wondered what he would do if anyone ever actually came to get one of the hubcaps. Knowing him, he'd check their other wheels to make sure they matched. A shepherd of misplaced things.

"Leave it outside, anyway. Don't belong in here."

I cracked the door and balanced the hub on the handrail of the stairs.

"You drink coffee?" Marcus asked.

"Not really."

"Well, it's a good morning to start." He opened the cabinet over the stove and brought down a jar of instant. "Why the fuck are you up so early?"

I bent over and unlaced my boots. "Just am."

"Sometimes the drink will do that to you."

"I wasn't drunk."

"That's one of those things that when you have to say it, it means the hundred percent opposite." He pulled two mugs from the cabinet and spooned the instant coffee into them. "It's okay to be drunk sometimes. Just don't drink and drive. More than a few anyway. You don't have to be ashamed of it."

I sat down on the couch. "But I wasn't."

Marcus reached under the sink and found a can of wet cat food. Spooky mewed. He opened the can and put it on the floor and she began to eat. "Having a beer don't make you a bastard. Sometimes it just brings it out of you."

I didn't say anything back. I knew he was talking about my dad. I didn't like talking about him with Marcus. I knew his hatred of him stemmed straight from his love for me, but he was still my father, even if most of the time it felt like I had no father at all.

The water started to boil, and Marcus poured it over the instant coffee crystals. He came from the kitchen carrying the two cups and handed one to me. I smelled the coffee. Warm, buttery and dark. I took a sip. It tasted nothing like the smell. Just bitter.

Marcus added no sugar or milk. I swallowed it down. Marcus smiled and sipped his own. "Life is just time between drinks," he said. "Coffee in the morning, liquor at night." He sat down beside me, his big leg covered in thick dark hair brushing against my jeans.

I took another small sip of my coffee. "You have to work today?"

"On at eleven. You coming to Meemaw's tomorrow?"

"For what?"

"Super Bowl Sunday," Marcus said. "I know you didn't forget."

Marcus finished his coffee and I finished half of mine, poured the rest down the sink drain. We headed back to my house. I drove the Ranger. It was the first time I'd driven since I got out of the leg cast and I was nervous on the gas and touchy on the breaks. Marcus spat directions. Put on your signal. Let off the gas. Get your hands ready to turn. I could tell he was getting frustrated. It was like our very first lesson all over again. Finally, we pulled onto Lantana Lane and into the driveway. I got out and he lumbered over to the driver's seat. "See you tomorrow," he said.

"Maybe."

"No. I'll see you."

I opened the front door and smelled bacon. Heard it sizzling in the pan beneath the sound of old country music on the radio. Twangy guitar and a nasally voice. I closed the door, took off my boots, and went to the kitchen. Mom stood in front of the stove wearing black sweatpants and a baggy long-sleeved T-shirt, swaying her hips and poking at the bacon with a spatula. "You're home just in time," she called, not even turning around. "I felt like making breakfast."

Half the linoleum flooring was pulled up and the table was

pushed into the corner. The stereo from my room sat on top. Mom must've brought it out. "Smells good," I said.

"Toast in the oven. How's Marcus?"

"He's Marcus."

"Ain't that the truth."

"Can I help with anything?"

"Yes," Mom said. "But not breakfast. Eat first. Then you can help me pull up the rest of these floors and ride with me to Molly and Easton's to get the new ones. They're going to let me borrow their trailer to haul them."

"You know how to pull a trailer?"

She turned the knob to kill the burner beneath her bacon. "I figured we could learn together."

"I know how. I've pulled Marcus's boat trailer. I can even back it up all right."

"Then you can teach me." She pulled a baking sheet of toast from the oven and set it on the stove beside the pan of bacon. The bread was slathered with butter and topped with yellow cheese just starting to burn black on the edges. She pulled two plates from the cabinet and handed me one. "Fix your own."

I put a few pieces of bacon on the plate and a piece of toast. "No eggs?"

"We're out."

Mom fixed a plate too and we ate there in the kitchen, standing up. When we finished, we left the dirty dishes in the sink and went right to ripping up linoleum. After a few squares, we worked out a method. Mom cut the edge with her razor. I slid the pry bar underneath and edged up the corner, then Mom sliced at the glue while I pushed on the pry bar until the sticky tile came all the way up. We didn't talk much at all, just focused on the work and the music. After a little while, I went to my room and found one of the CDs Marcus had brought me. Put that on the stereo instead of the country music Mom had been playing. I was hoping somehow it was the band we'd seen the night before. It wasn't. Not even similar. Too noisy. I couldn't even understand the words. After two songs, I changed it back to the radio.

Once we pulled up all the tiles, we moved the kitchen table into the front room to make way for the new flooring. Mom swept the yellow plywood. I washed the breakfast dishes and put them away. We both took quick showers and dressed to work. I put my knee brace on under my jeans. It was bulky and itched when the Velcro straps rubbed against my skin, but it gave me some support and made me worry less about stepping wrong or twisting it or something. Mom's clothes were starting to fit looser on her, like she was losing weight, but she hadn't mentioned anything about trying.

Molly and Easton were in front of the house they were building when we turned into the drive off Katy Hill Road. Molly waved her hand and it was almost like she'd been standing there all morning, just waiting on us to pull in. She was a short woman with thick legs, curly blonde hair, and a nose that turned up slightly. Easton stood beside her, tall and skinny, his T-shirt barely reaching his belt buckle. He had dark circles around his eyes and a carpenter's pencil stuck behind his ear. Mom rolled down the window and returned Molly's wave. Followed the driveway to the head and parked the Jeep. She patted my knee gently and got out of the car, closing the door behind her. Molly came walking over, smiling and already talking happily in a high-pitched voice. She hugged Mom. Easton stayed standing where he was. I got out of the Jeep and walked around to Mom and Molly, staying a few steps away.

"The house is gorgeous," Mom said.

"I'm starting to come around to it. Still needs a lot of work, but we're getting there. I say *we*. Easton's done most of it himself." The house was only one story, but it was very wide. Dark green siding and a black shingled roof. Perfectly square windows with vinyl storm shutters lining the front, three on either side of the door. It looked just like Marcus's trailer, only enlarged and more permanent.

"You must be Grady," Molly said. "I feel like I already know you."

I nodded my head and smiled. Didn't know what to say. It felt strange, showing up to somebody's place to meet them, give them money, haul away their stuff. I looked over at Easton. He had his head bent down, toeing the grass with his boot.

"Come on," Molly said. "I'll give y'all the nickel tour." She walked up the front steps and we followed. Easton went around the back of the house. Molly walked us through the living room, bright and open, still smelling of paint. Into the kitchen, unused gas range, marble counters so clean I could see my reflection in the stone. Whitewashed wooden cabinets, but the doors hadn't been installed. The floors were a dark brown like oak with a matte finish. They'd look all right in our house. Not perfect. Down the hallway, Molly pointed into bedrooms, two of them, cold and empty, waiting on baseboards and trim.

"One of these will be the nursery," Molly said. "When we need it."

Mom touched her shoulder. "Soon."

At the end of the hallway, we came to the master bedroom. It was painted a different shade than any of the other rooms, light blue, almost silvery, like a fish. "I can't wait to sleep here," Molly said.

"Of course not," Mom said.

"At the end of my shifts, when my feet are aching, I just think about coming home to this. Taking off my shoes and lying flat on my back in a soft bed, in this room."

"It's your own little sanctuary."

"Just wait until you see this." Molly crossed the room in three steps, pushed open the bathroom, and flicked on the light switch. Inside was a large round tub with a gooseneck faucet and jets in the side. The rest of the bathroom was unfinished. No sink, no toilet, no mirror. Just the enormous white tub. "My one demand," Molly said.

"Wow," Mom said. "That really is something."

Outside, Mom pulled the Jeep around to the backyard and me and Easton hitched up the trailer. The flooring was already loaded in cardboard pallets and secured with two thick ratchet-strap. When we were done, Easton grabbed one of the pallets and shook it. The whole trailer rocked. Even the Jeep wiggled on its springs. "Ain't going nowhere," he mumbled in a deep, gravelly voice.

"Thank you."

"Ain't no problem." He pulled the carpenter's pencil from behind his ear and tapped his knuckles with it. "Just take care with the trailer. I'll be around for it tomorrow. Need it back for work Monday."

"Yes, sir."

He put the pencil back behind his ear and walked away, around the edge of the house. Mom and Molly were standing by the back stairs. I went over to them and they stopped talking when I got close.

"Anyway," Mom said. "We really do appreciate this. The floors, letting us borrow the trailer, everything. And what a beautiful home. You're going to be happy here." She reached into her pocket and pulled out a stack of crisp new bills, folded in half, and offered it to Molly.

She smiled and shook her head. "No. I want you to have them."

Mom's cheeks flushed red. "I want to have them too," Mom said. "And I want to pay you for them."

Molly put her hands in her pockets. "Me and Easton talked, and we want to give them to you. We already accounted for them. They're extra. We're just happy to see them go to good use."

I felt my face getting hot too.

"That's very sweet of y'all," Mom said. "But that wasn't the deal." She still had the money held out in front of her. "Here," she said. "Take it."

"You're doing us a favor, getting rid of them." Molly walked up the stairs. "We won't hear nothing else about it. See you at work."

Mom put the money back in her pocket. "Thank you," she said, low, resigned.

"No, thank you," Molly said, and went inside.

Me and Mom got in the Jeep and she drove carefully around the house and out of the yard, the trailer rattling behind. I looked for Easton to wave goodbye but didn't see him anywhere. Mom pulled onto Katy Hill Road going toward Highway 76, looking in her rearview to make sure the trailer was okay. When she turned onto Highway 76 toward home, she started to talk, like she'd been wanting to make sure we were out of hearing distance from Molly and Easton.

"That isn't what I meant to happen. You saw I had the money."

"They were just trying to be nice."

"We don't need anyone's charity," Mom said. "Never have. That house is nice. He's done a fine job. But you better believe she's going to make it tacky with furniture and decorations. She's got no taste."

We passed a brick house, mailbox out by the highway, red flag tipped up, holding a note. Mom wasn't overly used to kindness, so when it came to her, she didn't trust it. I adjusted my knee brace under my jeans.

"Does it hurt?"

"Not right now," I said.

❖

Like me, Mom was fine at pulling the trailer forward but shaky at backing up. Took her a couple tries to back down the driveway, but eventually she got it. Together we unloaded the pallets of flooring off the trailer and carried them inside. Stacked them in the kitchen. It was almost two o'clock and Mom had a shift at three. She opened the top box and looked at the flooring, rubbed her hand across the surface. "Maybe we can start laying them tomorrow before we go to Meemaw's."

"Maybe we can just skip Meemaw's," I said.

"It's the Super Bowl. You don't want to watch?"

"I'm just not that into it this year. I don't even know who's playing."

"It's football," Mom said. "It's your family."

I didn't say anything. Didn't want to tell her that neither of those two things seemed very appealing, especially not together. It meant questions about my leg, how I was doing, would I be ready for next season. Like I had any answers. Like I wasn't asking myself the same thing every day.

"Listen," Mom said. She bit her bottom lip and looked down at her watch. "I don't have long, but I wanted to ask you about this anyway. I talked to Coach Hendrickson."

"When?"

"He called me the other day."

"Why would he call you?"

"He's worried about you. He said you haven't been to weight training since you've been back at school."

I looked down at the floor, the grungy old plywood. It wasn't so much getting caught that bothered me. I knew eventually I would. But now I'd have to start going.

Mom turned and walked to the front room, gesturing with her hand for me to follow. She knelt on the floor facing the recliner and pointed for me to sit in the chair. I did.

"He isn't mad. He knows it's hard. He wants to help you."

"Then why didn't he tell it straight to me? Why'd he have to drag you into it?"

"I'm your mother."

"He calls us men. Maybe he ought to treat us like it."

"You're fifteen. I don't care what he calls you. You aren't a man. You're a kid. He's your coach. You were cutting class. He called me. That's how all this works."

I looked down at my lap.

"He didn't do anything wrong. Neither did you. I get it. I'm not mad. He's not mad. You shouldn't be. It's all just a big accident. It's bad luck that's happened to you, Grady. I'm sorry. I wish I could take it away."

"It doesn't feel the same."

Mom tucked a strand of hair behind her ear. "It isn't," she said. "It won't be. It's different. You have to get used to it. That's what happens. Things change, and we have to get used to it."

"What if I don't want to anymore? What if I've changed, too?"

Mom bit her bottom lip. I could tell she was trying not to cry. "Do me a favor," she said. "Go to weight training on Monday. Give it a chance. Give yourself a chance. I don't care if you never play football again." She paused. "But I know you love it. And I don't want to see you give up something you love just because it's hard."

I nodded. I was scared if I spoke, my voice might shake.

Mom stood and kissed me on top of the head. "I'm sorry. I love you," she said. "I have to get ready for my shift."

�֍

After Mom left, I stayed in the living room watching television. Show analyzing the Super Bowl matchup. New England Patriots versus the Atlanta Falcons. Show previewing super bowl commercials. Budweiser beer, Ford trucks.

Hambone texted. *Let go HUNT.* I ignored him. He wouldn't be happy when I told him I was going to weight training. Maybe that'd be okay. I could just cut him off all at once. No more hunting. No more sitting on our bench every morning, dipping snuff. Hanging out with him was a good way to kill time. Maybe I'd killed enough.

A show came on about super bowls from the past and I turned the television off. I went to YouTube on my phone. I wanted to look for the band I'd seen with Marcus the night before, but I didn't know what they were called, or the names of their songs or anything. All I knew was the drummer's name was Harrison. I figured I'd search something broad, knowing I probably wouldn't find that specific band, but maybe something else cool, something Marcus didn't even know about that I could show him. I typed in *South Carolina rock band.* The first thing that came up was a video of a band called 2nd South Carolina String Band playing a song called "Zip Coon." I clicked the link and the song began to play: banjo, flute and fiddle. There was no real video, just a sepia toned picture. Eight men in what looked like a Civil War camp, wearing kepi hats, sporting curled mustaches, holding instruments. I couldn't tell from the picture if it was actually old, or just made to look like that, but the sound quality was too good to be authentic.

> *Old Zip Coon, he's a learned scholar*
> *Sings possum up a gum tree and coonie in a holler*
> *Possum up a gum tree coonie on a stump*
> *Over double trouble, Zip Coon will jump*

After the first verse, the image switched to an old cartoon drawing of a tall man with dark skin and curly hair dressed in fancy clothes and a top hat. One hand on his hip, almost teasingly, the other twirling a set of spectacles attached to his neck with a gold chain.

The song ended and another video started to load, but I clicked off before it could play. I checked the time. It was only four o'clock. Marcus was still working. Mom wouldn't be home until close to midnight. I thought maybe a couple pain pills would help me pass the time. I could feel a little aching in my knee. Went to my bedroom and got the bottle from my sock drawer. Found the owl feet there, hidden away. I pushed them all the way to the corner and covered them with a pair of underwear so I wouldn't have to look at them or touch them. Shook two pills from the bottle and swallowed them back. I hoped they'd work. If not, I could take one more. I still had twelve left. I went back to the front room, turned on the TV, and flipped through the channels, waiting on the haze to settle over me. After half an hour, I couldn't find anything worth watching and barely felt anything at all from the pills. I took out my phone and texted Hambone. *We going after Old Zip Coon?*

In less than five minutes, he'd texted back. *U know it. Pick you up round 6.*

When we got out to the old Allendale Plantation land, it was almost dark. Sky still blue, but barely. Hambone drove the winding, narrow dirt roads until he came to a recent cutdown on the edge of the swamp. Hambone's uncle had sold the pines to the paper company. Hambone pulled the Frontier to the edge of the road and parked. I felt Merle stand up and move around in the dog box bolted to the bed, shaking the truck slightly.

"I brought you something," Hambone said. "To make up for the other night. I was just messing around. Trying to have a little fun. I wasn't trying to piss you off."

"You didn't," I said. "Just forget it."

He reached into his pocket and pulled out a blue Altoids tin. "I brung you these." He held the tin out toward me and opened the lid. Inside were pills of various shapes and sizes. Long tablets like horse pills, smaller green ones shaped circular and stamped with letters. Multicolored capsules. One little white tab shaped like a pentagon. They were all mixed together, rolling around in the shiny silver interior of the tin. A Geometry lesson in miniature.

"Where'd you get these?"

Hambone grinned, showing his sharp eyetooth on one side. "I told you, my momma's got a drawer full."

"What are they?"

"I can't pronounce the names. But I know how they make you feel."

I reached across the cab and closed the lid on the tin. "Not tonight." It was one thing to take my own pills out the bottle they came in from the pharmacy. Ones the doctor signed for me to have. But taking random pills like that that, all jumbled up, pilfered out of somebody's medicine cabinet, that was something else entirely. "Just beer."

Hambone slid the Altoids tin back in his pocket and opened his truck door. The cab light came on. He pulled a box of twenty-two bullets out of the console. "Okay, but they're yours." He started loading his rifle. "Whenever you want them, just say the word."

We turned Merle loose and drank cans of Bud Light on the tailgate while the dog sniffed for coons. Getting ready for him to pick me up, I planned on telling Hambone I was going to start going back to weight training. Thought I'd tell him I didn't really want to. Mom was making me. But I couldn't steer the conversation around to it. Anytime I tried to bring up school, he changed the subject real quick, said he came hunting to forget about all that bullshit.

After about forty-five minutes, we'd downed three beers each and Merle was treed way across the cutdown. We set off for the kill, trudging through the briars, guns on our shoulders. I whistled the tune to "Old Zip Coon."

VIII.

Meemaw cooked since it wasn't her birthday. She made chili in a humongous pot, so much we all could've eaten it every meal for three days and still not finished. Homemade biscuits, light brown and silver-dollar sized. A mound of cheddar cheese grated by hand, piled on a platter. She was standing near the stove when me and Mom came in, leaning awkwardly against the counter because her back was sore from standing, but she refused to sit. Marcus, Aunt Gail, and Peter were around the table, but they weren't eating. Mom and I were late, like always. We'd been laying the new floors and lost track of time, then Mom took forever in the shower.

"Don't worry," Meemaw said. "We waited. The game hasn't started." She stood up straight and winced a little bit. Forced herself to twist it into a smile. I went over and hugged her. She kissed my cheek.

"Would y'all hurry up with the pleasantries?" Marcus said. "My stomach is barking. I ain't ate all day."

"Sorry," Mom said. "It's my fault."

Aunt Gail rolled her eyes. "He's fine. Just trying to get your goat."

"Fix a bowl," Meemaw said, waving at Marcus. "What are you waiting for, come on, hurry up."

Marcus pushed back from the table, stood, and shuffled over toward the pot. He flicked my ear when he came by me and I punched him soft in the belly. I walked to the edge of the kitchen, where it opened into the living room. The gas logs were burning, and it felt good because it was rainy and cold outside. Shorty sat in his rocking chair in front of the television watching all the pregame festivities. American flag, celebrity singing the national anthem, Air Force flyover. The team captains jogged out to midfield and the referee showed them the coin he was going to flip, explained what the symbol on each side meant.

The Super Bowl meant nothing to me, not just then, but always. Too much extra stuff that had nothing to do with football. Ceremonies, commercials, parties. The game was a sideshow. It didn't matter who won. The following day, men on sports talk would discuss which players were switching teams, which team was the favorite to win next year. Vegas would begin accepting bets. Even the players always seemed underwhelmed. Last game of the season, win or lose, so what's the point? No more challenges, no one else to beat. The miracle isn't winning a Super Bowl, it's making it to the league at all.

Mom came up behind me, tapped my shoulder, and handed me a paper bowl. "Come on," she said. "Meemaw's waiting. You know she insists on going last."

I fixed a bowl of chili and piled it high with cheese. I took it to the living room where everyone else was getting settled. Aunt Gail and Peter sat on the couch against the wall, Meemaw's spot on the corner waiting for her. Marcus was perched on the recliner near the fire. There were two foldout chairs to the left of the couch for me and Mom. Everything arranged around Shorty in his rocking chair, the center of our familial circle. I sat and stirred the cheese into my chili. The teams were lining up for the kickoff.

"Who you pulling for, Shorty?" Marcus asked.

"Patriots," Shorty said.

"New England? Over Atlanta? Sounds like treason."

"I like the way they play the game. Respectful. None of that extra bullshit, the dancing and boo-hooing and all the rest." As he spoke, Shorty stared straight ahead at the screen, spoon full of chili trembling in his hand.

"Reckon some people find that entertaining," Peter said. "The flashy types."

"Disgusting," Shorty said. "Disgraceful."

The Patriots' kicker booted the ball off the tee and the other players ran downfield. The crowd screamed. The ball sailed out of the back of the end zone for a touchback and all the players ran to the sideline. The broadcast cut to a break.

"Y'all, hurry up," Aunt Gail called to Mom and Meemaw in the kitchen. "Commercials are on. They're supposed to be funny."

By halftime, we were all about to bust from eating too much chili and the Patriots were losing 21-3. Shorty was irate. When Lady Gaga came out for her halftime performance wearing sequins and eye paint like a cat, Shorty said, "Turn this jip-jap shit off my television."

"But this is my favorite part," Aunt Gail said.

"We'll leave it on," Meemaw said. "We'll just mute it."

Shorty grumbled.

"What's the point?" Mom asked. "She's going to sing."

"It's a compromise, honey," Meemaw said. "What more do you want?"

I stood up and took my bowl to the kitchen to throw it away. Peter followed behind me. He went to the stove and scooped a third helping of chili into his bowl. "Man, this stuff is good," he said. "My mother used to make chili, but it was never this good. Not spicy enough. Hard to beat your Meemaw's cooking." He shoveled a spoonful into his mouth and swallowed, hardly chewing. "How's the knee treating you?"

I put my bowl in the trash can. "Okay, I guess. It's getting there."

"Going to have a big season this fall? They say junior year is when the recruiters really start looking."

"Hope so. Guess we'll see." Marcus came in from the living room with an unlit Pall-Mall in his mouth. He threw his bowl away. "Good god, Peter," he said. "You're eating more? You're going to fart in your sleep and blow my poor mother to Oz."

Peter held back a laugh, cheeks full of chili. Marcus went out the back door to smoke and I followed him, thankful for the diversion. It had stopped raining, but it was still cold and damp. Marcus walked over to his Ranger, lit his cigarette, and pulled a Natural Light from the cooler in his toolbox. "You want one?"

"Sure."

He handed me a beer. "If Peter said something stupid, he don't mean nothing by it. He can't help it sometimes."

"Nothing like that."

"Hopefully your stepdaddy one day will be smarter than mine."

"I don't know why you keep talking about that."

Marcus took a long drag from his cigarette and smiled, blew smoke from his nostrils. "I'm a realist," he said. "I won't apologize for it."

We finished our beers slowly and went inside. The game was back on. Shorty was muttering cuss words under his breath. Atlanta had scored again on their opening drive. Now the Patriots had the ball and for the first time all night they looked like a competent football team. Brady completed a quick-out to Edelman and he took it for about fifteen yards. Shorty perked up slightly. Another quick pass, then a halfback draw for another first down. Shorty was quiet. The Patriots drove down the field and scored a touchdown on a pass to Gronkowski.

"I just love to watch those white boys catch the football," Shorty said.

"Little late," Meemaw said.

Shorty acted like he didn't hear her.

After that, the Patriots looked dominant, and the Falcons played like they were scared to lose, which is the one thing you can't be in football. You can be cruel, you can be dishonest, you can be selfish, you can be sloppy, but you cannot be scared.

"One day we'll be watching you play on the Super Bowl, Grady," Meemaw said.

"I don't know about that."

"I do. You've got it in you."

Mom patted my shoulder. "If he wants to, he can. Just has to put his mind to it."

Brady completed a pass to Hogan, the backup tight end, for another touchdown.

"Holy shit," Shorty said. "They're coming out the woodwork. I love to see those white boys catch the football."

✦

New England came back to win in overtime. We left Shorty rocking, prideful and devout in his rocker. It was a good while past midnight when Mom and I got home. The house was a wreck from us working on the floors. Kitchen table crowding the living room, pushed up against the couch. Hammers, nails and glue strewn across the kitchen floor. We had to watch YouTube videos to figure out how to lay the flooring—it was a delicate and slow-going process, applying the glue, lining up the grain, securing the nail in the edge so it didn't show—but we got about a third of the floor covered and it looked all right. Not quite professional, but close. The dark stain didn't match the cabinets, but Mom figured even if we couldn't get new ones for a while, we could sand and paint them.

"Thanks for all your help this weekend. We're a good team."

"I think it's going to look good," I yawned and wiped my eyes. "When we get to finish."

She put her arm around my waist and kissed my cheek. "Good luck at weight training in the morning. Don't forget. It might be tough at first, but you'll get through it. It'll be normal again soon. Try not to worry."

"Okay," I said. "I'll try." I went to my room, closed my door, and laid down in the dark. I tried hard not to worry, saying to myself over and over, *don't worry, don't worry,* but it was no use. I could barely fall asleep. When I was finally able, I dreamt a vivid, terrible dream. It was a Friday night before an away game. We went through the pregame ritual. The sandwiches, the bus ride, the prayer. We ran onto the field, under the lights, and I realized I was naked, my penis all shriveled up and pale. I stopped and tried to cover myself with my hands as the rest of the team, fully dressed in their jerseys and gear, ran around me. A roar came from the crowd in the stands. Marcus, Mom, Hambone, Lydia, the singer of the band from the bonfire—every person I ever knew—laughing and shouting my name.

I woke up with a headache and thought about taking a couple pain pills but decided against it. Since Hambone offered me his stash, I'd been worrying about that, too—how he knew what I'd never even admitted outright to myself—that it felt good to take the pills. That even though the pain in my knee was terrible, I was just as worried thinking that one day it might be gone. I'd have to either quit taking the medicine or find something else that hurt. I considered flushing the last of the pills down the toilet, but that seemed wasteful. Still hurt so bad sometimes. If I was going to start working out again regularly, getting into shape for next season, I'd probably need them.

Walking down the long hallway toward the locker room, brushing against the people I passed heading to class, some of them still reeking of the weekend, I felt like I was going to barf. I wished that Hambone would turn up and ask me where I thought I was going, make me sneak out to our bench. I would've done it. I cut my eyes down every corner, looking for him, but he was never there. Probably outside already, packing his can of Copenhagen, waiting on me to show.

When I finally got to the locker room, I stood up tall, pulled open the door, and went inside without hesitating. The smell was the same, strong and overwhelming, the scent of a past life. Body spray, old socks, ammonia from the cleaning solution. Quiet, just the sounds of clothes pulled on and off, mumbled good mornings. I went straight to where my locker had been, and there it was still. Name and number written on a laminated card taped to the top. Green shorts and gray T-shirt on the rack. Black shoes waiting in the cubby. I put down my bookbag and changed. Coach Hendrickson was at the fold-out table in his office, behind the Plexiglas partition, wearing a striped polo shirt. He was pecking at his laptop. He looked up from his work and saw me sitting in my locker, getting ready to put on my shoes. He nodded to me and I nodded back.

I had my knee brace packed in my bookbag, but I decided not to wear it. No need to call attention to my injury, my absence. I went straight to the gym after I changed, thankful I could get away from my locker before Quinton came to his beside me. Seabrook was already in the gym with a few others. He was bent over, stretching his quads. He looked up as I came through the door. Smiled and jogged over to meet me.

"Where've you been, man? Fucking missed you."

"Vacation."

"Yeah," he said, slapping me lightly on my belly with the back of his hand. "Looks like it. Been hiding out at the Shoney's all-you-can-eat buffet."

I laughed. "Probably still outrun you." I was thankful he was ragging on me. It felt normal, like I could fall back into my place in things.

"I don't know, man," Seabrook said. "I been grinding since the season ended. Working on my forty time."

"Guess we'll find out soon enough."

He cuffed me on the shoulder. "Glad you're back, man."

"Me too."

Coach Ellis came in, bald head shining, whistle already pressed between his lips. The rest of the team followed him in from the locker room. Quinton and Fritz were the last ones through the gym doors, shirtsleeves rolled up, exposing their strong arms, eyes still heavy-lidded with sleep. We fell into lines. Coach Ellis blew his whistle. Everyone started to stretch. I'd forgotten the order of the stretches and had to watch Seabrook to remember, but no one really noticed. My muscles were tight in the leg I'd hurt, and everywhere else, too. Hips, lower back. Felt almost like they were ripping. I was sweating when we moved to calisthenics, but it felt good and productive, the looseness in me, the sweat draining out those wasted months.

We lined up on the edge of the court under the basketball hoop, footsteps echoing across the gym. Seabrook was in the first group in the far line. I was more toward the middle, farther back. Coach Ellis blew his whistle and the first group ran high knees across the court. A voice came from behind me in line. "Damn, you're sweating so heavy already?" It was Quinton. "That ain't a good look."

In the line beside us, Fritz snickered. I wondered if they'd purposefully fallen in near me, or if it was just chance. I ignored them, but there was something in Quinton's voice that made it hard, like he was finally able to say the things he'd always wanted to, and I just had to take it.

When my turn came up and Coach Ellis blew his whistle, I ran the high knees full force, lifting my knees up as high to my chest as I could, pumping my arms. I couldn't find the rhythm to it. The music. It was pure work. Every time my left foot hit the floor, pain shot up my leg. I gritted my teeth and ran through it. On the other side, I filed to the back of the line and Coach Ellis blew his whistle again. Quinton's group came crossing. He ran smooth and effortless, his knees coming up almost to his chin, graceful and limber. He was silent, smiling as he finished his strides, and took his place in line behind me.

I was sore just from finishing the warmup. Muscles and bones. Sweating through my T-shirt as we filed out of the gym toward the weight room. Seabrook put his arm around my shoulder as we walked. "Takes time," he said. "But you'll get it back."

In the weight room, the workout was written on the board like always. Upper body: bench press, military press, triceps extension, rear-delt fly, curls. Four sets of six. I went to my and Seabrook's usual station, avoiding my reflection in the mirrors. Coach Ellis cranked up AC/DC's "Hell's Bells" on the stereo. I got the station set up for the bench press, laying the bench flat, lowering the bar, and sliding on two forty-five-pound plates on either side. My knee was aching, and I pulled up the leg of my shorts to look at it. Already swollen. I wanted to go outside and find Hambone. Listen to him philosophize about how stupid football was. Maybe nod my head this time.

Seabrook came up to me from the other side of the weight room. "Shit," he said. "I should've told you. Since you been gone, I had to lift with Quinton and Fritz."

"Good thing I'm back now."

He cracked his knuckles. "Yeah, but I don't want to leave them hanging."

"There's two of them."

"I know, but still. They'll push us. It'll be good."

It was hard enough being in the same room with Quinton. I didn't want to be any closer to him than I had to. He always tried to act like he was better than me, but now it was even worse, it was like he knew it was true. And maybe I did too, and I hated that, and I hated him for making me feel it so strong. But I didn't know how to say any of that, so I just shrugged.

"Whatever you say."

We took the weight off the bar and put it back on the rack,

then went across the weight room to Quinton and Fritz's station. They had already started their first set, Fritz on the bench and Quinton spotting, two forty-five-pound plates and a ten on each side of the bar. Fritz finished his six reps, filling his chest with air and blowing it out mechanically, then threw the weight back on the rack and stood up off the bench, rolling his shoulders and watching his muscles move in the mirror on the wall.

"We figured you'd be done with us now," Quinton said.

"Yeah," Fritz said. "Now that your b-b-bitch is back."

Seabrook didn't respond, just laid down on the bench and hefted the weight off the rack. I tapped Quinton's arm to move out of the way so I could spot Seabrook. He cranked out his set fast and easy. Stood and nodded to Quinton. Quinton laid on the bench and Fritz came around to spot him. His set was like Seabrook's, effortless, barely more than a warmup.

My turn came. I laid on the bench and grabbed the bar. Seabrook came around to spot me. The steel was warm from the others' hands. I spaced my arms out carefully and pushed. The weight felt good in my arms, down to my chest. The first three reps were smooth and easy. Last three, less so. Felt myself shaking. I hoped Seabrook and the others couldn't tell. I finished and stood, pulled back my fingers to stretch my forearms.

"I never seen someone get weak so fast," Quinton said. "Wasn't even your arm you hurt. You're going to have to switch to baseball or something more easy."

"I did the set, didn't I?"

"Sh-shit," Fritz said. "Barely."

"Let's see about the next one." Quinton took a five-pound plate off the rack and put it on the bar.

Fritz did the same to the other side, then laid on the bench. Eminem's "Lose Yourself" came playing through the speakers.

"This lame-ass shit, every day," Fritz said. "L-l-let us play something." He took the weight off the rack and started his set.

"Y'all watch that game last night?" Seabrook asked. "Pretty crazy."

"Shit is rigged," Quinton said. "How many times the Patriots got caught cheating? Recording people's signals, deflating footballs and everything. They're getting their ass whooped, then they come out of halftime looking brand new? Hell no."

"Brady and Belichick, man. You can never count them out."

"You're right about that," Quinton said. "Because they cheat."

Fritz finished his set and Seabrook took his place. I got in position to spot him, my arms hanging heavy and dead like they were filled with sand. Seabrook cranked out his set, no problem. Quinton did the same. My turn came again faster than I expected. I laid down on the bench and stretched my shoulders.

"Need me to take off the extra weight?" Quinton asked, "I don't want you to hurt yourself."

Fritz laughed. I wrapped my hands around the bar and pushed. I could tell right off I wasn't going to be able to do the whole set. Arms numb, wrists weak. I brought the bar down quick anyway. Let it bounce off my chest, then pushed it up for my first rep, blowing air out of my mouth. Same for the second, arching my back to get it all the way up. On the third rep, I stalled halfway up. Seabrook put his fingers under the bar and gave me a nudge up. I fought through, pausing for a breath at the top, arms fully extended.

"I told you to let me take some weight off," Quinton said. "I begged you."

My eyes were blurry and fresh sweat was beading on my forehead. I brought the weight down, bounced it off my chest, and got it halfway up again. Seabrook gave me another spot with his fingers again. I held my breath and pushed as hard as I could, but I still couldn't finish. My vision started to shake. Finally, Seabrook grabbed the bar with both hands and helped me get it up, onto the rack. I sat up, panting hard. The Eminem song was still playing, accented with the sound of plates knocking, bars being dropped on the rack. Seabrook rubbed my shoulders. "Good effort," he said.

Fritz giggled. "Y-y-yeah," he said. "G-good try."

"Come on," Seabrook said. "Ease up. It's his first day back."

"I know that," Quinton said. "That's why I told him I'd take off the extra weight. No trouble at all. He didn't have to embarrass himself like that."

Anger churned in my ears, hot and wet, mixing with adrenaline from the set. I gritted my teeth, stood up from the bench, and spun around so I was facing Quinton. "I ain't embarrassed. I been out six months. What's your excuse?"

"I don't need one," he said, taking a step closer to me. "I did the reps."

My backbone was hot. My nerves felt tender and sensitive. This was what I had been worried about since the moment I got hurt on that field in Gadsden. It was always leading to this. Pain, embarrassment, weakness. But now that it was finally here, I felt a lightness almost like relief. I opened my mouth and spoke. My voice sounded distant and strange. "If anyone ought to be embarrassed, it's you. Fucking senior. I'm a sophomore and I beat you out last summer. I stole your fucking job. If I'm as weak as you say I am, what the fuck are you?"

"Hey, come on," Seabrook said, touching my shoulder. "Chill, let's get a sip of water."

The others in the weight room were quiet, watching us. Music blaring. Coach Ellis must've stepped into the hall.

"No," I said. "He's going to fucking answer me. He was riding the fucking pine until I got hurt. If I'm so weak, how'd I beat you out?"

Quinton smiled. "You didn't beat shit. You know Coach always looking out for his boys."

"D-d-damn straight," Fritz said.

"What you mean *his boys?*"

"Don't play dumb," Quinton said. "You know he's got his boys. Especially the ones he's trying to get with their momma."

Sound and space blurred around us. Sweat ran cold down my spine. I took a step forward and got right up in Quinton's face. He was slightly taller than me. Had creases at the corners of his eyes. I smelled his breath. Mint chewing gum and tobacco smoke.

"What the fuck did you say to me?" I asked through gritted teeth.

He held back a grin. He wasn't afraid. He was joyous. "I said you were only starting because Coach is trying to slip it in your momma."

I balled up my right hand and swung it at Quinton as hard as I could, but he leaned out of the way and I missed. He planted his right foot, pushed off, and drove his fist into my jaw, rocking my whole body back on my heels. Before I could catch my balance, he hit me again, this time on the bridge of my nose, between my eyes. I fell on my back. Quinton jumped on top of me, pinning me to the ground. His fists fell on my face again and again like a hard, heavy rain. I never even got my hands up. I just laid on the floor, staring up at him between flashes of darkness and pain, and I knew that as glad as I was to be there, finally, after all the waiting and worrying—some vague, violent prophecy fulfilled—gladder still was he.

IX.

I waited alone in Coach Hendrickson's office, a dark curtain covering the Plexiglas partition facing the locker room. Held a bloody rag to my nose. The left side of my face was swollen. Didn't hurt yet, just felt big, the skin pulled tight. It was hard to see out of that eye. Seabrook came in with a bag full of ice from the training room and handed it to me. I took it and pushed it against my face. He kept standing there like he was waiting for me to say something, but I didn't and after a minute he went away.

The office was plain, just the fold-out table and a few matching chairs. Pages from the McCleod County Gazette tacked to the wall—big games, playoff berths—print too small to read. No pictures of family, no posters, just white walls and white tile and news clippings. Faint smell of institutional cleaning solution. Fluorescent bulbs humming overhead. The ice burned my face.

I'd never been in Coach Hendrickson's office before, but I'd seen other people called in, the curtain pulled over the window. Back then, I'd envied them. The chance to speak to him alone, hear his wisdom, even if punishment was the price. Now that it was my turn, I just wanted it over with.

A few minutes later, the door swung open and Coach Hendrickson came in, toweringly tall in the stark little office, the dark cologne smell of him like a shadow in the room. He closed the door behind him, took up a folding chair, placed it in front of me, and sat so close our knees were almost touching. I dropped the bag of ice and the bloody rag on the floor, kicked them under my chair. Still wearing my workout clothes, I wished I was able to change. I felt exposed in the thin material, stiffening now with sweat, especially with him in his usual polo tucked into khaki pants. Leather boat shoes on his feet. He stared hard into my face and I held his gaze. Green eyes ringed with darkness. It looked like he was wearing eyeliner. The thought was so funny to me at that moment I had to hold back a smile.

Coach Hendrickson's face tightened and twitched. "You find this situation comical, son?"

"No, sir."

"Neither do I. First day back and you get in a fistfight with your teammate." He paused. "Doesn't look like it was much of a fight though. He doesn't have a mark on him. Looks to me it was just a plain old ass-cutting."

I lowered my head. Studied the gold-black speckles in the tile.

"You want to tell me what got into you?"

I thought about what Quinton had said about my mom. "No, sir."

"Sit up, son. Straighten your back. Look me in the eye."

I felt myself getting mad again. Hands tingling. Breath

shortening. I was starting to recognize its coming. I looked up at his face. Stared through my unswollen eye at the gold chain glinting on his neck, holding that holy cross. The notion that Quinton might be right set my jaw to shaking. About me, about my mother, about everything. "Can I go?"

Coach Hendrickson took an exasperated breath. "Go where?" he said. "This team is your family. You're home now, son. There's nowhere to go."

My face was numb from the fight. I felt woozy and afraid. Afraid everyone might be telling the truth, finally, for once.

"So, here's how this is going to go." He scratched the back of his hand. "You put me in a bad spot, but we're not going to drag this out and let it fester. No sense in all that. You're going to go back to that weight room right now, shake your teammate's hand, and tell him you're sorry. He'll do the same and we'll put all this behind us for good. Understand?"

I met Coach Henrickson's eyes, knowing how I must look, all swollen and bloody. Suddenly I wanted to tell him exactly what Quinton said. See how he'd react. Then maybe I'd know the truth. But he didn't look concerned. Didn't even look mad. He was bored. It was clear. He didn't care what happened. He just wanted it to be over because it inconvenienced him.

"No," I said.

"Excuse me? Did he knock something loose in your brain? I didn't ask you anything. We've had this conversation before. When I tell you something, it's not a suggestion. It's a command."

I stood. Eyes hot, cheeks wet, salt burning my abrasions. I shook my head and walked out of his office and into the locker room. It was empty, the rest of the team still in the weight room. I wondered if Quinton was with them, deep in the rhythm of triceps extensions and rear-delt flies. My brief appearance, our fight, nothing more than a slight break in the waves. I went to my locker and checked the time on my phone. Ten minutes until classes changed. I had messages from Hambone. Didn't read them. I stripped off the workout clothes and wiped my eyes dry with my T-shirt. Changed into my jeans and hoodie. Quickly laced up my Wolverines, all scuffed and muddy. I wore them every day now, hoping they'd give me a purpose, or at least make other people think I had one. My heart was beating fast. I expected Coach Hendrickson to come after me, but he didn't. The curtain over his window stayed closed. I slipped on my bookbag and walked quietly out through the door, down the hallway, staying clear of the weight room.

I moved fast, peering into the classrooms through the skinny windows in the doors. Teachers standing at whiteboards. Students hunched over desktops, scribbling on lined and hole-punched paper. The scene was common—humble and civilized—but the faces all looked foreign.

I realized I was heading for Hambone. Walking toward the door that would lead to our bench. I didn't know what he could do for me. Probably nothing, but there was nowhere else to go. I took my phone from my pocket and read the messages he'd sent.

Waiting

Where fuck r u

home sick?

I started typing to tell him I was on my way. Before I could send the text, I heard a classroom door open behind me. I walked faster. Raised my shoulders to try and hide my face.

"Grady," a voice said in a hoarse, scratchy whisper.

I stopped, but I didn't turn around. Footsteps fell lightly on the tile, echoing off the steel lockers. I focused on a single locker up ahead with multicolored sticky notes all over the face.

"Grady," the voice said again.

I turned around. It was Lydia. She was wearing dark jeans, dirty white Converse sneakers, and an oversized flannel shirt with black-and-red checkered print.

"Shit," she said, seeing my face. "I thought that was you. You're all fucked up."

I turned back around and began walking away. Felt my eyes getting heavy with wetness again.

"Wait," Lydia said, coming up behind me. "I didn't mean it like that. Hey, it's okay. It's going to be okay." She put her arm around my waist. "Come on." She led me down the hallway, past the locker with the notes. Bible verses were scribbled on them. I didn't recognize the verses, but I could tell by the names at the bottom: Matthew, John, Mark. Numbers that looked like time. 3:11, 10:18. I breathed in the smell of Lydia's hair as she led me. Warm coconut and the faintest hint of cigarette smoke. She didn't say anything, just kept her arm around my waist, guiding me down the hall and out to the student parking lot, between rows of dented cars. Paint peeling, parking decals hanging from rearview mirrors. Lydia stopped beside her Oldsmobile. She pulled a single silver key from her pocket and shoved it in the passenger door to unlock it for me, then went around to the driver's side. I got in, put my bookbag in the backseat, and closed the door, hinges ringing with rust. The inside of the car smelled like mold masked with perfume, but it was clean. Carpets freshly vacuumed, wrinkled dashboard rubbed to a shine. Lydia got in and shut her door. She cranked the car, shifted into reverse, and turned her head to look out the rear window. I watched the tendon flex tight beneath the smooth brown skin of her neck. She backed out of her parking space and drove through the rows of cars, out of the lot, onto Highway 76. I didn't know where we were going. I didn't care.

❖

We rode for a while in silence. It was a heavy, cloudy morning outside. Fog lingered in the ditches. My breathing slowed and the tension in my chest and muscles waned. Lydia was heavy on the gas, but she'd ease off when she got going too fast and just let the Oldsmobile coast, so we kind of rocked back and forth between fast and slow. I was worried talking might break the spell, like Lydia would realize I was in the car with her and slam on breaks, turn around, take me back to school. But eventually the silence got too big to ignore.

"What class were you in?" I asked.

"Economics," Lydia said. Both hands on the wheel. Eyes fixed on the road.

"You left your stuff."

"It's fine. All I had was a notebook. It'll be there."

A mile or so later, she flicked her turn signal and turned left onto Oceda Drive. I still didn't ask where we were going. I was just thankful to be in motion. We passed a hand-drawn sign advertising cheap satellite internet and a house with a black-and-tan dog chained to a sweetgum tree in the front yard. I studied my face in the sideview mirror. Dried blood. Nose smashed wide. Faintest hint of a bruise starting to show around my eye socket.

"You think that's bad," Lydia said. "You ought to see Ronald some Saturday night. You'd think after twenty years of getting drunk and talking shit he might learn how to fight, but no. He don't even wake me up when he comes in anymore. I leave medicine on the bathroom counter when I go to bed."

"My first time."

"I can tell," Lydia said, grinning, cutting her eyes over at me briefly. "But that's okay. Nobody is good at nothing the first time."

The Oldsmobile ran quiet, but there was a tick in the engine.

Some wires hung down below the steering wheel, coated with red and blue plastic, their gold ends frayed and exposed. Lydia made a left on Sheep Island Road. I'd never been down that road before. We passed a property scattered with broken-down lawnmowers, an old man with a white beard picking his way through the maze.

"Y'all always live down here?" I asked.

Lydia nodded. "Since I was a baby." A few minutes later she slowed the car and pulled into her yard. "Good," she said. "He's not here."

The trailer where Lydia lived was small, and the siding was coming off in places, but brick stacked around the foundation made it look permanent. Two green plants in mismatched pots stood on the steps leading up to the front door. Lydia turned off the Oldsmobile and got out. I followed her up the stairs and she twisted open the door and we went in. All the lights were off, and the heater wasn't running. Deer heads with thick horns hung on the walls. Lydia pointed to the couch, brown like leather, sagging in the middle. "Right there." She flicked on a lamp and I sat down. She walked through the kitchen and down a narrow hallway. Another light came on. Sound of drawers being opened. A cabinet being rummaged through.

Sitting on the middle cushion of the couch, I studied the room. Plain wood coffee table laid with hunting magazines, an ashtray overflowing with yellow butts, and a thick hardback book with a red cover, the dust jacket taken off. Across the room, a flat-screen television stood on a square pressboard table. A fox squirrel was mounted on the wall above it. Gray hide, long tail, dark black hood. Its teeth were bared and it was looking back toward the couch, toward me.

Lydia came back, arms loaded with medicinal supplies. She dropped it all on the coffee table and sat down on the couch beside me.

"Why are you doing this?" I asked.

"What?"

"Taking care of me."

She wrinkled her nose. "You're hurt."

"But you were mad."

She rolled her eyes and reached across the coffee table. Picked up a cotton swab and the bottle of hydrogen peroxide. She wet the swab with the solution and leaned in close to me. I closed my eyes. She rubbed the cotton around my eye, cold and wet. She blew on my skin and I smelled mint toothpaste on her breath. I was stirred by her closeness. Adjusted the way I was sitting on the couch. She laid down the swab and I opened my eyes.

"I wanted to see you," I said, glancing again at the squirrel on the wall. "I wanted you to come over. Before. I just. I don't know."

Lydia took up a tube of Neosporin and squeezed some of the cream on her pointer finger. Leaned forward again and rubbed it gently on my wounds. "I know how y'all are. Act like fools. Running around, picking up heavy metal, beating the briars, fighting. You're proud of that." She pulled back and wiped her finger on her jeans. "Then you get hurt and you're ashamed. What did you expect?" She stood, went to the kitchen, and got two cans of Mountain Dew from the refrigerator. She came back to the couch and handed me one, put the other on the coffee table.

"But the way it happened. On the sideline. You were there."

"It doesn't matter. You think everybody remembers where you were standing? No one even noticed." She shook three Tylenol pills from a bottle and handed them to me. "I know it feels like you're at the center of the universe when you're under all those lights. Pushing and growling and carrying on. But get over yourself."

I cracked the can of Mountain Dew and swallowed the

Tylenol, tiny and smooth compared to the pain pills I'd gotten so used to taking. Lydia kept standing. Arms crossed, neck flushed with shades of pink.

"Well." I took another sip. "I'm sorry."

"Forget it."

"No," I said. "And thank you. For fixing me up."

"I'd do it for anybody."

I looked down at my boots.

She came back to the couch and sat beside me. "Bad news is, I ain't a miracle worker. It's gonna get uglier before it gets better."

Me and Lydia spent the rest of the morning and the early afternoon watching television, sitting close on the couch but not touching. We watched *The Price is Right* and I told her about how I watched it every day when I was laid up, how good I'd gotten at guessing how much things cost. She was better, though. She knew how much everything cost. When *The Price is Right* went off, we moved to the kitchen and Lydia fixed us lunch while I sat at the kitchen table against the wall. She fried thick pieces of bologna in a cast-iron skillet that was already sitting out on the stove. Toasted white bread and lathered it with mayonnaise and yellow mustard. Laid on the hot bologna and slices of American cheese. She brought the sandwiches over on paper towels and we ate. I told her it was the best sandwich I ever had and I meant it. She said it was because of the skillet. It was her momma's, passed down from her grandmother. It had never been washed, only wiped out and seasoned with oil at high heat. It was like every meal ever made in it added up and contributed to the next.

"Where is your mom?" I asked.

"Gone," Lydia said. "Left us. Left town."

"My dad too," I said.

Lydia nodded, didn't say anything else. Even though she was only a year ahead of me, she felt much older. The things she could do. The way she talked. Even the way I could tell she was thinking something and wasn't saying it. She had a certain wisdom about her. It made me wonder about all those times she called me to ask questions. How to check the oil in her Oldsmobile. It seemed unbelievable that I could ever know something she didn't.

After lunch, we went back to the couch and watched a rerun of an old dating show. Eight women competed in physical tests to earn a one-on-one date with a middle-aged musician neither of us had ever heard of. At some one point, Lydia laid down on the couch and put her feet in my lap, still wearing her Converse. I didn't know whether I should touch her somehow. Maybe take off the shoes and rub her feet. Eventually I just settled for resting my hands on top of her shins. It made me so nervous I couldn't focus on the show.

Lydia never asked me about the fight that day. Who it was with, what started it. I almost wished she would. It was a heavy burden to haul alone. And confusing. I wanted to lay it all out and let her tell me whether I was right or wrong. Pass judgement. I wanted to believe things were that simple, though I was starting to understand they weren't. But more than all that, I wanted just to sit there in that trailer with Lydia watching daytime television and eating bologna sandwiches—outside of place, outside of time, outside of consequence—forever. I kept my mouth shut.

Later in the afternoon, the sun finally breaking through the clouds and coming in through the windows, my cell phone vibrated in my pocket. I took it out. It was Mom. I stared at the screen, the three letters of her name, until they lost all their meaning. I just kept staring until the phone stopped vibrating and the screen went black.

"Who was it?" Lydia asked.

"My mom."

Lydia took her feet off my lap and sat up. "You're not going to answer it?"

"Don't feel like talking."

Lydia nodded. "What time is it?"

"Little after three."

"Ronald might be around soon."

"Guess I should go."

She didn't say anything, which I knew meant yes.

The whole ride home in the Oldsmobile, I was quiet, shaking my leg. Mom called again two more times, but I still didn't answer. I hoped she was working, but when Lydia pulled into the driveway, the Jeep was already there.

"Shit."

"It's better," Lydia said. "Just get it over with." She reached over and touched the side of my face gently.

I got my bookbag out of the backseat. "Thank you."

"For what?"

"Everything." My eyes were starting to fill up again.

Lydia nodded. "Call me if you need me."

"Thank you." I got out of the car. Halfway to the steps, Mom opened the front door. She stood there in the opening wearing her scrubs, her cell phone clutched in one hand, the door handle in the other, her face pale and splotchy. Lydia backed out of the driveway and pulled onto Lantana Lane. I turned and waved. She wiggled her fingers through the window as she drove away.

"Who was that?" Mom asked. Before I could answer, she was

firing more questions. "Where have you been? What the *hell* is going on?"

I walked to the house and brushed past her through the door. I went straight for my bedroom, but before I could get there, she'd slammed the front door and come quickly up behind me. She grabbed my arm and tried to turn me around.

I snatched away. "Don't touch me," I said, keeping my voice low and measured.

"I was worried."

"Too late for that." I turned and started heading again for my bedroom. She didn't stop me. I walked down the hallway, past the crooked picture frames, the photo of me in my uniform, stamped *SAMPLE*. It seemed fitting. Like that person had never been real.

"What did I do?" Mom called.

I tossed my bookbag on my bedroom floor and closed the door behind me. Just stood there, back to the door. My room stunk. Tang of sweat and unwashed laundry, the dirty clothes piled up in the top bunk of my bed. I wanted to pull the bed over and smash it on the floor. Beat the wood till my hands were bloody. My whole body felt like a hot coal glowing in a pile of cinders. I turned and swung the door back open, stomped down the hall. I found Mom in the kitchen, just standing there, looking down at the floor, still half torn up, plywood exposed.

"You want to know what you did? Well, me too. So why don't you tell me."

She turned around and took a step toward me. "Honey, your face."

"Who told you?"

She rolled her eyes. "I don't know what you're talking about."

"About the fight. You were calling me. You already knew. Did he tell you?" I felt my voice rising. I thought it would make me feel better to yell, help the anger subside, but it did just the opposite. "Did he fucking call you?"

"It's been a bad day, baby. Try to calm down."

"What did you do?" I was screaming now, and I felt the wetness on my face again. Mom was crying too, looking down at the floor and pulling at a hair tie around her wrist.

"He said he was better than me. He said I was weak. He said I was only starting because of you. Because Coach Hendrickson wants to *fuck* you."

She shook her head. "I'm so sorry."

"Stop saying that."

"I thought it would be good for you to go back."

"Answer me. What did you do?"

She looked in my eyes. "I'm sorry." She was sobbing, her face twisted and ugly. "I didn't mean for it to be like this."

It should have upset me to see her like that, but it didn't. It made me feel powerful, like finally my words had meaning. It made me angrier. "What are you sorry for? Tell me exactly what you're sorry for."

"We went on some dates," she said, voice garbled with tears. "Three dates. I shouldn't have done it. He said it was okay. I should've told you. But I wasn't seeing him before. Not until after he came here. After you were hurt."

She stopped and I didn't say anything. "It had nothing to do with you. I promise. It had nothing to do with you." She paused again. "I'm so sorry."

I watched her sob. She didn't try to hide her face or wipe her tears, she just stood there shaking and sobbing. I turned and walked out of the house, leaving the door wide open behind me. I walked down the driveway, onto Lantana Lane. My legs seemed to swing themselves. She didn't follow me. I flipped my hood up.

Boots slapping time on the asphalt. A truck passed, a silver F-150. It slowed when it got near me. I lowered my head and kept walking.

My first instinct was to call Marcus, but as soon as I thought it, I realized he'd known. He'd tried to tell me. It made my heart beat harder to understand it. Felt like I couldn't get a good breath. I stepped off the road, crossed the ditch, and walked into the woods. The trees were young, and the ground was dry. Thick briars and brush at the edge, but open once you got in a little bit. Mostly pines, ground covered with soft brown needles.

I saw a glass beer bottle slightly buried. Picked it up and threw it as hard as I could at a tree. It just glanced off the bark and skittered crookedly out of sight. I found a lonely white oak that had gotten blown over in a windstorm. I sat down on the trunk and tried to calm myself by not thinking any thoughts. Just looking around the woods, all ears and all eyes. Empty senses. I wished I was a snake. No knees. Hard scales. Slithering through the pine needles, warm earth beneath my belly. Subsisting on the weather. Or maybe buried, hibernating in a hole. I could shed my skin. Have a whole new hide, itching with possibility.

Heading off like that, upset and alone, reminded me of a time when Dad was still living with us. I must've been six or seven. He hadn't come home Friday night before I went to sleep, but I found him Saturday morning, laid on his back on the couch, snoring. I tried to wake him, but he wouldn't open his eyes, or even stop snoring. I shook his arm and whispered his name, but still he wouldn't wake. I sat on the floor in front of the couch and watched cartoons, some old ones that came on the local channel. I didn't really care about them but whenever Dad was home on the weekend mornings, he would turn them on and tell me to come watch with him and he would laugh. But he didn't wake up. He kept snoring. I turned the volume up as loud as it would go.

He still didn't wake up. A few minutes later Mom came out of their bedroom, stepping through the hall.

"Why in Jesus do you have that turned up so loud?" she asked.

I pointed with my thumb at Dad behind me. "Snoring."

She went to the couch and tapped him on his chest. "Wake up." He didn't stir. She tapped him harder. Still nothing. She started shaking his shoulders with both hands. Then somehow, she was straddling him on the couch, screaming, shaking him, and I was sitting there on the floor beside them. Finally, he startled awake and pushed her off him, onto the floor. They both stood up and they were yelling in each other's faces. The cartoons still blaring. I got up and walked to the kitchen. I called Aunt Gail's house on the cordless house phone. Marcus was still living there. I asked to talk to him and when he heard what was going on, he didn't even ask anything. Just told me to go to my room and get dressed. He'd be there in ten minutes.

When he knocked on the front door, Mom and Dad got quiet. I heard mumbling. Marcus opened my bedroom door. "Come on," he said.

I followed Marcus out of the house, past Mom and Dad sitting on the couch, silent. We went outside and got in the Ranger. He had that thing forever. He drove us down to Henry's and bought us burgers. After that, we went out to the lake and skipped rocks, our reflections rippling on the water.

No matter the question, the answer had always been Marcus. Now it wasn't. Somehow his knowing and not telling was worse than Mom's doing. The feeling wasn't loneliness. It was heavier. Absolute. Maybe not a feeling at all, but a condition. A state of being. My phone vibrated in my pocket. I took it out and looked at the screen. Mom. I laid it beside me on the tree trunk and let it rattle.

X

A sliver of moon shined on the old Allendale Plantation
land. Me and Hambone weren't even pretending to hunt.
Didn't have any guns. We were leaned against the hood of his
Nissan Frontier, drinking cans of Bud Light quick as we could.
Parked in an open cutdown, we had the doors of the truck open.
Dome light glowing yellow. The weather was chilly and wet, one
of those cold soup February nights. Hambone wore jeans and
a long-sleeved T-shirt beneath a hooded canvas coat. He was
simmering, just steady sipping beer and digging in the sandy dirt
with the toe of his boot.

"We could slit the tires on that fucking hoopty of a Chevrolet
he drives."

"No," I said.

"Why not?"

"It ain't worth it."

"Shit if it ain't."

Hambone had answered the first time I called and come straight to get me. I met him at the corner of Lantana Lane and Highway 76, so we didn't even have to go near the house. I told him about Quinton, but not Mom. He was mad at me for going back to weight training. For not telling him. I saw him grit his teeth when I told him on our way out to the Plantation. Muscles in his jaw bulging. But he didn't say anything about it. He honed it all in on Quinton.

"We can't just let him get away with it," he said.

I drained my beer and crushed the aluminum can to a wrinkled blue disk beneath my boot. Sailed it like a frisbee across the cutdown, out of sight. I went to the bed of the truck and got another from the cooler. "Need one?"

"Yeah."

I went back to the hood with the beer. Gave Hambone his. Cracked mine and took a sip.

"Fucking coon," Hambone said, opening his can. "I can't believe you swung on him. But hey, spade's a spade. Merle would be proud of you, even if you did get your ass kicked."

I remembered the dog standing in the dark swamp, baying up a tree, fur rippling down his backbone. The way Hambone reveled in the kill. He was fueled by hatred, ruled by violence.

"We could throw a dead one in his backseat," Hambone said. "He'd know who it was. Make him and all the rest of them think twice about fucking with you again. With any of us."

I just shook my head. "It's not about that."

"Hell if it ain't."

I took another long drag of Bud Light to calm the sickness I was feeling in my belly. Just the suggestion that I would do something like that made me see myself differently than I thought I was and wanted to be. I'd made a mistake. Acted outside of myself. And now it was all just out there floating around in a swamp of uncertainty for other people to make their own meaning of, their own little history. I'd stepped off the dry, hard-packed land into muddy water. Now, Hambone was trying to call me out even deeper, where the water was over our heads, where I realized he'd been leading us all along.

"How about those pills?" I asked, changing the subject to something he was always interested in. Getting fucked up. "You bring 'em?"

Hambone grinned. "You feeling some pain?"

"More than you know."

He pulled the Altoids tin out of his back pocket and laid it on the hood. Opened the lid. "There you go," he said. "All-you-can-eat buffet."

"What's what?"

He fingered around the tin and brought out two pills. One long white tablet that looked like my pain pills, and one tiny round blue one. "Just swallow these," he said. "They'll get you there."

I stuck out my empty hand and he put the pills in my palm. I shook them around a little bit to see if I could read a brand or something on them, but there was nothing. I tossed them into my mouth and chased them with a gulp of beer.

"That'll fix it," Hambone said. He fished around the tin and got a couple pills for himself and threw them back. Closed the tin and put it back in his pocket.

I stared across the cutdown, slash piles like little mountains in the night. Sprawling limbs and rough-cut stumps, all pushed together. Probably there were rabbits in them sleeping. Maybe a bobcat. Coincidental homes. I was already feeling a little bit wobbly, but still waited impatiently on the pills to hit. The whole idea being not to feel anything at all.

"You know, I went out for football one time," Hambone said. "Back in middle school. My dad made me."

"You didn't like it?"

"Wasn't nothing to like. It wasn't real. It wasn't me. Stuck spinning in a dream. I only went one day. Couldn't have gone back if I wanted to."

I nodded and drank a sip of beer.

"It was after school, the first day of eighth grade. I went down to the locker room and changed into shorts and a pair of brand-new cleats my momma had bought me. All the rest of them, they were in their pads, all decked out, helmets on. Mud and grass stains all over everything. Wished I'd at least put on the cleats and scuffed 'em up in the yard or something." He pushed his hair back from his forehead. "They'd all been practicing for weeks. See, my dad, he knew the coach. Something from work. He'd talked to him and figured this whole thing out. So, I sat there in the locker room, listening to their jokes. Then we went out to the field and I just stood there. Whistles blowing, people yelling, pushing me one way and another."

"What position did they put you at?"

"I don't even know," Hambone said. "Nobody ever told me. I just stood out there in the middle of the field, no pads on, squinting in the sunshine. My dad wasn't home when I got there. He came in real late, but I'd waited up for him. I told him what happened. He said don't worry. You'll figure it out. That was his advice. I said fuck if I will and never went back."

I waited for Hambone to say more, but he didn't. I wanted to tell him I'd seen other boys like that. Come out late, no clue what's going on. Stand around for a day or two. Then disappear. Pass them in the hallway at school and hardly even recognize them until they drop their head down, slump their shoulders. I wanted to tell him he wasn't the only one, but I didn't know if that would make any difference.

"You feeling anything yet?" Hambone asked.

"Just cold."

"Same. We ought to build a fire."

Hambone got a lighter from the glovebox of his Frontier. We closed the doors and struck out across the cutdown. Pulled the smallest pieces of wood we could find from one of the slashpiles and stacked them together. Shoved in some dead leaves and twigs, a few pinecones. Hambone flicked his lighter and held it to the pile. The leaves caught and smoked. They burned bright orange and the twigs withered black, but the bigger wood never caught. We just stood there staring at the pitiful, smoldering pile.

"Well, that was short-lived," Hambone said.

We rearranged the wood and added more leaves and pinecones. Lit it off again. The leaves sparked. The wood hissed and started to burn.

"There we go," Hambone said.

We stood on opposite sides of the fire, close to the flames. I felt the warmth in my Wolverines. Easing up my jeans. Smoke billowing. Dark earth smell of it. The pills were starting to work. My mind was swimming. Muscles turning soft and heavy in my skin. I closed my eyes and thought about Lydia. Her legs on my lap. Taste of greasy, hot bologna and smooth, salty mayonnaise. Imagined that was the taste of her.

I opened my eyes and Hambone was watching me. His face shifting and shimmering through the smoke. "You feeling it now?" he asked.

I nodded.

He flashed his teeth in a smile, and I saw Merle in his face. Lips curled back. Beady black eyes. I half expected blood on the corners of his mouth. But then it was gone. He was just Hambone again. He walked to the slash-pile and gathered more wood. Came back and arranged it carefully on the fire.

"You look ancient," he said. "Lit up by the flames. Face beat black and blue. Some kind of warrior." He cleared his throat and spat on the fire. "Does it really hurt?"

"Not too much. Medicine helped."

"That's right," Hambone said. "That's what I like to hear."

We went back to the truck for beer. The fire burned behind us distant and dim as a cigarette cherry. I opened the door to the cab and fished my phone out from under the passenger seat. I'd turned it on silent and shoved it under there on our way out to the Plantation. I had a dozen missed calls from Mom. More from Marcus. Bunch of texts.

Call me back plz

Where are u. I am WORRIED!

Call me

Where u? Pick up.

Answer the fucking phone

I'm sorry

I'm a terrible mother

Let us know ur ok??

I cleared them all without responding and put my phone back under the seat. I was glad they were worried. I hoped they were out riding around, looking for me. But probably that was too much to expect. Probably they were sitting at home, punching numbers on their phones. I thought about the stuff Marcus said at Meemaw's about a stepdaddy and how he knew that Friday before when we went out to the river that Mom was on a date and I swore to god if he was there I would've driven my shoulder into his chest and watched his fat ass fall to the ground, wheezing.

Quinton was right. Had known all along. Watched me standing like an idiot under the gleaming floodlights, taking the opening handoff and tucking the hot football like pride into my chest. Like I'd earned something.

I slammed the truck door and turned around to face the flames in the distance. Hambone came around from the back of the truck. "What a measly fire." He handed me a Bud Light and stood beside me.

"That's about how I feel right now." I cracked the beer and took a sip.

"Yeah? You need some more medicine?"

"I don't know."

"That means yes," Hambone said. "Come on." He grabbed my forearm and led me to the hood of the truck.

"I'm feeling all right."

"All right ain't good enough." He sat his beer on the hood, took the Altoids tin out of his pocket, and found two more of the long white pills. Laid them on the hood beside his beer. "You really want to feel better, you don't eat them." He put the Altoids tin back in his pocket and pulled out his knife. Flicked open the blade. Same one I'd used on the owl. I felt the cold steel in my hand. A physical memory. Sawing off the owl's feet. Pushing the blade through feathers and bone. Hot red guts in my hand. Hambone took the knife to one of the pills and shaved off thin slices, then turned the blade and chopped. Over and over until it was ground to a lumpy white powder. He did the same thing to the other. My ears were ringing with nervous blood. Knee aching in the damp cold. Hambone used the blade to arrange the white pill dust into two short, sloppy lines. I knew he meant for us to sniff it up.

"You ever done it like that?" I asked.

"Sure," Hambone said, folding his knife and putting it back in his pocket. "Nothing to it. Burns for a second, but it's worth it." He smiled. "After this, you won't feel a bit of pain. I promise. You won't even remember what pain is."

He leaned over the hood, plugged one side of his nose, and sucked up a line of the powder. He stood up straight, stumbled backward a step and laughed. "Holy shit. There it is." He picked up his beer and took a swig. Wiped his nose with the back of his hand. "Now your turn."

The blood was rising higher in my ears. Sound of river running toward sea. I felt nervousness and excitement tingling in my joints. I stepped to the hood. Blue metal can of Bud Light clutched in my hand. I bent over. Fire burning in the cutdown. I pushed one nostril closed. Hambone watched over my shoulder. I breathed in the dust.

It burned hot and raw in my sinuses. I stood up tall and felt the medicine moving behind my eyes. Pops of hot sugar at the back of my neck, then flowing like warm, sweet-smelling oil down my spine. I realized I was starting to get a hard-on. Reached down to adjust my jeans.

"Told you," Hambone said.

I turned around to face him.

"Like drinking momma's milk," he said. "Fresh from the tit."

Then we were riding the dirt roads of the old Allendale Plantation land, bouncing over ruts worn by the winter rain. Hambone drove and I sat in the passenger seat. We had the windows cracked, cold air blowing in. Pinches of Copenhagen tucked into our lips, passing an empty beer can back and forth to spit. Hambone tuned the radio to a rap station. Coon tunes, he called it, laughing, cutting his eyes over at me. He was dropping more crumbs. I didn't want to follow. He cranked up the volume. Bass notes buzzed in the door speakers. Man rapping about how even a small lighter can burn a bridge.

I stared straight ahead. The high beams on the truck were like the head lamps we wore in the swamp. They cut too narrow and short a swath of sight. Felt like at some point we'd outrun them and fall into the dark. Into nothing.

There were birds. Whip-poor-wills. Ruffled and brown, the size of a baseball. They flew from one side of the road to the other, picking bugs in the light. It was like they were following us, the way seabirds follow a shrimp boat. Profane symbiosis. I raised my hand to my face and touched the skin around my eye, swollen and blackening. I pushed on it. Felt nothing. Hambone let off the gas and turned the wheel to the left. Swerved onto a different road I hadn't even seen. More dirt, trees, darkness.

"Now we're in for some real fun," he shouted over the music.

I took a deep breath, closed my eyes and bobbed my head to the music. Man's voice so strangely smooth saying lord forgive me, things I don't understand. Clean electric guitar chords. Loud, heavy drumbeat.

"Here we go," Hambone said.

I opened my eyes. In the road ahead stood a small, still lake. Surface like a mirror, reflecting the truck lights. Hambone stayed steady on the gas. Both hands on the wheel. I looked over at him and his jaw was clenched.

We hit the hole. Muddy water rushed over the windshield. Some seeped in through the windows we had cracked open and stuck to the sleeve of my hoodie. It stunk, stagnant and rotten. Hambone pushed harder on the gas and the motor choked loud through the water. The back tires spun, shooting a rooster tail of mud out from behind us. The Frontier lilted side to side. Hambone yelled over the music. No words, just sound, but somehow still meaningful. I felt myself smiling. Heart beating fast. In seconds we were on the other side. Hambone eased on the brake, turned down the radio and flicked on the windshield wipers to clear away the mud. Steam rose from under the hood.

"Holy shit." I leaned forward in my seat. "I thought we were done for."

Hambone laughed. "What, we were gonna sink? Scared you might drown?"

"I don't know."

"Just a bog hole." He hit the gas hard and the truck lurched forward. "There's more further down."

We kept on the dirt road with the radio playing low. Swamp to our right, oozing. Every stand of muddy water we rode up on was a new beginning. Another chance to show our power over nature. Hambone approached each with fresh eyes, a different set of skills to employ. He handled the wheel with extreme precision, working the pedals like an organ player. Kept the truck swaying in time.

I sat amazed in the passenger seat, just riding the current and flow. Sucking the sweet wintergreen snuff and spitting carefully into the can. On that road there was nothing but joy. My other life was somewhere in the darkness, I couldn't see. Didn't care to. Medicine humming down my backbone and in every bog hole the realization that we might not make it. Might get stuck somewhere in the middle or get water in the fuel tank. Strip a gear in the rear axle or bottom out on a rut. Might sink beyond discovery. Adrenaline. The risk itself was the reward.

Hambone stopped between holes and put the Frontier in park. The windshield was caked with mud. The wipers weren't doing any good, just smearing it. He spun the wiper switch off, opened the door and climbed out. Fished the wad of dip from his mouth and slung it on the ground. Spat leftover strands of tobacco from his teeth. The temperature had dropped a little bit more. I could see Hambone's breath. I had no idea what time it was. Thought about checking my phone but decided against it. Didn't want to see any messages that had come in. I got out of the truck and walked around to where Hambone was. We stood beneath the sharp white moon suspended above us like a sickle blade. Looked at the mud spattered on the steel body of the truck like paint layered on a canvas.

"Beautiful, ain't it?"

I nodded. "We turning around?"

"Hell no," Hambone said. "There's two more holes between here and the next crossroads." He took off his jacket and put it on the seat of the truck. "That'll take us right back to the cut-down where we started. Maybe our fire's still got some coals." He pulled his T-shirt over his head. Chest thin and pale, slightly sunken in the middle. I could see the bones of his breast plate. A long, crooked scar ran across his belly. He saw me looking and I turned away. He put the jacket back on over his bare body and used his T-shirt to clean the windshield best he could. Not perfect, but you could see through it now. He tossed the tee-shirt in the bed when he was done and came back by me. "You in a rush to get home? Your momma going to be mad?"

"She doesn't give a fuck," I said.

He grinned. "She ain't seen your face yet?"

"She saw it. She don't care." I took out my wad of snuff. Dropped it on the sandy ground. "Let's quit talking about it."

"I was just asking. Don't get all bitchy. You want to captain the last couple holes?"

"What?"

"Do you want to drive?"

I picked tobacco off my gum and wiped it on the leg of my jeans. "Sure."

"Come on then," Hambone said.

I climbed in behind the wheel and Hambone got in on the passenger side. Showed me where the lever was to adjust my seat. "You know everything else, right?"

"I know how to drive." I shifted into gear. Let off the brake and stepped lightly on the gas. The back tires spun in the sand before catching. The throttle was more sensitive than Marcus's Ranger.

"You sure?"

I ignored him. Focused on the road shrinking in the dark black distance. Hard to decipher through the mud-smeared windshield, fog beading in the corners. A whip-poor-will fluttered across the headlight beam. Disappeared into the trees. Felt almost like I saw a contrail left in its wake, a wisp of smoke and ice.

"Give it some gas, granny," Hambone said. "No speed limit out here."

I pushed a little harder on the pedal. Glanced at the needle on the dash climbing. The steering wheel vibrated in my hands. I felt every rut and rock in the road. I let all the sensations breathe through my bones. Kept my eyes fixed straight ahead.

The next mud hole appeared in the distance. Surface of the shallow water shimmering like a mirage in the road.

"All right," Hambone said. "Just stay steady on the pedal as you get up to it. Don't slow down. Keep the motor turning."

I nodded.

"When you get deep in it, jam down on the gas. Let the back tires float. And just bounce the wheel back and forth. Give it a little wobble. Let it dance."

The hole grew as we got closer to it, spreading across the road. Black as the sky, shining mirror-image stars. We hit it. Water flooded the hood, splashing over the windshield. I pushed a little harder on the gas and the exhaust growled as it exhaled mud. I spun the wheel to the right, felt the tires spin. It was like the Frontier was briefly sliding on an unearthly plane, without gravity, without friction, without velocity. I cut the wheel the other way and the tires caught. Blew mud out from behind the truck before grinding forward. I straightened the wheel. We emerged from the other side of the hole. Sound of water sizzling on the engine block. I let off the gas and let the truck coast slowly.

"Jesus." I turned on the windshield wipers. "It's like a whole different universe."

"You're sailing now, captain." He reached across the cab and patted the top of my head. "Not bad for a greenhorn."

I laughed. Stomped the throttle and we were back barreling through the night. Condensation spreading from the corners of the windshield. Mud smeared across the glass. Another whip-poor-will flitted across the road, dipping low over the sand, twisting its body and tilting its wings. Rising as it disappeared on the other side of the road.

"Did you see that?" I asked.

"That bat?"

"It wasn't a bat. It was a whip-poor-will."

"Bullshit," Hambone said.

"No. It was. I swear." I kept my hands on the wheel. Glanced down at the speedometer, hovering at fifty. Peeked in the rearview at the dust billowing behind us in the dark. I tried to figure out how I knew the birds were whip-poor-wills, to call back to a time I'd seen one before and someone told me what it was, maybe Dad or Marcus, but I couldn't. I tried to remember a book I looked at as a kid, one of those big heavy ones with a hard cover and thick pages. But there was nothing. No memory. No book. I just knew.

A blur of brown came streaking into the road from the woods and I thought, here comes another one. Hambone yelled, and as he did, I realized the blur was not a bird at all, but a deer. I snatched the wheel to the left to avoid the animal and the Frontier shot sideways off the edge of the road, into the trees. Sound of metal smashing. I was thrown forward, chest hitting the steering wheel, knocking out all my breath. My head smashed against the windshield. My vision went blurry. The engine made a weak, wheezing sound for a few seconds before stuttering and falling silent. One headlight shined crooked through the trees. I held very still and caught my breath. My ears were ringing, and I tasted blood in my mouth. Ran my tongue around and felt a gash on the inside of my cheek where I must've bit it. I slowly squeezed my hands. Moved my legs. Nothing hurt too bad.

Hambone was crumpled in the floorboard. His back was to me, but I could see his shoulders moving as he breathed, pulled in air.

"You okay?" I asked. My voice echoed in my head, like I'd talked under water. He didn't answer. I asked him again, but he still didn't respond. I got out of the truck and walked around to his side. I was dizzy. Held onto the truck for balance. I looked in the window. Hambone was all curled up, hugging his chest, pale skin shining under his coat. I opened the door. "Are you okay?"

"I don't know," he said. "I think."

"Can you get out?"

He unfolded his arms and used them to push himself up off the floorboard, back into his seat. He stretched his legs slow and swung them out. Slid stiffly out of the truck.

"Nothing broke?"

"No." He put a hand on my shoulder and we walked carefully from the edge of the woods to the road. Turned back and looked at the Frontier. The hood was smashed all into the cab, the silver steel wrinkled and torn like a beer can. Fluid dripped onto the ground, and the windshield had a broad crack down the center.

"Oh, fuck," Hambone said.

"I'm sorry, man."

"My dad."

"I didn't know what to do."

"What the fuck."

"I'm sorry."

"I should never have let you drive."

I walked back to the Frontier and reached inside the cab. The key was still on. I turned it off and the headlights went out. I got in and put my foot on the brake. Tried to crank the truck. The engine didn't even turn over. "Nothing," I said.

"What the fuck."

I got out of the truck and felt dizzy again. I held the door to steady myself. "I hit the hell out of my head."

"I wish you'd have killed us," Hambone said. "I wish we'd have gone ahead and died."

Me and Hambone sat cross-legged in the road, facing each other, trying to think what to do. Faces barely lit by the moon. We were getting cold, and without guns or the truck, the woods felt dark and deep.

"Can we call your dad?" I asked.

Hambone drew circles with his finger in the sand. "He paid ten thousand dollars for that truck."

"It was an accident."

"He don't give a shit. He's going to make me pay."

"You got money?"

"No," Hambone said.

I thought about the scar on his belly. It didn't look clean enough to be from surgery, all jagged around the edges. The pills and the beer were starting to wane. My stomach felt sick and my head was aching on both sides above my ears. I couldn't hold a clear thought for long.

"Why don't we call your mom?" Hambone said.

I didn't respond.

"That's what I thought."

"We'll just stay out here."

"Not a chance." He looked over his shoulder, vaguely toward the woods. "Anyway, what good would that do? We somehow find a way to fall asleep on the dirt, in the cold, then what? The truck is magically going to be fixed in the morning? Your magic fucking birds you're so obsessed with you can't see a hundred-and-fif-ty-pound deer running out in front of us are going to come fix everything?"

"You got no ideas."

"There's no ideas to have. You fucked us, Grady. We're fucked."

I stood up and walked back and forth across the road. "How is it my fault?" I said. "It was an accident. You'd have done the same thing. The deer ran out. I just happened to be driving."

"That's all that matters," Hambone said. "Not what or if or why. Just happened."

I got my phone out of the truck. Somehow it was still intact, under the seat where I'd left it. The clock on the screen said quarter past midnight. I cleared out the missed calls and messages without reading them and called Marcus. He answered on the third ring. No emotion in his voice. I tried to keep it out of mine too, but it was hard. I was relieved to hear him, angry I had to call him, thankful he'd answered. I told him I needed a ride—nothing about the wreck—and I handed the phone to Hambone to give him directions on where to find us.

While we waited for him to come, me and Hambone walked a long way down the road, past the last mud hole I'd driven through, and hid the Altoids container in a hollow log in the edge of the woods. Both of us were scared to go any deeper into the trees without a light or a gun.

We were back by the truck, sipping beers to stave off the soreness when the headlights of the Ranger appeared in the distance. Two yellow lights, little suns, growing broader and brighter as they approached. We killed the beers and threw our cans in the woods. Marcus shook his head when he saw us standing by the wreck. I watched him through the window. The Ranger had mud stuck to the wheel wells and on the bumper, but nothing like what was on the Frontier. He must've gone slow and careful through the bog holes.

I climbed in the truck first and slid over to the middle seat. Hambone got in after me and shut the door. My leg and shoulder were pressed against Marcus. I tried to tense my muscles and hold myself away from him, but it was impossible in the tiny cab.

Marcus didn't ask any questions about the wreck, or what we were doing. He just asked where Hambone lived. Hambone said he'd rather not go home. Marcus said he didn't give a shit what he'd rather, and that was it. Hambone navigated Marcus down the dirt roads, off the old Allendale Plantation land, and onto Highway 76. Every time we hit a bump, my arm and leg brushed against Marcus.

✢

Hambone's house was in a gated community near the lake, off Cane Gully Road. The house was three stories and there was a jacked-up Nissan Titan on mud tires with shiny black rims parked in the driveway. Right beside it, a green Dodge Challenger. Marcus didn't even pull in, he just stopped at the curb. Hambone opened the door and got out.

"You going to be all right?" Marcus asked him.

"I don't know." He looked feral, all disheveled and still shirt-less beneath his coat.

"Usually that means yes," Marcus said. "If you weren't, you'd know for sure. But call Grady if you need anything."

Hambone nodded and shut the door. I scooted away from Marcus into the seat where Hambone had been by the door. Marcus waited until Hambone was inside before pulling away from the house. He drove without talking. Windows up and the defrost on. He turned off Cane Gully onto Mudville Road. My whole body was starting to get sore. My thighs, the back of my neck. Head was still throbbing. A motorcycle passed us going the other way, its single headlight flickering from the unevenness of the road.

"You ought to see yourself," Marcus said. He scratched his patchy red goatee. "You think that truck was in bad shape. Wait till you get to a mirror."

I ignored him.

"Who was driving? I hope you aren't that stupid, but from the looks of it, you probably are." He flicked off the defrost. "You been drinking. I know that. What else? Something, I can tell."

"What do you care?"

"Don't give me that bullshit, Grady. I didn't know."

"You're a liar."

"No, I'm just smarter than you. I could tell something was

going on how she was acting. I didn't know it was your fucking coach."

"I don't believe you."

"I don't give a shit." His voice was rising. "I don't care if you believe me or not. But whatever I did or didn't know, you can't just take off and not answer your phone, man. All the shit I seen."

"Don't act like you care."

"Fuck that," he yelled. He'd never yelled at me before. "Don't come at me with that shit. I'll black your other eye."

We were both quiet. The only sound was the rubber tires rolling over the asphalt, the motor humming as it spun.

"We going to your place?" I asked.

"Not a chance," Marcus said. "You're going home."

XI.

I lay in bed and let the sun creep in through the blinds and make bright lines on the carpet. Stared up at the slats of the top bunk. Ran my hand over the wood. I felt like I hadn't slept at all. Just tossed back and forth. Hips sore, back tense from the wreck.

My bladder forced me up. I swung my legs out of the bed and stood. I was dizzy, like my head was stuffed with cotton. I moved to the bathroom as gently as I could so Mom wouldn't know I was awake.

The night before when I came in, she was sitting on the couch. Kitchen table still out of place, pushed into the corner of the front room. Her eyes were red, face still splotchy. She held tight to a coffee cup. Looked at me when I came through the door. I avoided her gaze. Walked straight to my room. I'd expected her to follow me, but she didn't.

I kept the light off in the bathroom. Sat down on the toilet to be quiet. Didn't flush, didn't wash my hands. Back in my bed-room, I went to the fish tank. Sprinkled in flakes. The bass swam to the surface and sucked in the food, making little bubbles. It had stopped growing and its color was fading. Fins looked brittle and thin. It probably needed a light. Water filter. Another fish for company. I'd half-assed tried to keep it alive because Marcus gave it to me. Meant for it to make me feel better. But probably it was better off dead. I eased the lid shut and went back to my bed. Laid down and closed my eyes, like the longer I stayed in my bedroom, the longer I could stave off consequences. For the fight, the leav-ing, the wreck. Maybe after a while it would all just disappear.

I thought about Lydia the day before. Her soft fingertips applying Neosporin under my eye. That dusty trailer, animals watching from the walls. The weight of her legs on my lap. It felt like something I'd imagined, some strange daydream. I got my phone off the floor and texted her.

Hows school? Get ur notebook?

She responded almost immediately. Like she was waiting on the text.

Rite where I left it. Ur not here?

No. Glad u didn't lose it.

Class. Talk later.

My stomach made a hollow, empty groaning sound and I felt my guts twist. I realized I hadn't eaten anything since Lydia made us lunch the day before. My mouth watered at the thought of food. I sat up and put my phone back on the floor. Listened care-fully for Mom stirring somewhere. Clank of a hairspray can from her bedroom, clatter of the coffee pot. Nothing. Maybe she had an early shift. I stood and went to the door. Put my ear to the crack. Still quiet. I got a T-shirt from my dresser and pulled it on. Opened the door and went down the hallway to the kitchen, floors partially lain. No sign of Mom. Little in the fridge but jars of pickles and jalapeños, bottle of ketchup, packets of take-out grape jelly and soy sauce. Found a few strawberry Pop-Tarts in the cabinet. I got one and warmed it for thirty seconds on a paper towel in the microwave. Took it to the couch and started to eat with the television off. The filling on the inside was warm and sweet, but the pastry was a little bit stale. I ate it anyway. Went back to the kitchen and put another pack in the microwave. While I was waiting for it to warm, I heard the front door open and close. Mom came into the kitchen. She wore black leggings, a T-shirt, and walking shoes. Neck sweaty, cheeks red. The microwave dinged, announcing it was finished.

"We need to talk," Mom said.

I got the Pop-Tart out of the microwave, hot in my hands.

"You hear me?"

I tried to walk out of the kitchen, holding the hot Pop-Tart out in front of me. It was steaming. Mom blocked the way, standing with her legs and shoulders wide.

"Move."

"I said we need to talk."

"Move." The Pop-Tart was burning my hand. "I've got nothing to say to you."

"Then you're just going to listen. However mad you get at me, however shitty of a mother you think I am, that's fine, but we don't leave. We don't abandon one another. Not you and me."

I tried to go beside her out of the kitchen, but she slid over and stiffened her body, making herself strong so I'd have had to really push to get by her. I turned and slung the Pop-Tart on the floor. Red strawberry filling burst all over the surface. Some splattered on the wall. Pastry crumbled and rolled across the kitchen. I turned back around. Her face was slack, lips slightly parted. I tried again to leave the kitchen and this time she let me. I went to my bedroom and slammed the door behind me. Mom didn't follow me. She didn't even speak.

Standing in my room, the silence and stillness behind me, I realized that my mother couldn't make me do anything. And while that should have felt good, it didn't at all. It felt scary and dangerous. It was all the stupid things I'd ever do welling up inside me all at once like water in a cloud, growing heavy with nothing to stop it and no one to blame it on. Just waiting to pour. It was understanding that, ultimately, we were just two people living in the same house, spinning in the same circle, making our own choices that kept bumping into one another. Mom had no power over me, and I hated her for that.

I turned on the television sitting on my floor to distract myself. Flipped through the channels, not really looking for anything, just not knowing what else to do. I came to ESPN. They were broadcasting the Super Bowl parade for the Patriots in Boston. I sat on the edge of the bed and watched. Gronkowski standing on top of a bus, shirtless, clutching cans of beer over his head, pale muscles rippling. Brady wearing a dark coat and white scarf, clutching that silver trophy. Holding it like a child, like it belonged to him. The camera cut to the fans lining the cold gray street. A man held a sign printed with a drawing of a hand, middle finger up, a huge diamond-studded ring below the knuckle. It reminded me of what Quinton said about how the Patriots cheat. He was right about everything else. Probably right about that too.

Mom threw open my bedroom door, talking loud and fast. I sat up in my bed and rubbed my eyes. Pushed too hard on the bruises without thinking and winced. I'd dozed off. Mom kept talking. I sat up on my elbows. "Can't understand you," I mumbled. "Start over. Slow down."

"I said I just got off the phone with Edward Daniels."

"Who's that?"

"The man who owns the truck you wrecked last night."

I sat all the way up in the bed. Checked my phone.

"Are you kidding? I'm talking to you. Put the fucking phone down."

I was checking to see if Hambone texted, but he hadn't. I turned the screen off. "What'd he say?"

"So you did wreck the truck." Her voice got quiet, barely more than a whisper. "Grady, god damn it."

"What did he want?"

"He said you were drinking." Her voice started rising again, slowly growing shrill. "Trespassing on his family's land. Vandalizing it."

I stood up and walked over to my dresser. Hadn't mentioned anything about pills yet. I rubbed my hand over the wood. Dust. "Weren't trespassing."

"He said you totaled the truck."

"Deer ran out in front of us."

"Christ, Grady. He wants money. For the tow. Insurance deductible. A lot of money."

"Hambone was with me. It was his idea. They're rich."

Mom shook her head. "That's always how it is."

"I got to talk to Hambone."

"Edward said he doesn't want you hanging around his son anymore. Said you're a bad influence. I'm so embarrassed."

I laughed. Things were all backwards. Jumbled up and wrong.

"You think it's funny," Mom said. "Who are you? Those bruises on your face." She pushed a strand of hair behind her ear. Started to cry. "I wouldn't want *my* son running around with you either."

Nothing I could say.

She looked at her watch. "I've got a shift." She wiped her eyes. "I've got to go."

I texted Hambone. He didn't respond, so I tried calling, but he didn't answer. I took a long shower. Just stood under the hot, egg-smelling well water and rubbed a bar of green soap across my chest over and over until I felt raw. When I finished, I toweled off. Wiped the fog off the mirror. The bruises on my face were darker than the day before, especially around my eye. Rimmed with purple, stretching to my forehead. Specks of red where the skin had torn. Streak of blue along my jaw. My head was aching. I couldn't tell if it was the fight or the wreck or the beer.

I dressed in jeans and a T-shirt. Opened my sock drawer for a pair. Mom hadn't done laundry in a while, so I only had a few left. My pill bottle rolled around on the bare wood bottom of the drawer. I rearranged some underwear to cover it up and accidentally exposed the feet from the owl I killed, stiff and scaly. I took them out and laid them on the dresser.

I felt like I needed to be dressed for whatever was to come, even if it was nothing, just to feel like I had purpose, so I took my Wolverines out the front door and knocked off the mud. Pulled on my socks and laced the boots to my feet. I went back to my room and checked my phone again. Still nothing from Hambone. I didn't know what I wanted from him. To tell me it wasn't true that his dad called, that Mom was lying again. Maybe his dad was just angry, and it'd all blow over. I didn't know. Thought maybe his parents took his phone for punishment, that's why he wasn't answering.

I turned the ringer up loud and put my phone in my pocket. Looked at the owl feet lying on my dresser. I wanted to get rid of them. Couldn't understand why I'd ever brought them home in the first place. Vulgar trophies of a kill I never meant to make. I imagined Hambone stretched out in his queen-size bed, the walls of his room hung with coon tails. I took up the owl feet and went to the kitchen. The Pop-Tart was still there on the floor. Mom hadn't cleaned it. Filling dried to the new floors, shining glossy beneath the overhead light.

I thought about burying the owl feet deep in the bottom of the trashcan. I opened the lid and looked in. Paper towels, Pop-Tart wrappers, coffee filter heavy with wet grounds. It wasn't right, wasn't enough, to put the feet in there with the garbage. I didn't want them away from me, I wanted them gone. Disappeared. I closed the trashcan lid and rummaged through the kitchen drawers until I found a lighter Mom used for candles. I took it and went out the backdoor we barely ever used. The hinges squealed when I opened it. I walked a few steps into the yard, stilted weeds ankle high. I flicked on the flame and held it to the feet. The hide on the toes blackened but wouldn't burn. I held it to the other end, where I'd cut the feet from the body. Dried blood and old feathers sparked and smoked but wouldn't catch. The smell was awful, like burnt hair. I gagged. Put the lighter in my pocket. I carried the owl feet inside and put them back in my sock drawer until I could figure out what to do.

Lydia called around three o'clock, after school got out. She didn't have to work the peanut cart that day, and she asked if she could come by and check on me. I said I was fine, but I'd like to hang out anyway, so she picked me up in her Oldsmobile and we rode together to her and Ronald's trailer off Sheep Island Road. We went inside and sat across from each other at the table in the kitchen, eating leftover boiled peanuts from a plastic Tupperware container out the refrigerator. No lights on, just the grayish late winter sun seeping in.

"Your face looks awful," she said, reaching into the Tupperware. A hemp bracelet hung off her skinny wrist. "That why you didn't come to school?"

I slurped the juice from a peanut shell. The salt burned the inside of my cheek where I'd bitten it in the wreck. "Kind of."

She was doing something funny with the peanuts. Cracking the shells and dumping the peanut meat on the tabletop. "What else?"

"Hambone wasn't there either, was he?"

"I don't keep up with him." Lydia pinched some of the peanut meat from the pile she'd made and put it in her mouth. Chewed slow. "Anyway, what's that got to do with you?"

I told her about me and Mom arguing after she dropped me off, and me and Hambone going out drinking and mud bogging on the old Allendale Plantation land, leaving out the part about the pills. I told her about the deer and how I'd accidentally wrecked the truck. Told her about Hambone's dad calling and Hambone not answering my calls or responding to my texts.

"Of course he ain't," Lydia said.

"You know him good?"

"Enough to know he's an asshole. He was in my homeroom in sixth grade. Smelled like a wet dog. Always begging me to kiss him."

I felt my face warm up. Hoped the bruises would hide it. "Did you?"

Lydia smiled. "Do you care?"

"I mean, I just wondered."

She laughed. "No, I didn't kiss him."

I cracked a peanut. Tried to act like I wasn't relieved. Lydia stood and went to the cabinet. "How about the fight, though?

Yesterday. I heard it was with Quinton." She found a yellow plastic cup with a fading red restaurant logo and filled it with water from the sink. "You still haven't told me nothing about that."

"I guess people were talking," I said.

"People are always talking" She sipped from the cup. Swallowed. "Don't mean it's true. Why don't you tell me what you think really happened."

"I was there. It was me. I know what really happened." I started rocking back and forth in my chair. "But it doesn't matter."

Lydia sat back down across from me. "You know how you saw it, but that's just one part of it. You're not the only one. Anyway, it does matter. Because I want to hear it. Isn't that enough?"

"He's been wanting to fight me all year. Since I beat him out. Since Coach made me the starter."

Lydia put the lid on the Tupperware. "That's two different things, ain't it?"

"I mean, I guess, but not really. That's just how it works."

"Exactly," Lydia said. "That's how it always works. But he did pretty good while you were out, didn't he?"

"Sure. I guess."

"Maybe he had a right to be mad."

"What are you trying to say?"

"I'm not *trying* to say anything. I'm saying it."

I shook my head. "He kept calling me weak. He said something about my mom." I looked down at the floor. "It's complicated. I can't explain it all."

"It's always complicated, Grady. This is real life. Maybe you're just now figuring out shit's complicated but some of us have known that our whole lives." She stood up, taking the peanuts off the table. "That's not an excuse." She went to the refrigerator and opened the door. She was wearing those jeans with the back pockets ripped off, the denim dark where the pockets should have been. "You know he's my cousin, right?" It was like she spoke into the fridge. The yellow light from the tiny bulb inside shone around her.

I quit rocking. I felt like I was going to be sick. Like I'd ruined everything. Again. There was so much about her I didn't know. Didn't understand. Even though I wanted to. "For real?"

"Yeah." She closed the refrigerator and the light went out. The kitchen faded back to gray. She turned around. "Second cousin or something like that. On my momma's side. I don't see them much anymore. But yeah. Same blood."

"I didn't know that."

"But if you did, you wouldn't have fought him, right? Or maybe if you did, you wouldn't be here right now. Wouldn't have ever really talked to me at all."

"That's not true."

"You don't know." Her voice started to crack. "You can't say how things would go."

I tried hard to think of something to say, to explain, to make her know that wasn't true. But I couldn't, and that made me think somehow she was probably right. "I'm sorry."

"Yeah, you are." She wiped her eyes. "I wish you weren't in my house right now."

"I wish I wasn't anywhere."

"Well, you are. You fucking are." Her face was shining. "You're here and I'm here and we're all fucking here. And sometimes that's okay and sometimes it ain't, but you've got to buck up and make the best of it because this is all there is."

"I'm sorry." My face was wet too.

"It ain't me you got to tell it to."

"I like you." I needed to say it. So for even just a second things could be a little bit clear. "I really like you."

"I know," Lydia said. "I really want to like you too. But you make it so damn hard."

We went back out to the Oldsmobile and Lydia drove us deeper down Sheep Island Road. Oak trees leaned tight against the asphalt, cracking the surface. Limbs stretched over top made a low, heavy canopy. I rubbed my hands back and forth over the tops of my legs. Lydia stared straight ahead through the glass, both hands clutching the wheel. On the gas then off, that tempestuous rocking.

The road took a sharp turn. Around the corner, the trees broke, and I saw a small clearing on the roadside. Clutch of battered trailers in a sandy lot. Lydia slowed down. There were five or six singlewides standing in various states of disrepair. Peeling shingles, plywood covered windows. Lydia pulled in without using her blinker, no other cars coming either way. In the middle of the lot, a few people were standing around a fire barrel, clutching tall cans and sitting on old picnic tables made of weathered wood. They all turned their heads to look at us in the Oldsmobile. Lydia put the car in park. Raised her hand in a wave. They nodded.

"Like I told you, I don't see them much since my mom left. But they know me." She pointed to the corner of the lot, where an oak tree on the edge of the woods cast some shade. From one of the long branches, a mattress was hung with rope for a swing. Three kids were riding on it, wrestling playfully as it swayed back and forth. Quinton stood near them, watching closely. He wore dark, baggy jeans and a red zip-up jacket. Held a Black & Mild between his fingers. He raised the wood tip to his lips and inhaled. Blew smoke from his nose. Seeing him made me more guilty than angry. He knew about things I was only just starting to notice. Had known them a long time. The bitterness I'd felt for him all year was turning more into shame. Probably had been all along. I felt it rising from my guts. Cold, nervous sweat beading on my brow.

"I think those are his sister's kids," Lydia said.

"What am I supposed to tell him?"

Lydia got out of the car without answering and shut the door behind her. She walked over to the people near the fire barrel. One of the older men took her under his arm and hugged her. I felt stuck in the seat, like my legs wouldn't move. I watched Lydia talking through the windshield, but I couldn't make out the words. I opened the door and got out. Put my hand on the roof of the car. The man who'd hugged Lydia looked at me from across the yard and nodded. I nodded back. Somebody else spoke and the man laughed. Lydia didn't look at me at all.

I shut the door of the Oldsmobile and walked across the lot, toward where Quinton was standing by the mattress swing. Smell of smoke from the fire hanging in the air, a mix of pine wood and something like plastic or rubber, a chemical smell.

Quinton looked over and saw me coming toward him. He shook his head. "What the fuck you doing here, Hayes?" He raised the Black & Mild to his lips and took a small puff.

I kept walking until I was a few steps from him. Not close, but close enough for him to hear me. "Wanted to talk to you."

"I don't care what you want. This is my home, man. You ought not be here. I got nothing to say to you."

A little boy stood up on the mattress swing, clutching one of the corner ropes for balance. Dark hair braided back. He looked like he was about seven or eight. "Dang," he said. "Who beat you up?"

Quinton laughed, smoke leaking from his lips. I put my hands in my pockets and looked down at the ground.

"Go ahead," Quinton said. "Tell him what happened."

I just shook my head.

"Y'all stay here," Quinton told the kids. He walked away from them and motioned for me to follow. We stopped near the edge of the woods, up near the road, so we were out of shouting distance from everybody.

"What you got to say, Hayes?"

"Nothing," I said. "Just forget it."

Quinton sucked his teeth. "Come on, now. You come all the way here. To my home. I'm with my family. Say what you come to say."

I looked back at Lydia, still hoping she'd somehow help me figure out the words. She was standing with the others around the fire barrel, not paying us any mind. I turned back to Quinton. "You were right," I said.

"About what?"

"Everything. All of it." I paused. "It wasn't my time yet."

Quinton licked his fingers and snuffed out the Black and Mild. Tucked what was left behind his ear. "No. It wasn't."

"I didn't know. And it's not like I chose it. I didn't ask for it. I just did what I was told."

"Don't none of us choose nothing," Quinton said. "But we still got to deal with it."

He looked over at the kids and I did too. They were all three standing up on the mattress swing, laughing loudly, their high-pitched voices drifting across the lot.

"You really going somewhere to play next year like they're saying?"

"It's looking that way. Finally."

"Carolina?"

He smiled. "We'll see."

We were both quiet for a little while, just standing there. I didn't know what else to say. I stuck my hand out to shake.

Quinton laughed. "Nah, man. It ain't that simple."

"Come on."

"I can't do it, Hayes. I just can't do it. You want to shake my hand and move on like nothing? Fuck that."

I lowered my hand.

"You want to get right? Be different, man. Be fucking different. That's all it takes."

I nodded.

"All right then," Quinton said. He walked away, back toward the mattress swing hanging from the tree, the kids slowly swaying back and forth.

The sun cast a strange light through the canopy of trees as me and Lydia rode away from Quinton's in the Oldsmobile. Lydia didn't ask me what I told him, or what he said. She just drove. I was quiet too, staring out the windshield at the road winding through the trees.

"It's hard to go there," Lydia finally said. "Without my momma. It's like I don't belong."

"Didn't seem like that to me."

"No. But it is. They don't like Ronald. They think he's the reason she left. I guess he is, but so are they."

"Where is she now?"

"Baltimore. But we don't talk. She don't talk to none of us."

I waited for her to say more, but she didn't, and the silence between us started to get heavy. "My dad's in Georgia. He's got another wife. Had another kid. He lives with them."

"Some people can have all the lives they want," Lydia said.

"Change them like socks. That's how I feel sometimes. Like a dirty sock, lost behind the washing machine."

We were quiet again, just the engine of the Oldsmobile grumbling.

"I'm sorry," I said.

"I know."

I reached across the cab and put my hand on her leg. I felt her muscles tense up. Expected her to move away, but she didn't. She let it stay there.

Lydia dropped me off at home. She had chores and homework to do before Ronald came back. Said she'd see me at school the next day. Mom wasn't home from her shift yet, so the whole house was dark. I went straight to the kitchen and turned on the overhead light. Squinted at the brightness of it. The Pop-Tart mess was still splattered on the floor, the filling hardened and brown. I found the broom leaned against the refrigerator and swept up all the crumbs. Got a kitchen rag from one of the drawers and wet it at the sink. Knelt on the floor and wiped up the filling. In some places it wouldn't come up easily and I had to scrape it off with my thumbnail. When it was clean, I rinsed the rag, wrung it out, and laid it on the back of the sink to dry.

I was sore and my head still ached, heavy and nagging around my ears, the back of my neck. I went to the front room, sat on the couch, and turned on the TV. Flipped through the channels until I landed on the chainsaw carving show, the same one I'd watched with Marcus. The man with the curly blond hair had slipped with his saw and grazed his shin, barely even cutting through his jeans, but it made some blood. He and another carver wrapped a rag around the cut and cinched it tight with duct tape. The show cut to an interview with him. *Blood, sweat and bar oil*, he said. *That's what carvings are made of.*

I changed the channel and kept flipping. Little bursts of sound between the silence. It was all the same. Tired stories. I was still flipping when Mom got home. She looked worn out, the skin around her eyes puffy and dark. Her purse hung heavy from her shoulder and she clutched a bottle of cheap white wine in her hand. She walked past me to the kitchen and didn't speak. I heard her purse clatter on the counter. Rummaging in drawers. Pop of the cork, liquid sloshing. She came back into the front room with a glass of wine poured to the rim and sat beside me on the couch.

"Don't you ever just pick something and watch it?" she said.

"I feel like I've seen it all."

"Imagine how I feel."

"Always about you." I offered her the remote. She shook her head. I dropped it in her lap. We both watched to see what channel we'd landed on, but it was just a commercial for laundry detergent. I made to stand up, but Mom put out her hand to stop me.

"Wait," she said. "I talked to Edward Daniels again."

"Okay."

She drank deeply from her glass. "He wants twenty-five hundred dollars."

I tried to calculate how much that was. What it could buy. How long it would take Mom to make. I had no idea. "I'll fix this," I said. "I tried to call Hambone. He didn't answer."

"I don't have it." She said it like she hadn't heard me at all.

"A deer ran out. It was an accident. It could've just as easily been Hambone."

"But it wasn't," she said. "It was you."

We were quiet. The commercial changed to one for frozen pizzas that taste as good as delivery. "I owe twice that for your leg," Mom said. "At least. I don't even know. Emergency Room. All the doctor visits." She took another long swig of her wine.

I didn't say anything. What could I say? The things that were happening, words couldn't fix them.

"I called your father," Mom said.

"What? Why would you do that?"

"I had no choice, Grady. I didn't want to. It was the last thing in the world I wanted to do, but what else? You won't talk to me. You disappear, go off acting up in the woods. I got people calling me, telling me you were drunk, you tore up their truck. Telling me I owe them money. Telling me you're a bad influence on their kid." She paused. "You're his responsibility too."

The way she said it made me feel like a pet they'd decided to buy together so long ago, a dog with a vet bill. "What did you tell him?"

"Everything. Well, everything I know."

"You told him about you? About Coach Hendrickson."

"Everything."

"What'd he say?"

She tilted her cup to her lips and sipped heavy from the wine. "He said he's going to come here. To check on your wellbeing, I think is how he put it. And to set things straight."

"What does that mean?" I asked. "Where will he stay?"

"I haven't thought that far ahead."

I looked down at my lap. I hadn't seen him in so long. I wished it wasn't like this. I wished he wanted to visit. Still, I was excited I might get to see him, regardless. "Do you think he'll really come?"

"Do you want him to?"

"I mean, kind of. But not really. Not like this."

"Me neither," Mom said. "Knowing him, that probably means he'll show."

PART THREE

XII.

I sat on the front steps of the house, watching cars pass on Lantana Lane. There weren't many, but they all had their windows cracked open, their radios playing Friday afternoon music. It was the warmest day we'd had yet that year, an early taste of spring. Mom was inside cooking, the smells slipping out from the door I left cracked open, salty and rich. Dad was on his way. I had a feeling that it was going to be a good evening even though it shouldn't have felt that way at all given the reasons he was coming.

Me and Mom had been over a week preparing. Dad was staying with us. He said that was the only way to get everything all the way straightened out. I never thought it would happen, but I figured maybe it meant they were getting over some of the old things, and either way I'd get to see more of him.

Mom finished laying all the flooring in the kitchen alone.

There were cracks in places along the walls, the subfloors peeking through, but it didn't look bad, and she was proud of herself. She took the old pictures in the hallway down and replaced them with newer ones she had printed at the drugstore. One of me and her together in front of Meemaw's Christmas tree. One of me and Marcus standing in the yard, holding catfish in our hands, slime running down our wrists. No school pictures, no football.

I cleaned my fish tank, picked up all the dirty clothes in my room and vacuumed the carpet. Mom brought home an end table from the Habitat for Humanity store to set my TV on. I wiped and polished my Wolverines with leather cleaner I found in the hall closet. I was wearing them, dark brown and dimpled with wax, that afternoon.

I stood up and went inside to the kitchen. Mom was at the stove, frying pork chops in a pan of shallow grease. A pot of thick brown onion gravy simmered beside it, and on the back burner sat a pot of white rice, steaming. "Smells good," I said.

"We'll see."

That was about as much as we spoke those days, like both of us were waiting on Dad to come and settle things between us. Hear us out and tell us who was right and who was wrong. I checked the time on my phone. It was almost 4:30. Lydia was supposed to come at 6:00 for supper. She had to work the peanut cart and wanted to give Dad a chance to get here and get settled first. We'd been hanging out just about every evening after school or when she got off work. She was helping me catch up in Geometry. She took it the year before and remembered almost everything.

I went back out to the front steps and stood, watching the road for Dad. Tapped my boot on the wood. Couldn't hold still. I breathed deep and slow to calm myself. Since the wreck, I'd been getting headaches. They started out dull behind my eyes and spread over my ears, around the back of my neck. I'd tried taking my pain pills, but they didn't help. They didn't seem to do much of anything anymore. But if I kept myself from getting too worked up, just stayed even, I was all right. I wanted it to be a good night.

A little after five, I heard the rumbling of a loud muffler coming down Lantana Lane. I walked down two steps and stopped, just perched there halfway down. Dad's truck came around the corner, the same Dodge he had when I was kid, a 1985 Power Ram. He'd spent a lot of time and money on it. New motor, new headers, new exhaust. I could hear the iron muscle. He'd gotten it painted, shiny black, and put on chrome wheels and knobby mud tires. It was beautiful and mean. He turned into the driveway. On the front of the truck, below the grill, he'd bolted a rebel flag license plate. I watched the white stars shimmer on the red and blue background as he came down the drive. Stars and bars. I couldn't look in the cab. I was suddenly embarrassed to be standing outside, waiting for him. Dad stopped and put the truck in park. Killed the engine. I took another deep breath and looked up from the flag, through the windshield. He was sitting behind the wheel, smiling with his mouth closed, a wad of snuff tucked into his bottom lip. He had a thick, dark beard and he was wearing wraparound sunglasses with dark lenses. My heart was beating hard. I lifted my hand and waved, still standing on that second step. He nodded, then he turned his head and looked down at the seat beside him and said something. A tiny hand appeared above the dash, waving. He'd brought Rebecca, my half-sister.

Dad climbed out of the truck. He wore jeans and steel-toe boots with the leather peeling off the toe. Button-down shirt with the sleeves rolled up, showing his muscled forearms. He stretched his back and spit his chaw on the ground. Wiped his mouth. "Beautiful evening," he said. "It was raining back home."

I was still standing on the stairs. "Yeah. It's nice."

Dad walked around the front of the truck and opened the passenger door. He leaned in. I could hear him talking softly to Rebecca. He unlatched her seatbelt and helped her out of the truck. She wasn't wearing any shoes and her feet were dirty. She had on a smock dress stained with blue from some kind of candy. She was smiling, showing those tiny sharp kid teeth. Dad held her hand and they walked to the steps.

"You remember Grady," Dad said. "Your brother."

Rebecca came up the stairs and wrapped her arms around both my legs. She only came as high as my belly button. She squeezed me as tight as she could in a hug. "Hey, Grady," she said.

I patted the top of her head. "Hey, Rebecca."

She went up the other two steps to the door and Dad came behind her. I wasn't sure if we were going to hug. He reached his hand out, so I thought maybe we were going to shake, but instead he pinched my belly where it had started to poke out a little bit over my jeans. "Getting big."

I looked down at my boots.

He took off his sunglasses and put them in his shirt pocket. "Good to see you," he said. "Can we go inside?"

"Sure. Mom's in the kitchen."

"We got a bag in the truck, if you wouldn't mind."

"Okay."

"Some beer on ice in the cooler. Maybe bring a couple of those in too. One for you, if you want."

"I'm good."

He nodded and went up the stairs, taking Rebecca with him

inside. I went down to the truck. He'd left the passenger door open. The bag was on the floor of the cab, a green and yellow duffle, from back when he was at Sandridge High. He used it every time he took a trip. It was stuffed full and heavy. I put the strap over my shoulder and shut the door. The cooler was in the bed, packed with fresh ice. I stuck my hand through the ice, cold up to my elbow. Grabbed a can and pulled it out. Miller Lite, the only brand I ever saw him drink. I tucked it under my arm, got two more from the cooler, and went inside.

Dad was standing at the threshold between the front room and the kitchen. Rebecca was beside him, holding onto the tail of his shirt. I went past them into the kitchen and put the bag and the beer on the table. Mom was still standing at the stove, her back to us all, steam from the food rising up around her. Dad reached over and got a beer off the table. He cracked the can, tilted his head back, and took a long, gulping drink. He must've downed half the can in one sip. "Ahh. Thank you, son."

"Where should I put your bag?"

"I guess there ain't but so many options."

"I didn't realize you were bringing Rebecca," Mom said over the sound of pork chops frying.

"You mentioned that already," Dad said. "She wanted to see her brother." He took another sip of his beer.

"Y'all can have my room. I still got the bunk beds."

"I ain't going to take your bed. Rebecca can sleep on the top and you can keep the bottom. Let the siblings stay together. I'll be just fine on the couch. What you think about that, sweet pea?" He leaned over and kissed Rebecca on top of the head.

"Do we have to go to sleep now?"

"Not yet," Dad said. "We ain't even had supper yet."

✤

Dad and Rebecca went to my bedroom to get the top bunk set up for her. She wanted to lay out her blanket and free her stuffed pig from the duffle, get him situated. Dad wanted her to change into clean clothes for dinner. I stayed in the kitchen with Mom. She was taking a batch of pork chops out of the pan and laying them on a baking sheet lined with paper towels to soak up the grease. "What time is Lydia coming?" she asked.

"Six. What time is it now?"

"Almost five-thirty."

I wanted to call and tell Lydia to forget it, to just stay home, for her sake and mine, but it was too late.

"She's brave for coming," Mom said. "She must really like you."

"We're just friends."

"I know. But still."

Mom had never really met Lydia before. She'd seen her when she picked me up or dropped me off, but that was it. When Lydia offered to come, it seemed like a good idea to have her here with me, but now I realized how bad it all could go. I sat down at the table. Tapped my heel on the floor and tried to stave off the headache I could feel coming behind my eyes.

Mom looked over at me from the stove. Her face was concerned, but somehow still hard. "He's here because of you. Remember that. I called him, but it was your doing."

I massaged my temples with my fingertips. "I know."

Lydia called when she turned onto Lantana Lane and I went outside to meet her. She pulled into the driveway and parked behind the Dodge. Got out of the car and shut the door. The sun was beginning to set, and the air was cool. I could smell the pine trees across the road starting to put on fresh needles. Lydia bent over and looked at herself in the sideview mirror. She wore dark jeans and a purple shirt with the neck cut low and wide, showing her tan collarbones. That strand of fake pearls fastened around her neck like always. Her hair was fixed in a braided ponytail, and she'd put on dark lipstick to match her shirt. She looked beautiful, but not like her normal self, and that made me more nervous. She carefully wiped the corners of her mouth. As I approached, she stood up straight and smoothed down the front of her shirt. "Is it too much? Should I wipe off the lipstick?"

"No. It's perfect."

She rolled her eyes. "Your bruises look good." She gently touched the side of my face. "They're fading fast now."

"He didn't mention them yet." We walked together toward the house. She stopped in front of the Dodge. I saw her see the rebel flag plate. "Some truck."

"He brought my sister. Half-sister."

"Does she look like you?"

"Listen," I said. "This is probably going to be miserable. I forgot how he was. How it is when he's here. I just—"

"Hey," Lydia said. "That's why I'm here." She winked and punched me lightly in the arm. It made me feel all scrambled up. "We'll get through it," she said.

I believed her. She'd been helping me get through things. The day after we went to Quinton's house, I went back to school. She texted me that morning to come get her from her classroom again if I needed something, but I didn't need anything. I went to weight training. I had to. I knew Hambone wouldn't be at our bench, and even if he was, I didn't want to see him. No one mentioned my face in the locker room, and Coach Hendrickson wasn't in his office. Me and Seabrook went back to lifting alone at our old station. Quinton and Fritz ignored us. I was still slower than I was before, still weaker than I'd been, but it felt good to be there, not hiding anymore.

"If you say so," I said. We walked up the stairs and went inside.

Dad and Rebecca were in the front room, sitting on the couch. Dad still had his boots on. He clutched a can of Miller Lite in his hand. He looked out of place, not just in our house, but indoors at all. I couldn't believe he'd ever lived with us, it seemed so strange to see him there. Rebecca was beside him, wearing a fresh smock dress, looking around like she was trying to find a toy or a book, wondering why she was there. Her feet were still dark with dirt.

"This is Lydia," I said.

She smiled and did a little wave down by her waist.

Dad nodded. "Pleasure," he said, and took a sip of beer.

"Your hair is pretty," Rebecca said.

"Thank you. You have beautiful hair, too. It's so long."

"Can you make it like yours?"

"I can try."

"Yeah, let's do it." Rebecca wiggled herself off the couch. "Come on, we'll go to my room." She looked at me and cocked her head. "I mean Grady's room." She ran down the short hallway and Lydia followed her. I was glad I'd cleaned up.

"She's a funny little thing," Dad said.

"I always think of her as a baby."

"I think the same thing about you until I see you." He took a sip of beer. "I'm surprised you're grown. Then I leave and you're just a little boy again. In my head, you know."

I didn't know what to say to that, so I just stood there, wondering where to look, what to do with my hands. They felt gangly and wrong.

"That boy really did a number to your face. How long ago did y'all fight?"

"A week and some."

"I thought it was longer," he said. "Still. Them bruises are deep." He drained his beer and held out the can. "Get me another?"

I took the can and went to the kitchen. Threw the empty away and got a fresh one from the fridge. Mom looked over at me. "Where's Lydia?"

"Braiding Rebecca's hair."

She nodded. I went back to the front room and handed Dad the beer. He cracked the can and foam bubbled up from the lip. He slurped off the foam and took a pull. "It was a colored boy you fought, wasn't it? That's what your momma told me."

I nodded.

"Y'all fighting over her?" He nodded to my bedroom.

"No. Just. A bunch of stuff."

Dad laughed a deep, low alligator laugh. "It's never really that complicated."

An excited squeal echoed through the house from my bedroom, followed by Lydia and Rebecca both laughing. It was a strange sound in that house, other people's laughter. Usually I was alone, or it was either just me and Mom. It made the house feel full and warm to hear it.

"Sister seems to like her."

"We're just friends."

"Good," Dad said. "That's good."

I nodded and went back to the kitchen to see if Mom needed any help. She had just taken the last pork chops out of the pan and turned off the burner. Her cheeks were red and the hair near her forehead was frizzy from standing over the heat. "Everything ready?" I asked.

"We need a vegetable," she said. "Shit. I just realized. Something green."

"Do we have anything?"

"Check the cabinet."

I opened the cabinet beside the refrigerator. Few cans of tomato sauce, a tall can of baked beans. In the back of the cabinet, I found two cans of corn. Pulled them out. "There's these."

"Yellow," Mom said. "That'll have to do."

Rebecca came running from the bedroom. I heard her little feet thudding against the carpeted floor all the way down the hall. She came into the kitchen. Her long hair was pulled back and tied in a loose, crooked braid. "Look at me. Look. Am I beautiful?"

"You're marvelous," Mom said.

Lydia came into the kitchen. "She wouldn't hold still."

"You did a great job," Mom said.

"Thanks. Thanks for having me."

"Of course."

Rebecca ran out of the kitchen to the front room. "Daddy," she said. "I'm marve-ous."

"Always," I heard him say. "Always. Come here. Come hug my neck."

Mom warmed the corn in a small pot and we all gathered in the kitchen to eat. We only had four chairs, so Rebecca had to sit in Dad's lap. He sliced a chunk of meat off his pork chop and put it on her plate. Cut it into small pieces. She ate clumsily with a fork clutched in her fist. I sat beside them and Mom and Lydia sat across from us.

"When did you get these floors?" Dad asked.

"Brand new," Mom said.

"Who'd you get to put them in?"

"No one. I did it myself."

"Thought so."

Mom stared at him.

"They look great," Lydia said. She was sitting up very straight. "And this gravy is delicious."

Mom put down her fork. "They're certainly better than the cheap linoleum that used to be in here."

"Sure," Dad said. "They're fine floors."

"Daddy," Rebecca said. "Can I have some ketchup?"

"Do you have any?" Dad asked.

I stood up quickly. "Let me check." I went to the fridge and looked at the condiments in the door. Found the bottle of Heinz, almost empty. Took it back to the table and handed it to Dad. He shook it and squirted the runny red sauce on Rebecca's plate.

"Thanks, Grady," she said.

"Sure." I ate a forkful of rice and gravy. It was like salty mud in my mouth. I swallowed and shoveled down another forkful, thinking if I could just finish my food the night would be over.

"Lydia," Dad said. "I didn't catch your last name."

"Right," she said. "It's Proveaux."

"No shit." He took a slug of beer. "Your old man Ronald or Curtis?"

Lydia wiped her mouth with a paper towel. Some of her lipstick came off and you could see the lighter color of her lips beneath. "Ronald," she said. "You know him?"

"I went to school with them both."

"I'm full," Rebecca said.

"Better eat your corn, honey," Mom said.

I put my head down and sawed at my meat.

"What's old Ronald up to these days, huh?"

"Not much," Lydia said. "You know, just making it."

"What's he do for work?" Dad stabbed a piece of pork, rubbed it in gravy, and put it in his mouth. A drop of gravy ran down his chin and stuck to his beard.

"He's a peanut man. He's got his own cart. He sells boiled peanuts."

Dad smiled, his cheeks puffed out with pork. He looked over at me, that glob of gravy glistening in his beard. He swallowed. "Well, I'll be damned," He took a swig of beer and wiped his chin with the back of his hand. Wiped that gravy away. "Never would've guessed that. Good for him."

"Yeah, it is," Mom said. She still wasn't eating, and her hands were balled up tight on the tabletop. "He's an entrepreneur."

"I don't know about that," Lydia said. "But it ain't bad work. Not much overhead. A trailer and a propane burner. We're the only two employees and we make our own hours. Peanuts are cheap. You can mark them up two or three times." She stopped and took a sip of water from her glass. "It pays the bills."

"Sounds like you've got a mind for business," Mom said.

"Peanut business, at least," Dad said.

"I'm done," Rebecca said.

"Here, let me help you." I took Rebecca's plate and carried it to the trash. Scraped the food scraps into the can, then took the plate to the sink and dropped it in the basin.

"That was yummy," Rebecca said. "Can I go play now?"

"Sure," Dad said.

She got up from Dad's lap and ran to my bedroom. I sat back down at the table.

"It really is delicious," Lydia said.

"Fine supper," Dad said. He leaned back from the table and belched.

After dinner, me and Lydia played a couple games of Trouble

with Rebecca on my bedroom floor. She'd found it in a pile of old board games in the hall closet. I didn't remember the rules, but she said she had it at home and told us how to play. It was the first time Lydia had ever been in my bedroom. Not the way I imagined it would happen, but I still felt strange and exposed. When she leaned forward to push the popper to roll the die, the front of her shirt came down and I could see down it, her small breasts tucked into a lacy, cream-colored bra, but I made myself look away every time because Rebecca was there and it seemed dishonest.

Between the third and fourth game, Lydia sat up and looked around. "Is that a bass in your fish tank?"

"Yeah. Marcus brought it to me when I broke my leg."

"It's lonely," Rebecca said.

"There were two at first, but one died."

"Lonely fish," Rebecca said. She reached back and patted her braid. It had gotten even messier. "Your turn, Lydia. You won the last one."

After our fourth round of Trouble, Lydia had to go home. Rebecca hugged her and told her she loved her. Lydia said good-night to Mom and Dad and we walked together into the yard. The night was clear and dark. Half moon shining. A soft, chilly breeze coming from over the pines. We walked down the drive-way, past the Dodge, and stopped in front of Lydia's car.

"I'm sorry," I said.

"For what?"

"My dad."

"Don't apologize for him," Lydia said. "He isn't you."

I wanted to kiss her. For saying that, for being there, for all of it, and she must've seen that in me.

"Don't," she said. "Please don't."

I held out my arms. "Thanks for coming."

She hugged me and I held her until she pulled away. She walked to the driver's side of the Oldsmobile and opened the door. "Hang tight," she said. "Two days and it'll be over." She got in the car. I watched her back down the driveway and I waved as she drove off, until she was out of sight on Lantana Lane.

Inside, Dad was on the couch. He had a pint bottle of Crown Royal on his lap. I could hear my TV playing in my bedroom and figured Rebecca was in there watching. Mom was in the kitchen. I heard the sink running. Dad nodded to the seat beside him. I sat and he unscrewed the cap off the bottle. Offered it to me. "After-supper nip?"

"No, thanks."

He smiled and took a swallow for himself. Screwed the cap on and laid the bottle back on his lap. "Some little girl you got."

"We're just friends."

"Right. You ever met her momma?"

"No," I said. "Her and Ronald ain't together."

Dad smirked. "Ain't surprised. He used to run around with a half-breed. Bet anything that's your girl's momma."

I didn't respond. He sounded like Hambone. I felt trapped in it all. The meanness.

Dad unscrewed the cap of his bottle to take another swig. "I ain't just here to visit, you know. I'm here to bring some order." His speech was slow and measured. "I was you, I'd be pissed off too. Your football season got cut short. That's hard. I been there. I understand. Then come to find out your momma's running around with your coach." He shook his head. "I never been there," he said. "My mother was a good woman."

He stopped to take another sip from his bottle. "To be honest, it pisses me off too. That she'd do that to you. But she ain't my concern anymore. You still are. And just because you had a hard time, you're pissed off, you can't go getting your ass kicked by colored boys. Getting fucked up and wrecking other people's trucks. You can't be messing with girls like that one you brung here tonight. I'd say she's white trash, but she ain't even white. Just plain trash." He laughed at his own cleverness. "Get your mind back to football. Get your ass back in shape." He reached over and lightly slapped my belly. "There's a future in that. There'll be plenty of time for all the rest later."

My blood was hot. My teeth hurt from gritting them and my hands were shaking in my lap. "Is that all?"

"Yeah. For now. We'll settle the shit about the truck tomorrow."

I stood and went to the kitchen. Mom was washing the last of the dishes. I found a rag and started to dry the ones she'd stacked on the counter.

"You okay?" she whispered.

I just nodded my head and wiped hard at the dish I was drying.

I laid wide awake in my bed, staring at the blank television screen. My head was full-on aching. Behind my eyes, over my ears, down the back of my neck. A steady throb. Rebecca snored lightly in the top bunk above me and I could hear Mom and Dad in the front room talking, voices hushed. I felt bad for leaving her out there with him, but I couldn't stand to keep my eyes open in that lit room anymore with my head pounding. Listen to him talk. She could've gone to bed if she wanted.

All my life I'd wanted a sibling, and since the day he left, I wished my dad would come home. Now here they were, a manifested family, and all I could think was two days and it'll be over. Just two days. I got up and went quietly to my sock drawer. Fished out my pill bottle and opened the lid. I only had about six left. It made me nervous. I shook two in my hand and swallowed them dry. Hoped they'd ease my headache even a little bit. Maybe help me fall asleep.

Rebecca woke me early the next morning, whimpering in the top bunk. I stood up and looked over the edge of the bed. She was curled up in the corner, squeezing her stuffed pig. Her hair was greasy and matted from sleep.

"What's wrong?" I asked.

"I forgot I was here."

"Come on. Let's watch some TV."

I stood and she crawled over to the edge of the bunk. I helped her climb down and got her situated sideways in my bed facing the television. I went over and flipped through the channels until I found a cartoon. It was about creatures that lived in the ocean with floating flowers in the background and tropical Hawaiian theme music.

"My mom doesn't let me watch this," Rebecca said.

"Why not?"

She shrugged.

"Well, do you want to watch it?"

She scrunched up her face and looked at me like she was confused. A smile spread across her face and she nodded. I left the show on and went back to the bed. Sat beside Rebecca facing the TV and pulled the covers up over our legs. The episode was about a mean, bullyish flounder. I remembered watching it years earlier. When the theme song came on, I sang along to it and Rebecca looked at me amazed.

"I used to like this show," I said.

"I like it too." She snuggled up against my arm. We watched

like that for a while until the show changed to one with real people instead of cartoons, something I hadn't seen before and neither of us really liked. Rebecca said she was hungry, so we snuck quietly down the hall. Dad was asleep on the couch, boots beside him on the floor, bare chest peeking out from beneath the knit blanket Mom had given him as a cover. We went past him to the kitchen. I got the loaf of bread out of the cabinet and put a few slices in the oven to toast. While it was warming, I fixed Rebecca a small glass of milk. She sat at the table and sipped at it. When the toast was done, I smeared it with peanut butter and laid it on two paper towels. Carried it to the table and we ate together silently.

As Rebecca was finishing her second piece, I heard a stirring in the front room and Dad came around the corner with one eye shut, wearing nothing but his boxer shorts. He was lean and strong, his chest only a little bit hairy. He had a perfect tan line on his biceps where his T-shirt sleeves ended, his forearms dark red and the rest of him pale.

"Daddy!" Rebecca squealed. She jumped up from the table and ran across the kitchen in her nightdress. When she got to him, she held up her arms and jumped. He caught her and picked her up to his chest. She put her arms around his shoulders and nuzzled into his neck.

"Good morning, sweet pea." He kissed her head.

I looked down at the table. Folded the crumbs of my toast up into my paper towel.

"Morning, Grady," Dad mumbled.

"Morning."

He put Rebecca down and stumbled off to the hall bathroom. She came back to the table to finish her toast. When Dad came out of the bathroom, I stood and threw my paper towel in the garbage. "I'm going to take a shower."

"What about me?" Rebecca said, her mouth full of peanut-butter toast.

"Dad's awake now," I said. "You're fine."

I came out of my room after taking a shower and getting dressed and Mom and Dad were at the kitchen table together, sipping coffee. Dad had a shirt on now, but he still wasn't wearing any pants over his boxers. Mom wore a hooded sweatshirt and plaid pajama pants. Hair pulled back in a ponytail. Rebecca was playing with the Trouble game by herself in the front room, just hitting the popper over and over again. I found a mug in the cabinet and poured it half-full of coffee. Sat down at the table and slurped. It was bitter and harsh, but I kept my face normal.

"Since when do you drink coffee?" Mom asked.

"Just every now and then."

"I've never seen you."

I shrugged. "I don't know. Sometimes with Marcus, mostly."

Dad leaned back in his chair and crossed his arms. "How is Marcus? Still pushing the limits of his waistband?"

"He's fine," I said.

"That's good," Dad said. "He's a good boy. A lot to love." He snickered at his own joke. Me and Mom both ignored him. "Anyway, about this truck. We're going to meet the Daniels fella and his boy at one o'clock. Get that all straightened out."

"Okay."

"Now, let me make sure I got my facts right." He leaned forward and sipped his coffee. "You and the kid are buddies. Y'all were out fucking around on his uncle's property. Drinking beer and mud bogging. You were shittin' with your mother."

"What does that have to do with anything?" Mom asked.

"It's a fact, is it not?" He looked at me. I nodded. "Okay then. You and the kid were riding around, just raising normal teenage hell. He let you drive. A deer ran out, you tried to avoid it, accidentally ran the truck into the ditch."

"Well, in the woods. Hit some trees pretty good."

"Right. Okay. Then Marcus came and got y'all, took you home. End of story. Correct?"

"Yes, sir," I said. He hadn't mentioned anything about pills. So far, no one had.

"Is there anything else? Anything at all? I don't want to get there and get surprised. That'll piss me off."

"No, sir." My palms were sweating.

"You're positive?"

"He already said that's it," Mom said. "That's all there is."

"All right then," Dad said.

In the front room, Rebecca was still playing *Trouble* by herself. I heard the dice clacking in the popper.

We rode in the Dodge down Highway 76, just me and Dad. Rebecca stayed at the house with Mom. The truck was so loud you couldn't really even talk or listen to the radio, which was fine with me. We were meeting Hambone and his dad in the BiLo parking lot at the corner of Highway 76 and Highway 52. I didn't know what the plan was, whether Dad was just going to give him the money he'd asked for or what. He had his wraparound sunglasses on. No seatbelt. One hand on the wheel, the other resting in his lap.

I was nervous that somehow Hambone's dad might've figured out about the pills. I didn't know what Dad would do if that came out, not just for the pills but for lying to him. I looked out the window and tried to take steady, measured breaths.

We pulled into the parking lot and I saw Hambone's dad's Nissan Titan parked in the back, all jacked up on big aftermarket shocks. I pointed to it, and Dad drove that way. He pulled into the spot directly in front of Hambone's dad and shifted the truck into park. There weren't many other cars in the lot. Few ladies in and out of the store with buggies full of groceries. A kid carrying a smiley-faced balloon. Dad cut the engine. "Come on," he said.

We both got out of the truck and walked to the front. I could hear the stiff wheels of the buggies rattling over the rough asphalt. Hambone's dad opened the door of his Titan and climbed out. He was lanky like Hambone, all rib bones and elbows. He had a narrow face and big ears that stuck out from under a camouflage hat. Wore khaki pants with a long-sleeved T-shirt and Reebok running shoes. I knew Dad noticed that.

Hambone got out on the passenger side. His hair was cut since I last saw him, short and neat. It made him look not like himself. Tame. Even a little bit scared. He had a bruise on the side of his neck that ran down and disappeared under his shirt. I wondered if it was from the wreck or something else. He gave me a look like *I know this is shitty and I don't like it but there's nothing I can do*. I tried to give him one back like *I get it, but you're still an asshole*.

Hambone's dad took a step toward Dad and stuck out his hand. "Edward Daniels," he said. "Good to meet you."

Dad ignored his hand. Left him standing there with it all stretched out. "Let's hold off on the pleasantries," he said. "Since from what I understand you ain't been too pleasant on the phone with my ex-wife."

Hambone's dad slowly lowered his hand. His face turned red and he started to talk, then stopped. "That ain't it at all, see," he finally said. "I was just trying to get this rightfully sorted out. You know how things get twisted over the phone."

"Oh, is that all?" Dad shook his head. "That ain't what it sounded like to me."

He took a step closer to Hambone's dad so they were standing real close. Me and Hambone stayed off to the sides. Hambone's dad poked out his chest and pulled his bony shoulders back. Me and Hambone looked at each other like *this isn't what I was expecting*, then we went back to watching our fathers.

"No," Dad said. "It sounded to me like you were trying to intimidate a woman."

"Now, listen, I ain't going to stand here and be accused of something," Hambone's dad said. His eyes were darting around. At me, at Hambone, at the other people further off in the parking lot.

"Well," Dad said. "There you are standing. And here I am accusing."

I started to feel dizzy, like the sunlight had gotten brighter and the parking lot was shaking. My headache was coming back strong. Seeing Dad like that filled my belly up with pride but it also made me feel like I might throw it all up. I looked at Hambone and I could tell he felt mixed up in the same way, embarrassed by his dad but also enthralled that someone was making him look weak and small.

"I'm just asking you to do the right thing," Hambone's dad said. He took half a step back. "Your son was trespassing."

"Bullshit. Yours took him there."

"He was driving without a license."

"On a private dirt road."

"And he wrecked my truck. I'm expected to foot the bill for that?"

"I didn't come here to argue." Dad took off his sunglasses and slowly folded them up. He turned around and looked at me. "Hold these, Grady." He tossed them to me and I caught them.

They were heavy in my hands. It felt like a job he'd given me, an important part of the undertaking. I wasn't just standing by anymore. It made my head throb harder.

He turned back to Hambone's dad. "I came here to say fuck you for threatening my ex-wife. That's it. You ain't getting a dime from us. If you think we really owe it, call yourself a fucking lawyer. And if you speak to my son or my ex-wife disrespectfully again, I'll fuck you up." He pointed at Hambone standing on the other side of the Titan. "You hear that, boy?"

Hambone nodded. "Yes, sir."

"Good. You're my witness." He lowered his hand. "You been warned. Understand?"

Hambone's dad shook his head. "This ain't right."

Dad spat on the asphalt. "Maybe not. But it's the way it's going to be. Come on, Grady." He turned and went toward the driver's side door.

I looked at Hambone. I was still holding Dad's sunglasses with both hands. I gave him a look like *what a clusterfuck* and he gave me one back like *what are you gonna do*. I turned around and climbed into the Dodge. Hambone turned around and climbed into the Titan.

Dad cranked the engine and shifted into reverse. He backed out of his parking spot and navigated through the lot. "Give me back my glasses."

I handed them to him. He grinned as he took them from me. "Got that settled," he said. "Told you we would."

I nodded. I didn't know what to say. It didn't seem like things were over so much as they'd changed. We came to the exit of the parking lot and Dad eased on the brake. He put his sunglasses on, looked both ways, then peeled a tire out of the lot.

"Now he's got to go home and change his britches. Chicken-shit bastard. Calling your momma up." He fished his can of snuff out of his back pocket and packed a wad in his bottom lip. Rolled down his window and spat. The air blowing in was pretty warm, but it still had that little hint of late February bite.

Hambone's dad hadn't mentioned the pills, which meant he probably didn't know about them. Didn't know Hambone stole them from his mother's drawer. Didn't know there was an Altoid's tin full of them hidden on the side of a dirt road on the old Allendale Plantation land. There was no reckoning coming for the pills. I understood that then. Nobody cared. Nobody knew to care. Either I'd keep up with them—eating them, snorting them, whatever else—or I wouldn't. Either the pain in my knee would go away—and the headaches and the sleeplessness and the boredom—or it wouldn't. I rolled my window down too and stuck my elbow out. Dad pushed down hard on the gas. The engine growled and the muffler blew loud dark smoke as we motored back to the house it was hard to believe we ever used to share.

XIII.

It was still early in the afternoon when we got back to the house, but Dad took to celebratory drinking anyway. He got a beer out of the fridge and propped the front door open to let in the light and the spring-like weather. He sat on the couch and flicked on the television. Tuned directly to a NASCAR race. It wasn't a race from the primetime series. Those came on Sundays. It was a race for younger, up-and-coming drivers. You could tell by the second-tier sponsors on the cars and the small crowd in the stands. He always made me watch racing with him when I was younger, and I hated it. Maybe it was a sport like he said—maybe the drivers were skilled athletes, withstanding high temperatures for hours, fighting g-force in the corners, and shifting gears at exactly the right moment—but you didn't see any of that. You just saw hunks of expensive metal painted with advertisements ringing around an oval. I couldn't imagine anything more boring.

I stayed in the kitchen with Mom and Rebecca. They were mixing dough for biscuits. Mom had her cell phone out looking at instructions online. She'd never made biscuits before. My head was throbbing, so I just sat at the table and tried to keep still and quiet. Rebecca was stirring the dough in a big plastic bowl, gripping the wooden spoon she was using with both hands like it was a boat paddle. She was covered in white flour. Her cheeks. The front of her dress.

"How'd it go?" Mom asked.

"Fine, I guess."

"He won't bother y'all no more," Dad hollered from the front room. He chuckled to himself. "No, I don't believe he will."

Mom looked at me and I just shrugged.

"How long do I keep stirring?" Rebecca asked.

"That's probably good," Mom said. "That's probably just exactly enough."

By the time we sat down for supper, all four of us around the kitchen table like some incongruous family, Dad's tongue was fat with beer. There was biscuits and baked chicken with vinegar sauce and white rice and a pot of butterbeans with ham chunks and onions. Vinegar chicken was one of the things Mom cooked best, and one of my favorite meals. My plate was loaded down with a big breast and a heaping pile of rice and beans with vinegar sauce and chicken drippings ladled over the top.

"Great god," Dad mumbled, gesturing toward my plate. "You eat all that, we're going to have to roll you out the kitchen." He wasn't eating anything. Just sitting there with a can of Miller Lite on the table in front him. Only sustenance he needed.

"Y'all skipped lunch," Mom said.

"He's making up for it now."

"Try one of my biscuits, Daddy," Rebecca said, holding out the Tupperware bowl full of bread wrapped in a clean kitchen rag.

"Not now, sweet pea. I'm not hungry."

"But I made them."

"I know. I'll try one later."

Rebecca scrunched up her eyes and sat the bowl down.

"Here," I said. "Give me one." I reached across the table and got a biscuit. Took a bite. It was dry and clumpy. "Wow," I said. "That's the best biscuit I ever had."

Rebecca grinned wide, showing her sharp teeth.

"There you go," Dad said. "He'll eat enough for both of us."

I looked over at him and he was grinning, just staring straight ahead. I put my head down and started eating. Quickly downed everything on my plate. Half because I wanted to and half just to spite him. Sopped up the juice with another biscuit and went back for a second helping.

I'd forgotten how it was to live with him. How he watched and listened to everything. The way you had to always look out the corner of your eye to make sure he didn't disapprove of whatever you were doing or saying. Nerve-wracking weekends when he was heavy drinking, hoping he'd be happy, hoping you didn't somehow set him off.

"How's your coach doing?" Dad asked as I was polishing off my second plate. I looked up. Realized he was asking Mom.

"I'm not going to discuss it with you," she said.

"Do you call him that when y'all are alone? Is that your little pet name for him?"

Mom stood and took her dishes to the sink.

"That's women, Grady. It's just their nature." He drained his can of beer and sat the empty down hard on the table. It made a loud ringing sound. He looked at Rebecca. "But not you, sweet pea. You'll never be conniving, will you?"

"No way!" Her face was shiny with grease from the chicken. Her plate was empty but for a gristly leg bone.

"You promise?"

"Promise."

Dad laughed. He stood and threw his can away. Went to the front room and rummaged around in his duffle bag. Came back to the kitchen carrying his half-drunk bottle of Crown Royal.

Mom was still standing by the sink. "Don't you think you've had enough to drink?" she said.

"See what I'm saying?" Dad unscrewed the top and took a long pull. "Not even divorce and alimony can stop her trying to tell me what to do."

I stood and scraped my plate in the trash. Took it to the sink and put it in with Mom's. She scooted over a little bit. I turned on the faucet and began to rinse.

"Grady, do you know why women close their eyes when they're having sex?"

I ignored him.

"Because they can't stand to see a man having a good time." He laughed hard to himself.

"Rebecca, honey," Mom said. "Why don't you go get changed into your pajamas. I'll take your plate for you."

"Okay."

"She ain't your momma," Dad said.

"I know that," Rebecca said. "She's just Grady's. But I want to put on my pajamas anyways."

✤

Me and Mom washed and dried the dishes while Rebecca played with some old Tonka trucks Mom had found in the attic earlier that day. Dad sat on the couch spitting brown tobacco juice into an empty beer can and watching a show about alligator hunters in Louisiana. I could hear him every time they killed one, commenting on how small it was, how he'd seen a hundred gators twice that size. Mom and I didn't talk while we washed. Just stood there close together, hot steam rising from the sink. There was everything to say and nothing. I thought about why she left Dad. Considered it as a choice she made, not just something that happened to me. She made us a whole different life, and maybe it wasn't worse than the one we could've had with him. Maybe it was something she did for me, not to me. I dried the last dish and put it away in the cabinet. Closed it and rubbed the face of the wood.

"We should strip and sand these next weekend," I said. "Better match the floors."

Mom wiped out the sink basin with her sponge and turned the faucet off. "I've been watching some videos about it. I can try to adjust my shifts again."

I folded up the drying rag and put it on the counter. "It's a plan, then."

She nodded and rubbed my arm gently. "Good plan," she said.

When it got time for her to go to bed, Rebecca cried. She missed her mother and she was ready to go home. Dad stayed in my room with her for a little while with the lights off. Me and Mom were in the front room with the volume on the TV down low. I sat on the couch and massaged my head behind my ears, trying to keep my dull, constant headache from getting any worse. Mom sat in the recliner with her legs pulled up beneath her. The show about alligator hunters had gone off and one about a pawn shop was on. Men haggling over history and money. I could hear Dad talking softly to Rebecca and wondered what he was saying. After a little while, I heard him start to get aggravated. Raising his voice. Finally, he yelled something loud and came out, slamming the door behind him. Rebecca was bawling. He got a beer from the fridge and came to the front room. Sat down on the opposite side of the couch from me. He found the remote and turned the volume on the TV up loud to drown out Rebecca's crying. Cracked his beer and slurped up the foam. He'd already finished off the pint of Crown Royal and slowed the way he was drinking. Not gulping it down anymore, just sipping slow and steady. Keeping a low, grumbling rhythm like thunder humming in a distant cloud. Rebecca kept on, the sobs coming out in wet, choking bursts.

"Can I go talk to her?" Mom asked.

"She's fine," Dad said.

"I don't want her to be scared."

"Nothing to be scared of. Ridiculous. She'll wear herself out in a minute."

Mom shook her head and looked away from him, toward the TV screen. A young guy with tattoos inked on his neck was trying to sell letters his grandfather had written in France during World War II. The pawn man was bringing in an expert to tell him whether the letters were real and how much he should pay.

After a little while, Rebecca eased her crying. The three of us stayed quietly perched around the room, half-watching the TV, half just waiting for the night to be over. My phone vibrated in my pocket. I pulled it out and looked at the screen. It was Marcus.

How's it going?

I texted back. *Weird but ok.*

At the station tonite. holler if u need me. Call tomorrow.

ok

I looked up from the phone screen and saw Dad watching me. I put my phone in my pocket and turned my attention back to the TV screen. A commercial was on, but I pretended like I was paying hard attention to it anyway.

"Little late to be on your phone, ain't it?" Dad said. "You telling your girl sweet dreams?"

"It's Marcus."

"She's a pretty little thing. Surprising given her stock. Peanut man. Ronald never was the brightest of stars."

"They're kids," Mom said.

Dad took a sip of Miller Lite and smiled drunkenly. "You want to fuck her, that's one thing."

"Enough," Mom said.

"But don't be bringing her to supper no more, all right?"

I stood up quickly off the couch. My head throbbed and my vision went blurry. I felt dizzy and loose. I looked down at Dad. He raised one eyebrow and slurped his beer, like he was waiting on me to say something. Hoping for it even. I turned to Mom. "I'm going to bed. Aren't you ready?"

"Not yet." She was shaking her leg.

"Come on anyway."

"You go ahead."

"Please."

Dad spat into his can. "Said she ain't ready yet."

I shook my head and walked down the narrow hall to my room without saying anything else. There was something she wanted to say to him. Something she didn't want me to hear. I hated leaving her up with him for another night, but my head was hurting too bad to stay up or argue anymore.

I quietly twisted the door handle to my room and pushed the door open. Light shined in from over my shoulder and I saw

Rebecca curled in the top bunk, eyes open, her cheeks wet with tears. I went in and closed the door behind me almost all the way, leaving it a little bit cracked. Found a pair of gym shorts in my dresser and went to the bathroom to change. When I came out, Rebecca was sitting up on her knees, her head almost touching the ceiling. "Your fish makes spooky noises," she said.

"I never heard them," I whispered.

"Splashes. Like he's trying to get out."

I went to the tank and opened the lid. Sprinkled in some flakes. The bass came to the surface and sucked in the food. It made a little popping, swishing sound. "Like that?" I said. "He was just hungry."

"Oh," Rebecca said. "Okay."

I closed the lid on the fish tank and laid down in my bed. Put my cell phone on the floor and plugged it in to charge.

"Can we watch some cartoons?" Rebecca asked, her voice soft and strange coming from the top bunk.

"Dad will get mad. Just go to sleep."

She was quiet for a minute. I heard her sniff. When she spoke again, her voice was shaky. "I can't, Grady," she said. "It's too bad. I just can't."

I stood and looked at her over the railing. "Come on," I said. "Come down here with me." She crawled over to the edge of the bed and I helped her down. I got in the bottom bunk first and pressed myself all the way over by the wall, then she got in and laid down on her side, facing the room. We shared my pillow.

"I want to go home," Rebecca said. "It's scary here at night."

I wiped her face dry with the cover. "It's not scary."

"Is too," she said. "So scary."

I was quiet and she slowly stopped whimpering. I closed my eyes and tried to listen for talking in the front room.

"How long until morning?" Rebecca asked.

"If you can fall asleep, it's like no time at all."

She wriggled closer to me. "Okay. I'll try."

I rubbed her shoulder and softly hummed the melody of the theme song to the cartoon we'd watched that morning, just slower and quiet. After a few minutes, she started lightly snoring. I stopped humming, but I didn't feel sleepy at all. My head was killing me. It was starting to worry me, how it lingered in the back of my neck. Flared up at the worst times. Almost made my knee seem like an afterthought. But I wasn't going to say anything. Didn't want to see any more doctors. Run up any more bills. Figured it would go away eventually.

I turned over on my other side, my back against Rebecca's. Felt her steady breathing rising and falling against my spine. I closed my eyes and listened again for Mom and Dad's voices coming from the front room, but all I could hear was the TV still turned up loud.

The TV was still turned up loud in the front room, but I could hear mutterings coming from beneath it. Heavy movement rumbling the floors. I tried to focus on the voices—Dad talking deep and slow, Mom more high-pitched and frantic—but I couldn't make out the words through the noise. I laid there listening, my chest getting tight. I heard something loud like wood cracking and stood up out of bed. Crept quietly across my bedroom to the door, my eyes adjusting to the fresh woken dark. I slowly eased the door open and stepped out. TV light reflected on the glass of the picture frames. Noise. Voices. I balled my fists tight and snuck down the hall. Stopped just short of the end and peered into the front room.

Dad stood with his back to the flashing TV. He was leaned

over the couch with his shirt off. The TV flickered different colors on the bare skin of his back. The ends of his belt listed unbuckled from his jeans. He still had on his boots.

I scanned the room but couldn't find Mom. Then I saw her. She was on the couch beneath him, her back pressed against the seat and her bottom-half writhing on the floor. Hair tangled, mascara smeared on her cheeks, something thick and dark like blood dripping from her bottom lip. She was trying to speak, but her voice only came out in harsh, garbled gasps. Dad had his left hand around her throat. He mumbled through his teeth, low and rhythmic. "Fucking whore can't fucking tell me. Fucking bitch don't fucking know." He kept his right hand cocked at his side and punctuated each stanza of his drunken chant by punching Mom just above her hip. "Fucking whore can't fucking tell me. Fucking bitch don't fucking know."

Mom tried to kick him away, but her foot just glanced off his thigh. He tightened his grip around her throat and punched her harder in the side, his voice shaking from the effort. "Fucking whore can't fucking tell me. Fucking bitch don't fucking know."

I stood at the end of the hallway—watching, listening—until the noises of my body became louder than all the rest. Blood like the sound of a rain-flooded river. Heart keeping time. I felt myself perfectly in that place. Bare feet on the rough worn carpet of my home. I took a deep breath and tasted it was special, charged with the same mythical electricity as a Friday night football game. I stepped from the hall into the front room, the maw of our whole spinning little world. Fists still clenched. Wearing just my gym shorts and a T-shirt. Mom saw me first. Her eyes darted over to me and I held her gaze and everything she said with it.

Dad turned to see what she was looking at, still clutching her throat, still mumbling. Bloodshot eyes drooping at the corners, veiny and red against the dark blue of his irises. "Look," he slurred. "There he is. There's our boy."

"Turn her loose."

"It's fine," he said. "Everything is fine. Go back to bed."

"Turn her loose."

He let go of Mom's neck and stood up straight. Mom coughed and gagged. Dad turned his chest toward me. Looked down at my hands clenched by my sides. "What?" he mumbled. "You going to stop me? You mean to hit me?" He laughed and fumbled with his belt, struggling to refasten the buckle. "All you motherfuckers in here," he mumbled. "Don't none of y'all fucking know."

Mom stood up and put her hand on Dad's shoulder. "Just stop," she said.

He snatched his arm away. "Don't fucking touch me."

"Please," Mom said. She was crying now. "Please don't."

Dad stepped toward me. "You mean to hit me, boy?" He jutted out his jaw. "You going to try and tell me what I can and can't do too? In my own fucking house?"

"This isn't your house."

"Grady," Mom said. "Just go back to bed. I'm fine."

"Fuck if it ain't. This is always my goddamned house," Dad moaned. "Always." He took another step toward me, so close now I could smell the liquor and wintergreen tobacco on his breath. My head was clear and numb. My limbs felt solid and strong. He stuck out his chin, bristled with that dark beard, and tapped it with his own fist. "Right here," he said. I'll give you the first one."

I stared at him in his eyes. Shallow, red-ringed holes. TV blaring. Mom crying. Even still, I could hear the first crickets of the year calling outside, tricked into song by the warm weather.

"Come on, boy," Dad said. "I know you want to hit me." He tapped his jaw again. "Come do it. It's my fault. Everything is my fault." He lowered his voice, like he was telling me a secret. "You know what? You're right. I should've never bred that bitch."

I hated him. My belly sunk with the truth of it. The sight and smell of him.

"Come on, boy." He pushed me hard in the chest, but I kept my feet planted. Hands down by my side. "Come out here all bowed up. Don't be scared now." He slapped my face with an open hand. I felt heat from the blood coming to the skin. Shame for him. "Come on." He slapped me again.

I wanted to hit him. I wanted to lower my shoulder and truck him like I would a linebacker trying to meet me in the hole. I wanted to stand over him and stare down at him on the floor, broken, busted open.

But I knew he wanted that too. Wanted me to try, at least. So instead, I stepped past him. Cheek stinging, the sound of the slaps still ringing in my ears. I put my arm around Mom's shoulder. She put her face against my chest and sobbed.

Dad turned around to look at us. "She ain't hurt. Don't let her fool you. That's all the fuck they're good for."

"Get out of our house."

"What the fuck did you say?"

I pointed to the door. "Get out."

He gritted his teeth. "Make me."

I walked with Mom around him, toward the hall, watching his face and keeping her to the outside of me. I looked in his eyes as we passed him. "If you don't leave, I'll call the police."

He snorted and shook his head. "Guess that's what happens when you're raised by a woman. Turn out to be a pussy."

I didn't respond. Me and Mom walked down the hall. I heard him mumbling and laughing behind us. As we walked slowly toward Mom's bedroom, my door squeaked open and Rebecca stepped out through the crack, her little knees shaking beneath the tail of her nightdress.

"Come on," I said.

She stayed standing in the doorway. "Is something happening?"

I walked into Mom's room and turned on the overhead light. Mom went in and cleared the clothes and makeup and hangers off the bed and straightened the cover. I waved Rebecca over and she peered down the hall toward the front room.

"Everything's fine."

She ran across the narrow hall and came into Mom's room. Mom laid down in the bed, sniffling. She patted the mattress for Rebecca to climb up.

"What happened to you?" Rebecca asked, getting into the bed and sitting on her knees.

"Nothing," Mom said. "Everything is okay."

I heard the front door slam. I walked to the front room and looked outside. Dad had the driver side door of his Dodge open, standing in the dim cab light, still talking to himself. I locked the deadbolt. Hunted for the remote and turned off the TV, sending the whole house into silence. I went back to Mom's room. She and Rebecca were both lying in the bed. I closed the door behind me and turned off the light.

"How long until morning?" Rebecca asked.

"Not long now," I said. "Not long at all."

XIV.

I tried to sleep for a few hours on the floor beside Mom's bed, closest to the door. The morning came on gray and a flock of starlings lit in the edge of the woods across from the house, chattering noisily. I got up, went to the front room and looked outside. Dad was sitting awake behind the wheel of his Dodge, looking sober and pale. I unlocked the deadbolt and opened the door. Went and sat down on the couch. Dad came in and started packing his things into his green and yellow duffle. I watched him, but I didn't say anything, and I didn't move to help.

After he got everything packed, he carried the bag outside and put it in the truck. He came back and stood just inside the house, leaving the door halfway open. "Where is Rebecca?" he asked.

"Sleeping."

"Go get her."

"She's tired."

"She can sleep in the truck."

I went to Mom's room and carefully picked Rebecca up out of the bed. She grunted and snuggled into my arms. I carried her down the hall to the front room and out to the Dodge. Dad came behind me and opened the truck door on the passenger side. I laid Rebecca softly on the seat. She crossed her arms tight against her chest and wriggled closer to the backrest.

"Hold on a second," I said quietly to Dad. I went inside and picked up the knit blanket Mom had laid out on the couch for Dad to use. Took it outside and covered Rebecca.

Dad had already gotten in behind the wheel. "Thank you," he said.

I didn't answer him. I kissed Rebecca on the forehead, closed the door gently, and walked to the steps. Dad cranked the engine and started to back out of the driveway. I didn't wave. I didn't watch as he drove down Lantana Lane. I just turned and went inside. Listened to the sound of the muffler as it slowly faded away.

I went to Mom's room and peeked in through the door. She wasn't in the bed. I heard the shower running in the bathroom. I went across the hall to my bedroom, Tonka trucks parked crookedly along the wall, Trouble laying out in the corner, unboxed. I knelt on the floor and started picking up the pieces.

It was a long time before I heard the shower turn off in Mom's bathroom. She must've run the water heater all the way dry. She stayed in her room a good while after that. I got my bedroom in order and then just laid on the bed. Eyes dry from lack of sleep. Head feeling heavy from the constant headache.

After a while, I smelled coffee and went to the kitchen. Mom was sitting at the table with a chipped mug. Hair pulled back in a wet ponytail. She was wearing her scrubs. I sat across from her.

"Want a cup?" she asked.

I shook my head. I didn't want to pretend to like it. Mom's bottom lip was swollen and cracked at the left corner. She had dark bruises on her neck. She'd tried to cover them with makeup, but you could still see them clear enough to make out finger lines. It made me angry and sick to see them. "You're not going to work today," I said.

"I've got to."

"Mom."

"I'm fine," she said.

I leaned back in my chair and took a deep, loud breath.

"I'm fine. I promise. I'm fine." She had both hands wrapped around her coffee mug, like she was trying to warm them.

"Okay. Whatever you say."

She brought the cup to her lips and took a sip. "I'm sorry," she said.

"There's nothing for you to be sorry for."

"I didn't know what else to do."

I leaned forward in the chair and put my palms on the table. "There's nothing to do," I said. "It's already done. You can't fix it. We just go from here, best we can."

She put her hand to her neck. Pushed lightly on the bruises, like to check whether they were still there. How bad they hurt. It reminded me of myself.

"I'll stop seeing Jeff. Coach Hendrickson. If that'll make it easier for you."

I was quiet for a minute, thinking. What that would accomplish. Why it bothered me to begin with. "No," I said. "Not for me. If you like him. We'll just figure it out."

I think it was the hiding that was worse than anything, the idea that things were happening around me I didn't know about and couldn't understand, but that didn't seem such a scary thought anymore. Truthfully, I couldn't imagine playing football again anyway, slow as I was, as much as I hurt. Couldn't imagine myself in pads and a helmet, standing on the field beneath the floodlights, people in the bleachers looking down. Couldn't imagine holding tight to that ball like a rare, valuable egg. Putting my head down and letting boys blindly bang their bodies against mine. But I didn't say that. I swallowed it like a pill, another secret.

"I do like him." Mom sipped her coffee. "He's a good man, I think."

I nodded. Maybe he was. She'd learn one way or the other. I stood and pushed my chair in under the table.

"Where are you going?"

"Need a shower too."

"I'll be gone when you get out. But I'll be home tonight."

"Okay." I turned to walk out of the kitchen. At the threshold between the kitchen and the rest of the house, there was a jagged crack where the new floors ended and the old ones began. I stopped and turned around. "I didn't tell you before. These floors are perfect. You did a good job."

Mom smiled. "Thank you," she said.

I nodded and stepped across the crack.

Lydia texted while I was in the shower to ask if Dad had left yet. When I got out, I sat on the edge of my bed wrapped in a towel, water dripping down my back. I told her that he had, and I was thinking about doing some studying. She said she had some homework to do too. I asked if she wanted to work on it together. She said she did. She'd be over in an hour. I stood and dried myself the rest of the way. Dressed in a pair of Wranglers and a

T-shirt. It hugged tight against my belly. I stuck my hands up the hem and stretched it out and that felt better.

I opened my sock drawer for a pair of socks and saw the owl feet again. One all charred up from where I'd tried to light it on fire. I took them both out and put them on top of my dresser. Pulled out my pill bottle too. Unscrewed the top and counted the pills. Four left. They wouldn't last long. I wondered what I'd do when they ran out. If I asked Mom to get it refilled, she'd start asking questions. Maybe I could try to go without. The thought made me nervous. I put the bottle back in the drawer. Worry for another day.

I pulled on my socks and instinctively went to the closet to fetch my Wolverines. When I saw them, I thought about Dad the night before, bent over top of Mom, choking her, the sounds she made. Him standing shirtless, but still wearing his steel-toe boots. Cold sweat beaded on the back of my neck. I got my Nikes out of the closet and put them on instead. I picked up my boots and got the owl feet off the dresser. Dropped one long-taloned foot in each boot. Carried them outside, across the front yard, across Lantana Lane, into the woods.

I walked deep into the trees. Deeper than I'd ever been, carrying one boot in each hand, just looking, not knowing what for. I was half expecting to come to another yard, or another road, thinking I'd have to turn around, but it was just trees as far as I went, as far as I could see. I came to a briar thicket, dense and green and sharp even after the winter. I stopped and looked at the boots in my hand. Thought about doing something ceremonial. Maybe burying them. Instead, I just tossed them into the middle of the thicket. Spat once on the ground for good measure and started making my way back to the house.

✤

Lydia looked like herself that day. No lipstick, no fancy shirt. She wore jeans and a faded T-shirt with a pocket. Still that strand of fake pearls, but they always suited her somehow. We sat beside each other at the kitchen table with textbooks spread open before us. She didn't ask anything about Dad, and I didn't tell. There was no need. She knew how it was with fathers, probably even better than me.

I had a test in U.S. History that coming Wednesday. We'd been studying the Great Depression and the New Deal. Well, Coach Molina had told us to read the chapters about those things, and we'd watched a PBS movie about the Dust Bowl. I remembered Coach Molina standing in front of the class and trying to start a lecture. He told us that the Social Security Act signaled the beginning of the end of American democracy, but he started tripping over his words shortly after that and just went back to his desk. I couldn't find anything like that in the textbook at all. I asked Lydia if she remembered anything about Social Security.

"Sure," she said. "Cradle to grave."

"What?"

"That's what Social Security is."

"I've never heard that before."

Lydia crossed her arms. "I don't know what to tell you," she said. "That's what it is."

I got the feeling again like I wanted to kiss her.

"Stop looking at me like that."

My ears turned hot. I looked down at my textbook.

"It's just. It freaks me out. I mean, I like hanging out with you."

"Then what's the problem?" I asked, still staring down at the book.

"It's not worth it. We kiss. We fool around. It feels good. But then what?"

I looked up from the book. She was still sitting with her arms crossed. I shrugged.

"Exactly. You don't know. But I do. It's a whole storm of shit you can't even imagine. From everywhere. And it's not worth it. Just trust me, okay?"

"Okay," I said. And I did trust her. And I understood somehow that she wasn't exactly saying no so much as she was saying not yet.

Lydia uncrossed her arms and put her elbows on the table. Looked at me sideways. "How about Geometry?"

"Made an eighty on my last quiz."

"All right," she said. "Now we're getting somewhere."

We quit studying around two and Lydia showed me funny videos on YouTube. Her favorite was one about a man dressed up as a lady listing all the weird muffins she makes. I laughed but I didn't really understand what was funny about it. Marcus called. I wasn't going to answer, but Lydia paused the video we were watching and told me to pick up, so I did.

"Hello?"

"Did he leave yet, or is he fucking moving back in?"

"What?"

"Your daddy," Marcus said. I could hear music playing in the background, loud and scratchy.

"Oh, yeah. He left this morning."

"Why didn't you call?"

"I thought you were calling me?"

"Christ, you're worse than raising a sack of flour. I'm coming to get you."

"Lydia's here," I said. "We're studying."

"Even better. She can bring you over. See you in a few."

He hung up before I could respond. I sat my phone down on the table. "He wants us to come over."

"Both of us?" Lydia asked.

"Yeah. He's scheming something. I don't know what."

"Let's go." She stood up from the table.

"You want to?"

"Something to do, at least. Beats just sitting around inside all day."

"You know how Marcus is though."

She rolled her eyes. "He don't bother me."

Lydia rocked the Oldsmobile off Lantana Lane. Hard on the gas, then easy off. It felt like sitting in Marcus's jon boat, riding the wakes other boats make as they motor by. We took Highway 76 past Sandridge Fire Station, past the Methodist church. Left onto Black Tom Road. The wind blew in from the cracked windows. I studied my face in the sideview. Fading bruises around my eye, cheek puffy and red. My head felt like it was full of muddy water, heavy and dense. We passed a field being plowed by a man on a blue tractor. Smell of diesel and fresh turned earth.

"Peanuts," Lydia said, pointing with her thumb toward the field. "Georgia Greens. Won't plant until the middle of April. He's just getting the dirt ready now."

"You know him?"

"Not really," Lydia said. "But the last two years after he's harvested, he let me and Ronald come in and pick up the peanuts the tractor missed. Whole plants just laying on top of the dirt. We filled the bed of the truck up in an hour. Could've filled it five or six more times."

"They just leave it there?"

"Yeah, to rot. I wanted to go back and get more. I mean, they were free. Build a little dry shed behind the house to store them. But Ronald didn't want to seem greedy. Said we'd mess around and ruin a good thing. Peanuts just laid out there on top of the dirt. More than even the crows could eat."

We came around a deep corner in the road and I could see Marcus's trailer ahead. I pointed. "There it is."

Lydia let off the gas and flicked on her turn signal. Slowed to a crawl before turning into the driveway. The hubcaps leaned against the trailer skirting were gleaming in the sun. Marcus sat out front in a foldout camping chair wearing gym shorts and a cutoff T-shirt. He squinted at us as we pulled slowly down the drive, an unlit Pall Mall dangling from his lips. His red goatee was messy and long. Needed to be trimmed bad. Two other empty chairs stood folded-out on either side of him. Lydia parked behind the Ranger. "You got any idea what's going on?" she asked.

"No," I said. "Never."

We got out of the car and walked over to where Marcus was sitting. He stood as we approached. Took the cigarette from his mouth and hugged me around my shoulders. "Feel like I ain't seen you in forever, cuz."

I couldn't respond he was squeezing me so hard, but it felt good, and I wrapped my arms around him and squeezed tight too. He turned me loose from the hug and stuck his cigarette back in his mouth. Put his hands on both my shoulders and studied my face. "No more of that shit," he said. "I can't stand to see it on you."

I nodded. He let me go and turned his attention to Lydia, standing to my left and a little bit behind me. "Peanut Gal," he said. "Good to see you too."

"Call me Lydia." She stepped up and stuck out her hand to shake. "I insist."

Marcus grinned, lips curling around his unlit Pall-Mall, the filter getting soggy and limp. "Sure thing." He shook her hand lightly. "Now come on, sit, sit." He gestured to the camping chairs and sat back down in his. Me and Lydia did the same. Marcus pulled a blue BIC lighter from his pocket and lit his cigarette, drawing the smoke deep into his lungs and blowing it slowly out of his nose. "What a fine day in the country, ain't it?"

"Is that why you called us over? To enjoy the weather."

"Like that ain't a good enough reason," Marcus said. "Fucking-A that's why I called." He shook his head. "Peanut Gal. Excuse me, Lydia. We got to teach this boy about the more simple joys in life, don't we?"

"Got to teach him something."

Marcus laughed. He took another long drag from his Pall-Mall and nodded his head. "Guess so," he said.

Spooky came wandering from around the back of the trailer with her tail stuck up high and curled at the end. She made a wide circle around the chairs, strutting and stretching her back.

"There she is," Marcus said. "That noblest of backyard beasts."

Lydia wiggled her fingers near the ground and clicked her tongue. Spooky came over and smelled her hand and rubbed her teeth against Lydia's knuckles. Lydia pet the cat down her back. A little puff of black hair came away and floated slowly to the dirt.

"Shedding already," Marcus said. "Fuck Punxsutawney Phil. Spooky will tell you when winter is over around here."

Lydia laughed. She picked the cat up and stood her in her lap. "She's purring."

"Yeah, we don't get too much womanly love in these parts. I'm sure you're surprised to hear that."

Lydia giggled again. Her shirt was getting covered in cat hair. She petted Spooky behind her ears and the cat laid down in her lap. Marcus took one last pull from his Pall Mall and flicked the butt on the ground beside his chair. "Oh, there is one more thing," he said. "Almost forgot." He stood and walked up the rickety steps to his trailer. "Hold tight. I'll be right back." He went inside and the screen door clattered shut behind him.

Lydia tried to pet Spooky's belly and the cat bit her finger. Lydia squealed and drew her hand away. Spooky jumped down and trotted off behind the trailer again. Lydia held up her finger, drops of blood beading from two small tooth holes. "I was just trying to love on her."

"She got nervous," I said.

Lydia brought her finger to her lip and sucked away the blood. It made me about want to disappear from loving her so much.

The screen door clattered again, and Marcus came lumbering down the steps. He was holding something in his arms, long and bulky and covered by a tattered bath towel. He came straight to me and held the thing in front of me.

"What is it?"

"You ask too many questions," Marcus said. "Just pull the fucking rag off and find out."

I lifted the towel. Beneath it, laying in Marcus's outstretched arms, was a beaten-up acoustic guitar. The smooth curved body was made of light-yellow wood, the clearcoat peeling off in places. The rosewood fretboard was scuffed around the top and the strings were flaky with rust. I sat there in the camping chair, holding that ratty bath towel, staring at the instrument.

"Go on," Marcus said. "Take it. Give it a strum."

I dropped the towel and lifted the guitar from his arms. Held it in my lap. I ran my thumb down the strings and it made a messy, metallic sound. I looked up at Lydia. She was smiling. I pressed the top string at the first fret and picked it. Moved my finger down the neck, pressing the string down at every fret and plucking it. Marcus sat back down in his chair.

"Where did this come from?" I asked.

"One of the boys at the station was getting rid of it. He got a new one. Gave me a good deal. I thought you might want to learn. Give you something productive to do, at least."

"It's for me?"

Marcus looked at Lydia. "Don't catch on too quick, does he?"

Lydia raised her eyebrows and shrugged.

"Here, let me hold it," Marcus said. "I'll show you a G chord. It's the only one I know."

I handed him the guitar and he carefully arranged his fingers on the frets. Strummed the strings and the guitar made a half-hearted noise. "Probably needs to be tuned," he said. "Anyway, you got the internet. You can figure it out." He gave the instrument back to me and I held it flat on my lap. It was beautiful the way so many busted, hard-used things are beautiful. In its simplicity, its service, its history. "Thank you," I said.

"Learn how to really play," Marcus said, fishing another Pall Mall out of his pack. "That'll be more than enough thanks."

"I will."

"Glad I don't have to live with you while you learn," Lydia said.

"You'll change your tune when he can pick it though," Marcus said.

Lydia smiled. "We'll find out."

I kept the guitar in my lap the whole time we stayed outside, just talking easy, feeling the good weather on us. I ran my hand along the wood, fingered the strings, twisted the tuning pegs. Exploring potential. Clutching tight to an unexpected opportunity.

Marcus talked and Lydia laughed. I laughed too. I was groggy from not sleeping and time moved slow and steady like the afternoon would never end, but that was fine. Like there was nothing that came before and nothing that would come after, but that was just fine.

The sun began to sink down level with the pines and the moon started shining early through the blue, so they were both just hanging there in the same sky. A car pulled into Marcus's driveway, a clean, gold, 90s model Crown Victoria. Me, Lydia and Marcus all watched it approach without a word. The car stopped within shouting distance from us and the driver side door opened. A man got out and stood, most of his body hidden by the door. He was tall and his head was shaved clean. He looked to be around fifty years old, but I couldn't tell for sure. I'd never seen him before. "Sorry to roll up on y'all like this," he called. "Hope I didn't scare you. I lost a hub cap a while back. Think it's one of them leaned up over there." He pointed toward Marcus's trailer. "I seen y'all sitting out here. Figured I'd pull in and find out for sure."

Marcus stood and started walking toward the trailer. "Yeah, come on," he said.

The man closed his door and followed Marcus to the trailer. He left the engine running behind him. Marcus found a hubcap that matched the others on the Crown Victoria. Picked it up and flipped it over, like to inspect it. "This the one?" he asked, holding it out toward the man.

"Looks like it."

"Well, there you go," Marcus said.

"All right," the man said. "Hell yeah. Appreciate you."

"Just glad we found it," Marcus said.

The man nodded and walked back to his car. Marcus came back to where we were, but he didn't sit down. The man got in his Crown Victoria, put the hubcap in the passenger seat, and backed all the way out of the drive. He rolled his window down and waved to us as he drove away down Black Tom Road. We all three waved back.

Marcus sat back down in his camping chair. "Reckon that goes to show," he said. "You never can tell."

I looked over to the space where the hubcap had been. A break in the line of chrome, the torn skirting of the trailer exposed. "No," I said. "You really never can."

PUBLISHING
New & Extraordinary
VOICES FROM THE
AMERICAN SOUTH

HUB CITY PRESS is a non-profit independent press in Spartanburg, SC that publishes well-crafted, high-quality works by new and established authors, with an emphasis on the Southern experience. We are committed to high-caliber novels, short stories, poetry, plays, memoir, and works emphasizing regional culture and history. We are particularly interested in books with a strong sense of place.

Hub City Press is the publishing arm of the non-profit Hub City Writers Project, founded in 1995 to foster a sense of community through the literary arts. Our metaphor of organization purposely looks backward to the nineteenth century when Spartanburg was known as the "hub city," a place where railroads converged and departed.

THE SOUTH CAROLINA NOVEL SERIES (formerly the South Carolina Novel Prize) is open to all writers in South Carolina. It is co-sponsored by the South Carolina Arts Commission, the South Carolina State Library, and South Carolina Humanities.

PREVIOUS WINNERS

2021: Maris Lawyer *The Blue Line Down*

2019: Scott Sharpe *A Wild Eden*

2017: Brock Adams *Ember*

2015: James McTeer *Minnow*

2013: Susan Tekulve *In the Garden of Stone*

2011: Matt Matthews *Mercy Creek*

2009: Brian Ray *Through the Pale Door*

Janson MT Pro
11/15.3